Also By Donise Sheppard

Finding Home

Making Room

Welcome Home

Christmas in Bells

Scars

Dark Descending

Pride and Passion

Cozy Kisses

Love Like This

Nightshade and Moonlight

Phobia!

Merrow: Anthology

At Death's Door

A Bond of Words: 29 Short Stories

Flash Fiction Addiction

Magical Reality

A Haunting of Words

Love Dust

Flashpoint

Full Metal Horror

Second Time's the Charm

BlackHearts Anthology

Relationship Add Vice

The Altered Trilogy

Out of Left Field

Grace Between Us

DONISE SHEPPARD

RADIANCE

RADIANCE

An Imprint of Roan & Weatherford Publishing Associates, LLC
Bentonville, Arkansas
www.roanweatherford.com

Library of Congress Cataloging-in-Publication Data
Names: Sheppard, Donise, author.
Title: Her Mother's Wish/Donise Sheppard
Description: First Edition | Bentonville: Radiance, 2025.
Identifiers: LCCN: 2025937835 | ISBN: 979-8-89299-036-3 (trade paperback) |
ISBN: 979-8-89299-037-0 (eBook)
Subjects: BISAC: FICTION/Romance/ | Historical/ | American/
LC record available at: https://lccn.loc.gov/2025937835

Radiance Edition July 2025

Cover Design by Casey W. Cowan
Interior Design by Natalie Brianne
Editing by Staci Troilo and Deanna Adams

Her Mother's Wish is dedicated to my mother, Donna. I may not have always done as you wished, but I hope I've still made you proud.

Chapter One

MARY SMOOTHED HER SKIRT WITH shaky hands as the carriage traveled down the dirt path, bringing her aunt and uncle to their new home and pushing her farther from it. Mother stood beside her in a black mourning gown, hands over her bodice, staring at a fixed point behind the carriage.

The sun was starting to set, casting a golden light over the flowers in the front garden. Mary's anticipation grew as she looked at the roses, remembering a moment five years ago that she treasured dearly.

And now Andrew was coming to live with them. At least when he was two hours away, she could pretend she wasn't in love with him.

"Did you remember to set the gifts in Sarah and Andrew's bedrooms?"

"Yes, Mother. And I had a second wardrobe brought in for Sarah this morning."

"Excellent. Remind me to tip those boys tomorrow. I want to ensure they feel appreciated for their hard work."

Boys. Mary hid a smile. Her mother was only thirty-nine, and the youngest man on their staff was thirty.

Through the evening light, Mary admired how handsome her mother was, with her blonde ringlets and button nose.

Mary had inherited her father's looks, round face, and dark-brown hair. Only her gray eyes came from her mother.

The carriage came to a stop at the base of the porch stairs, and Henry, the footman, hastened to open the door.

Uncle Isaac stepped out first, promptly taking off his hat and revealing disheveled salt and pepper hair. He stretched out a hand to help Aunt Catherine from the carriage. She was dressed from head to toe in black, including her hat and traveling gloves. Mary had never seen her dress with such little color except at funerals and shortly after. Aunt Catherine had always been vivacious and colorful. As soon as her gaze reached the top of the stairs, Mother walked down to greet Father's sister-in-law, wrapping her arms around her in a tight embrace.

Andrew, their adopted son, stepped out next, donning a black traveling coat. His curly, black hair was cut short. He was taller and broader, even since her father's funeral six months ago. His skin was darker than his family's since his biological father was a Black man. Aunt Catherine had adopted him from her unwed cousin when he was born.

His joining their family had turned out to be one of the best things to happen to Mary. For as long as she could remember, Andrew had been her best friend. When she was five years old, they hid under one of the tables at one of her mother's dinner parties and laughed at the adults. It was there they promised to be friends all of their days.

When Mary was fifteen, their grandfather died. After his funeral, she was heartbroken. Andrew found her in a bedroom crying and wrapped her in a consoling hug. It was the first time it felt different when he hugged her. The first time she realized she needed him.

Andrew always had a way of bringing a smile out of her

when she was sad. That's why when Mother had told her he was moving in, some of the emptiness she had felt after losing Father had filled. How could her heart be empty when Andrew's presence and personality were big enough to fill it?

His eyes flitted up the stairs to Mary, and he bowed his head very slightly before stepping back to stand beside his mother. The footman took his sister's hand and helped her out of the carriage, her golden ringlets bobbing with the motion.

Mary hurried down the stairs to greet them.

"Oh, Mary." Sarah took both of her hands in hers and smiled. "I have so much to tell you. Mother has agreed to let me begin courting, and she's bought me several new dresses. Wait until you see them!"

"Are you sure you're ready to start courting? You're ready to be a wife and mother?"

"Oh, yes. It's all I've wanted since I was a girl."

As Andrew caught her eye, Mary could understand her desire for companionship. Children, however, were another story.

"Let's get into the house," Mother said. "Dinner will be ready shortly. We can get you settled." She addressed the footman as Mary led Sarah up the stairs. "Can you please see to it their belongings are delivered to their bedroom?"

"Yes, ma'am."

"Thank you, Henry." Mother nodded to him and followed her family into the house.

The candles were lit, but with evening setting in, the entrance hall was darker, casting shadows across the walls. Mary had always loved this time of day, but since her father's passing, she wasn't comforted by the warm glow of the flames.

"Your rooms are all ready for you," Mother said. "Mary, could you show your cousins where they'll be staying?"

"Of course," she said, eyeing the way Uncle Isaac's jaw

clenched when Mother spoke as if she were still the mistress of the house.

All of that would change soon. With Father gone, Isaac was the heir to his estate, and as such, he and Aunt Catherine would become the Master and Mistress of the house. Mother and Mary were now merely guests in their own home.

It was an odd feeling. Even Andrew's cheerful personality might not be enough to make her feel less awkward.

"I hope the trip wasn't too hard on you," Mary said as she led them up the stairs. "You must be tired after traveling for so long."

"It was lovely, actually," Sarah said.

"She and Mother spent the entirety of the ride singing," Andrew said. "I'd never been gladder than when the carriage stopped in front of Kline Manor."

Mary gave a short laugh and turned to him. When they were kids, they used to joke that Aunt Catherine sounded like a scared cat when she hit the high notes. The older they got, the more Mary would pretend to enjoy their singing to torture Andrew.

"I think Sarah is a wonderful singer. Perhaps she and Aunt Catherine can sing a duet for us after supper. You can play the piano for us. I dearly miss your playing."

He flashed her a small smile. "Perhaps for you, I can suffer another song."

Mary felt her cheeks flush as she flitted her gaze away from his hazel eyes.

"I would love to sing after supper!" Sarah exclaimed. "We shall see if Father agrees."

They arrived at the first room, Sarah's room, and Mary pushed open the door. "This is to be your room, Sarah. Mother has had it made up for you and even brought in a second wardrobe for your dresses."

Sarah eyed the flowers on the desk, the large four-post bed, and the two wardrobes. "It's lovely, but I don't care much for roses. I much prefer daisies or daffodils. Something with more color."

Mary frowned. Preference in flowers seemed such a mild complaint, hardly worth mentioning. Then again, her cousin had always been one to complain.

"What's the parcel on the bed?" Sarah asked, walking in. "A gift. For me?"

"Yes. Mother insisted on welcoming you both to our home and showing you how happy we are that you're here."

Sarah tore off the paper to reveal a notebook. "Oh. A book. I don't write much, but I suppose it's a kind gesture."

"That was very thoughtful," Andrew said, ducking his head. "We'll be sure to give her our thanks. *Won't* we, Sarah?" he stressed, narrowing his eyes at her.

Mary couldn't help but feel grateful he'd come to her rescue. "I'm sure she'd appreciate that kindness, thank you." She eyed Sarah, who had found interest in the wardrobes. "If you follow me, your room is just down the hall," Mary told him.

"Only one wardrobe for me, I see," Andrew said when she pushed open his bedroom door.

Mary's face fell. "We can have another brought up. We assumed you'd only need one. We thought Sarah, with all her dresses would—"

Andrew laughed and waved her off. "I was only joking. One wardrobe is plenty."

"Oh," Mary sighed a laugh. "Good. Well, I'll leave you to get settled. I'll see you at supper."

She turned to walk down the hall to her room, the last room on the second floor.

"Mary...."

"Yes?"

Andrew stood in the doorway, hazel eyes flickering across her face. "Thank you for your hospitality."

She bowed her head. "It's my pleasure. It is, after all, your home now."

"Yes. Quite right." He stared past her at the next door. "Your room is next to mine?"

"It is. Is that a problem?"

He swallowed but shook his head. "Not at all. I'd forgotten. That's all. I'm not sure I've ever been in your room."

Mary cocked her head. "No. I don't think you have. I'm afraid there isn't much to see, though. You might be disappointed."

"Nothing about you could disappoint me, Mary."

Her cheeks burned.

"I was merely wondering where to find you if I wanted to ask you for a walk around the garden, for instance."

Mary bit back a grin. "Well, you'll probably find that I'm already in the garden or the library. I'm usually only in my bedroom at night before bed or in the morning before breakfast."

"That's good to know."

Henry walked onto the landing, carrying luggage.

"Let me help you with that."

Before Henry could protest, Andrew had taken the bags from him.

"Thank you, sir."

Mary walked into her room to get ready for dinner. Mother wanted her to dress her best for their first night with Uncle Isaac as master of the house. She wondered if it would become a habit or if it only applied to special occasions. She made a mental note to ask Mother.

As she slipped into her nicer gown, she thought about how Andrew had spoken to her. Was his kindness intended to be as flirtatious as it was? He wasn't technically her cousin, after all. Not a blood relative. His birth mother was his adopted mother's second cousin, and Aunt Catherine had married into the family. Growing up with Andrew was no different than growing up with the boys from town, although, admittedly, she liked Andrew much more than she ever liked the others.

He was twenty-four now. Old enough for a wife. And she was twenty-one, old enough to start looking for a husband. Her mother had been married at seventeen.

Andrew would make someone a good husband someday, but could he really have his eye on her? He was charming and kind, but he was Andrew. She'd grown up with him. He knew every embarrassing secret she had. She could still remember daring him to eat a bug and him doing it.

Andrew was sweet and attractive, but he couldn't be thinking of her as a possible wife, could he?

She slipped off her black mourning gown and dressed for dinner, wondering if his flirting had all been in her head. Perhaps it had been her imagination because she was so desperate for love and affection since Father died. He couldn't possibly see her the way she saw him, could he?

Had she imagined it, though? The house had certainly been sad and felt lonelier, but would it really be described as desperate?

No. It was because now, without her father there, Mary was uncertain where her future was going.

A lot was going to change, and if Mary and her mother wanted to avoid homelessness and poverty, she had better start looking for a husband to care for them. Uncle Isaac wouldn't want to care for them forever. Even with the allowance of five thousand a year, her father had requested Isaac give them in his will, Mary and her mother would need more to continue living the privileged life to which they had become so accustomed.

Whether Mary was ready to be a wife or not, it was time to find a husband. Hopefully a good man. Perhaps, if she was lucky, Andrew could return her love, and she could marry her best friend.

Chapter Two

*A*T DINNER, UNCLE ISAAC TOOK Father's usual seat at the head of the table. Mary's heart sank. Father was truly gone, and Isaac was now the head of the house. Sarah and Andrew sat on either side of Mary, opposite Mother and Aunt Catherine.

"Of course, you two are welcome to stay as long as you wish, but I do say Mary will be married within the next few years."

Mary shot Uncle Isaac a look, then quickly stared down at her soup. She didn't want to discuss the prospect of marriage with him. She wanted her marriage to be more than a business arrangement. She wanted to be with someone she loved. She was going to be with him forever, after all.

"Thank you, Isaac. Your graciousness is most appreciated."

Mary's jaw clenched at her mother's words. It wasn't right for her to have to be so formal and courteous in her own home. He was speaking as though he were being kind and courteous, but if he were, he wouldn't expect Mother to act like a guest in her own home.

It was cruel women couldn't inherit their husband's estate after they passed.

"Oh, Elizabeth," Aunt Catherine started, turning to Mother. "Did you hear that Jeffry Lawson is finally looking for a wife?" She eyed Mary and Sarah across the table.

Mary quickly averted her gaze.

"Perhaps we should invite him to dinner this weekend to see if he is a good match for one of our eligible ladies?"

Jeffry Lawson was no catch. The only quality he had of a good husband was a proper upbringing. He was from a very prominent family in town. He wasn't handsome, which she could get past if he were at least kind, but the few times Mary had interacted with him, he came across as arrogant. She didn't like the way he spoke to his servants, or to her, for that matter, as if she hadn't had a proper education.

Andrew cleared his throat, and the women turned their attention to him.

"Perhaps Aunt Elizabeth has someone else in mind for Mary, Mother." He glanced at her. "Or perhaps Mary wants to make her own decision about who her husband will be. We ought not meddle."

Butterflies swirled in her stomach.

"Of course, you're right, darling. But I still think it would be nice to have his family for dinner. You never know if they're a good match." She glanced at her daughter. "He may just as well wish to pursue Sarah. She's a beautiful woman and would make a fine wife."

Mary would much prefer Jeffry to pursue Sarah, but she wouldn't wish him on her cousin either. Although, if he made her happy, who was she to say he wasn't fit for her? Sarah should be free to form an unbiased opinion.

Still, she couldn't help but wonder why Andrew had spoken up on her behalf. Had he seen the look of horror on her face when Aunt Catherine had mentioned Jeffry?

Or did he have something else in mind?

"I would like to meet him," Sarah chimed in, glancing at Mary. "If you don't have any protests, Mary."

"Oh, by all accounts, meet him. I'm not interested in marrying Jeffry."

Andrew caught her eye, and her heart began to race.

She couldn't have serious feelings for him. Could she? Everything she'd been feeling over the past few years had been growing, but she'd never stopped to consider that he might want to be with her.

"Then it's settled," Uncle Isaac said. "We'll invite his family to dinner on Saturday, and a few other families in town, as well. We'll properly introduce ourselves. We'll make it a party. What do you say, Elizabeth?"

"A party sounds lovely," she said in a soft, polite voice.

Mary knew she would rather be home alone while she was still grieving Father, but what could she say? This was Uncle Isaac's home now, after all.

After supper, they retired to the parlor, where Uncle Isaac poured himself a generous glass of whiskey, and Andrew sat at the grand piano. Mary couldn't help but watch as his fingers elegantly glided over the keys. He flashed her a grin as she sat down beside Mother on the sofa.

"Mary, will you sing with me?"

"Oh, Andrew. I haven't sung in years."

"Please? I remember you used to sing beautifully."

Mary felt her cheeks burn, but she shook her head. "Well, thank you, but I'm afraid you'll have to make do without me tonight."

Andrew frowned, his eyebrows creasing.

Had she disappointed him? He knew she didn't sing anymore.

"What about that duet you said I could hear?" she asked.

His eyes lit up. "Mother, would you and Sarah care to sing?"

Sarah and Aunt Catherine readily agreed and stood beside the piano and began to sing along with the music. Neither of them were particularly good singers, but when Mary saw Andrew cringe, it was worth suffering the sound.

"That was beautiful," Mary said as they finished. "I have no idea why you were complaining about them singing the entire ride here, Andrew. They're wonderful singers."

Aunt Catherine's mouth opened as she grinned. "You were complaining about our singing? And there we were, trying to make the ride more pleasant."

"I thought it was wonderful, dear," Uncle Isaac said.

Aunt Catherine sat next to him by the fire. "Thank you, Isaac."

As Sarah and Catherine began talking about Jeffry and the dinner party, Andrew began playing another tune on the piano. Mary turned to her mother.

"Are you all right with it all?" she asked. "There's a lot happening so fast."

She patted her hand. "I'm fine, Mary. Truly."

"Do you want me to meet with Jeffry?" she asked in a whisper, shooting a glance at her aunt and cousin. "As a potential husband?"

"Only if that's what you want. I know you have never cared for him."

Mary gave her mother a small smile, and the music stopped. They turned to Andrew, who was staring at Mary. His face was passive, and she wondered what could be on his mind. He wasn't near enough to have heard her conversation with her mother, but the way he was looking at her felt as though he had.

No, she didn't want to meet with Jeffry. She had her eye on someone else.

"Andrew, why don't you play something more upbeat?" Sarah suggested.

Andrew glanced at his sister, then shook his head. "I'm afraid I'm done playing for now."

"Oh, come on!" Sarah begged. "Mary, tell him to play something we can dance to."

His eyes met Mary's again, like he was asking what she wanted.

"You'll have to convince him yourself, Sarah. I'm about to go for my evening stroll around the garden."

"A stroll? At this time of night?" Uncle Isaac asked, glancing toward the window where the sun was already setting. "That's not safe for a lady."

"It is perfectly safe, Isaac. The servants keep an eye out for her."

Uncle Isaac raised his eyebrows but didn't respond.

"I can walk with her," Andrew suggested. "If you don't mind, that is. Then you can enjoy your walk, and Father's mind will be at ease."

"I suppose it would be all right," Mary said. "I would enjoy the company."

"Splendid."

"But who will play for us?" Sarah asked.

"Hush, now, Sarah. Let your brother be. Why don't you give it a go? You're getting better."

Andrew stood, and Mary took his outstretched arm. As they started down the hall, she heard several clunky keys on the piano, telling her Sarah had sat down on the bench and, indeed, had improved. She didn't envy her mother, trapped in the parlor with them.

"She really is dreadful," Andrew said. "But I suppose she tries."

"She's better than she was last year. My ears would have burst if Aunt Catherine hadn't stopped her when she did."

Andrew laughed as a servant opened the door to let them outside. Andrew nodded in thanks and ushered Mary down the stairs and into the garden.

"Thank you for telling your mother to stay out of my affairs."

He glanced at her as they started walking down the path. "Of course. Though, I do admit, it was partially for selfish reasons. I don't like the thought of you with another man."

Mary's heart leaped at his words. So she hadn't been wrong in thinking he might be interested in courting her.

"When Father first told us of Uncle Joseph's passing, my heart broke for you, Mary. I wanted to come to his funeral, but Mother was out of town and couldn't get home and Father insisted I stay and look after the estate."

"I understand," she said.

His eyes looked sad, darker than usual. "Still, I hate that I wasn't here for you. All I could think of was coming here, to Kline Manor, to make sure you were all right."

"I am as well as a woman can be after losing her father."

He stopped walking and turned to her as he sat on a bench, holding her hands in his as she sank down beside him. "Which is why I wanted to be here with you. When Father told me we were to move here, I'm almost ashamed to admit, I was glad."

"Glad?"

"Because it meant I'd get to be with you, even if only for a while."

Mary eyed him for sincerity. Everything he was saying was so kind and genuine, so unlike the sneaky boy who loved to joke around with her. There was a softness in his eyes telling her he was being sincere, and she didn't want to admit how much she liked this side of him.

"So, naturally, I'm not ready for you to marry someone else and move away. In fact, I can hardly bear the thought of it."

Her heart ached at the sadness in his voice.

She and Mother had never discussed the possibility of marriage with Andrew, but it seemed as though the thought had crossed his mind. It had certainly crossed hers. Andrew wasn't related to her by blood, and though she had only seen him once or twice a year, she was closer to him than she was Sarah.

They often wrote to one another during the year, where they would tell of all the adventures they were having, and all the trouble Andrew was getting into. She never wrote to Sarah. She wondered if their closeness was what had led to this moment.

He brushed a loose curl behind her ear, and her heart raced. She had never been touched so gently by a man. Goosebumps pebbled over her shoulders and arms, and she felt the sudden urge to lean into his touch.

The sudden idea that she was behaving inappropriately hit her, and she looked away from his hazel eyes.

"Have I upset you?" he asked.

"No. You have been very kind," she told him, blinking away tears.

He watched her for a moment. "Would you like to walk some more?"

Mary nodded. "I think I would if you don't mind. I rely on these evening walks to clear my head. And right now, my thoughts are dizzying."

"Then you must take my arm and let me lead you."

He stood and extended his arm. Mary gladly took it and leaned her head against his bicep, which was harder than she thought it would have been.

"Andrew?" she whispered into the night.

"Yes, Mary?"

"Thank you for your kindness. I am glad of your company."

Though she was unsure of what aspect he would be in her life, whether a cousin, a friend, or a husband, she knew she cared deeply for Andrew, and his kindness had been unexpectedly appreciated. She was glad he was there with her, even if his presence was making her heart and mind race.

Chapter Three

 OR THE THIRD TIME THAT week, Mary found her mother sitting at the writing desk in the library, pouring over a letter by candlelight. Mary pulled the curtains back, and the brilliant sunlight lit up the room, casting its rays over the woman in black.

"Is there anything I can get you, Mother?" Mary asked.

She glanced at her daughter, eyes red and swollen. "No, dear, nothing."

Mary narrowed her eyes at her.

"Oh, stop making a fuss. I assure you, I'm all right. It should be I asking about you." She dipped her quill in the ink and began writing again.

"I'm all right. Why do you ask?"

"You were out longer than usual on your walk last night, and I didn't get a chance to ask how it went."

Mary felt her cheeks burn. "It was pleasant."

Her mother eyed her. "Andrew was a gentleman?"

"Very much so."

Still, her mother stared at her as if expecting her to say more or something out of the ordinary. But after their talk, Andrew led her around the garden, talking of his plans at his father's company.

"I wondered, the way he was looking at you and had so quickly volunteered to accompany you on your walk, if perhaps he had ulterior motives."

Mary turned back to the window and looked out. Her mother knew more than she had thought. She wondered if everyone else had picked up on Andrew's change in demeanor. Andrew had all but admitted he had feelings for her.

"I admit, I, too, question his motives. I think, perhaps, he sees me as more than a friend, though I daresay I hate to assume anything."

"Yes. I was afraid of that."

"Afraid?" Mary wheeled around.

Her mother dipped her quill into the ink and began scribbling on the parchment once again. "Andrew is a lovely boy, Mary, but I'm not sure I could see you happy with him."

"Oh." Mary had thought about the prospect of marrying Andrew more than she cared to admit. He was kind and always made her laugh. She had no doubt Andrew would make her happy, so why did her mother? "Why do you say that?"

Her mother sighed and dipped her quill again. "Please don't think me awful. Andrew truly is a sweet boy, but you need someone more mature."

"Andrew is mature."

"That's enough, dear."

Mary narrowed her eyes. She didn't like the way her mother was speaking about Andrew. He was a great man, and yes, he liked to have a laugh, but it was part of his charm. Who would want to be with someone who was serious all the time?

"But I think if you gave him a chance, you would see—"

"Enough!"

Mary drew back at her mother's outburst. She hadn't shouted

at her since she was a girl, and that was for sneaking a frog into her mother's washroom.

She couldn't wrap her mind around why her mother would shout at her for wanting to have an input on whether Andrew would make a good husband for her.

But the hard look in her eye told Mary now wasn't the time. If she tried to reason with her when her mother was this angry, she'd never listen.

It would have to wait until later.

"I was just going to breakfast. Do you care to join me?"

"In a moment. I want to get this letter sent to your cousin with the morning post."

"My cousin?"

She walked toward her mother to try to see who she was writing, but her mother set the quill down and folded the letter. On the front, she addressed it to a Mr. William Connell.

"There. Annie?" She turned to the maid waiting by the door. "Could you ensure this is sent today?"

Annie accepted the letter from Mother's outstretched hand. "Of course, ma'am."

"Now, I shall accompany you to breakfast."

She stood and gave her daughter a strained smile.

"I do not believe I've met this Mister Connell," Mary said, following her mother from the library.

"You haven't, but with any hope, you will at the dinner party on Saturday. I've invited him and his family. I've not seen my cousins in some many years. His father married my cousin Eliza about ten years ago after his first wife, William's mother, perished."

"That's dreadful!" Mary said as they entered the dining hall.

"Indeed, but it worked in Eliza's favor. Your father and I went to the wedding. It was a beautiful ceremony, and William was such a handsome boy with a promising future."

Mary frowned as she took her seat. "You don't intend him to meet me as a prospective wife, do you?"

Her mother gently laid her hand on Mary's and sighed. "He really was a good boy, and he comes from a wealthy family. He would take such good care of you."

Mary opened her mouth to tell her that Andrew would take care of her, but Aunt Catherine and Uncle Isaac chose that moment to enter the dining room, followed closely by Andrew. She couldn't very well admit she wanted to marry him to his face.

"Breakfast looks lovely!" Catherine exclaimed as the servants set the table.

"Andrew, did you check on your sister?" Uncle Isaac asked.

"Yes, Father. She told me to get out of her room and let her sleep."

Isaac sighed. "She's going to keep some man on his toes."

Aunt Catherine laughed. "She's a free spirit, that one. Although I believe she'll grow up when she is married. If only a little."

Andrew looked at Mary, who felt her face flush.

"How did you sleep, Mary?"

"Quite well, thank you. And you?"

"Oh, very well."

Mother glanced at Andrew, then at Aunt Catherine. "Catherine, I hope you don't mind, but I invited William Connell and his family to the dinner party. The last I heard, he was looking for a wife."

Mary glanced at Andrew to see his eyes flicker from Mary to her mother before staring down at her plate, focusing on breakfast and avoiding his gaze. She felt embarrassed and hurt that her mother had taken the matter into her own hands instead of honoring what she had said about wanting Mary to be happy with her husband.

"Oh, how wonderful. The more the merrier."

"Well, perhaps you should draw the line at twelve, seeing as that's how many dining chairs we have?"

"Of course, darling," Aunt Catherine said.

Andrew sighed out a deep breath but didn't say anything. Mary chanced another glance at him and saw his face was hard, his eyes downcast.

He had suggested letting Mary and her mother choose her husband as an excuse as to why Mary shouldn't be with Jeffry. Now, however, with her mother extending the invitation to a potential suitor, Andrew didn't have an excuse. He had expressed to Mary that he didn't like the thought of her with another man, but she hadn't reciprocated his feelings. Perhaps he thought she was open to the idea of meeting William.

Her stomach churned. Had her mother mentioned William in front of Andrew on purpose? The way she was studying him suggested she had wanted to see his reaction.

Anger boiled in her chest at the thought. Surely her mother wasn't so cold?

"Excuse me, everyone," Andrew said, pushing back his chair. "I just remembered I haven't mailed out the paperwork Father gave me yesterday."

"Andrew...." Mary reached out, but he held his arm away.

He gave her a small, sad smile, then left the room.

Mary frowned at her mother before tossing down her napkin and following him from the room.

"Andrew!" she called to him halfway up the stairs.

He paused and turned toward her. She made her way up the stairs to stand beside him.

"I didn't know she was inviting him," Mary said softly.

He studied her with tear-filled eyes, and her heart ached. She'd never seen Andrew look so heartbroken.

"Please don't be upset."

His fingers brushed her hand. "I'm not upset with you, Mary."

"Just at the idea of me getting married?" she tried to smile and joke.

"The idea of you marrying someone who isn't me."

Her lip trembled as her breath hitched. That was an admission if she ever heard one. If she told him how she felt, they could talk with her mother and make her see it was what they wanted.

"Andrew, I—"

"Mary!" She jumped when she heard her mother from the foot of the stairs, staring up at the two. "Can I speak with you for a moment?"

Mary swallowed, wondering how long her mother had been standing there. "Uh...." She eyed Andrew. "Can we talk later?"

"Absolutely."

Mary reluctantly walked downstairs and glanced up to see Andrew was now walking toward his bedroom, watching them as he went.

"Everything all right?" her mother asked.

Mary narrowed her eyes. "I'm not sure. Andrew's quite upset. As am I."

Her mother pursed her lips. "I'm truly sorry for upsetting him, dear, but I really do believe William is a better match for you."

"For me, Mother, or for you?"

"For us, yes. Do you think I want you to get married and rush off with the first boy you meet? You need a good man with a great deal of money to make sure you have a good future. William is a good man and has more than enough to ensure your family will be taken care of."

"Andrew has money and a respectable job. He would take care of me and any children we have."

"Andrew is not an option, Mary."

Before she could respond, her mother turned on her heel and walked off. Mary sighed, feeling incredibly foolish.

She looked up the stairs, debating on finding Andrew and talking to him, but she couldn't bring herself to do it. Andrew wasn't an option? Mary couldn't wrap her mind around her mother's reasoning.

Whatever it was, she would find out, and she would make her understand it was what she wanted.

She walked to the library to read to take her mind off everything. She had just opened her book when she heard shouting from the hallway.

"Someone took my favorite clip!"

Mary set her book down and walked to the hall where she saw Sarah and Uncle Isaac.

"I want them found!"

"Now, darling, are you sure you didn't misplace it?"

Sarah glared at her father. "It was on my vanity when I went to bed, but this morning, the room had been tidied, and my clip was nowhere to be found."

Several servants and the rest of the family had gathered in the hall to see what the fuss was. Mary's heart sank when Isaac raised his hand to Samuel.

"You, sir. Do you know who cleaned my daughter's room this morning?"

Samuel glanced at Mother, who looked pale and worried, but nodded.

"Yes, sir. Miss Taylor cleans the girls' rooms."

"Right." He turned until his eyes landed on Mother. "Who is Miss Taylor?" he asked.

Mother cleared her throat and raised her hand to gesture behind him as Ruth stepped forward.

"Me, sir, but I assure you, I didn't touch her vanity. I merely tidied the floor and gathered her clothes for washing. When she woke, I helped her dress, then I left."

He stared at Ruth as if waiting for her to give something away.

"I don't believe it. She had to have taken it! Where else could it have gone?"

"It does look bad for you, Miss Taylor."

"Uncle Isaac, Ruth has never given me reason to believe she is the type to steal. She has been in and out of my room for years and nothing has gone missing."

He stared at her for a moment.

"What else could have happened to it?" Sarah demanded.

"If you allow me to help you search your room, perhaps we'll find it," Mary said. "It may have fallen behind the vanity. Or perhaps you tucked it in a drawer and forgot."

"I wouldn't have!" Sarah said.

"You would!" Andrew told her, from the top of the stairs. "You and Mary should search the bedroom before accusing someone of stealing. It's her reputation on the line, Sarah."

She glared at him. "But Father...."

He held up his hand. "He makes a fair point. Check your room again, and if you still don't find it, we'll go from there."

Sarah sighed, then turned on her heel and marched up the stairs.

Andrew smiled at Mary as she started to follow.

"Thank you," she told him as she passed.

"You're welcome. And good luck." He shot a glance toward Sarah, waiting by her bedroom door.

"I cannot believe Father didn't believe me!" Sarah said as she stomped into her room and sank onto her bed.

"Ruth truly is a kind person, Sarah. I think perhaps you are mistaken about what happened to your hair clip."

Mary walked to the vanity and rifled around the mess. There

were perfumes, broches, makeup, hairbrushes, and many hair clips.

"You have so many. What does your missing one look like?"

"It's silver with an emerald flower in the center."

Mary sorted through them, organizing the vanity and lining them up, and sure enough, at the bottom of the pile was a silver clip with an emerald flower.

"Is this it?" Mary asked, walking over to her cousin, who perked up from where she sat.

"Where did you find it?" she asked, mouth open with shock.

"It was on the vanity."

Sarah shook her head. "It wasn't. The maid must have sneaked in here and put it back when she knew I knew it was gone."

"How could she have done? She was downstairs cleaning the parlor when you began shouting. You would have seen her sneak by you and into your room."

Sarah shrugged. "I don't know how she did it, but she did. It wasn't there a moment ago."

Mary shook her head. "We should go tell your father we found it."

Sarah pinned a feather to her head with the clip, then turned to admire her reflection. "What do you think? Feather or no feather?"

Mary sighed and walked out of the bedroom without answering her. She loved her cousin dearly, but sometimes she wondered about her priorities. Mary adored Ruth, and Sarah had nearly gotten her dismissed from her position on her first morning in the house.

Her mother was waiting by the stairs, eyes wide with worry. "Did you find it?"

"Yes. It was on the vanity, under a pile of clips. She hadn't looked," Mary whispered the last sentence, not wanting to be caught speaking ill of her cousin.

Mother nodded. "I'll go and inform Isaac. Could you go and speak with Ruth? She's around back, distraught with worry."

Mary nodded, her brown curls bouncing. "Of course."

She found Ruth near the stables, sobbing into a handkerchief. Henry stood by her, rubbing her back. When she saw Mary, she stood quickly.

"Don't cry, Ruth. It was a misunderstanding."

"You found it?"

"I did. Sarah didn't look well enough. I knew you wouldn't do something like that."

"I need my job, Miss. Henry and I are having a baby. I can't afford to be out of work."

"You won't be. I assure you, I won't allow it."

Ruth started sobbing again and Henry pulled her against his chest.

Mary gave him a small smile. "Congratulations to you both. You'll make excellent parents."

She walked back into the house, wondering what she was going to do about her own life. Soon, she would be expected to marry and have a child. She might not be a good mother. She quite enjoyed her time alone, and a husband and child would ensure she'd never get it again.

Still, perhaps it wasn't about never being alone again. She looked up at Andrew's bedroom window. Perhaps if she married the right man, she wouldn't crave solitude quite so often.

Chapter Four

AFTER DINNER, ANDREW ONCE AGAIN insisted on joining Mary for her evening stroll. She didn't argue as he extended his arm. It was quite welcoming, in fact. She glanced at her mother, who gave her a stern, warning look before he led her through the door.

Mother might not have approved of Andrew, but Mary cared for him deeply. She was still eager to speak with him and hopeful that she could change her mother's mind.

Mary knew Andrew's mind was busy. He had avoided her eyes at mealtimes and found something to occupy his time after. Was he truly so upset by her mother inviting William to dinner?

He had expressed an interest in her. He'd told her he didn't like the idea of her with another man. Any man who wasn't him. Did he truly mean it? Was he prepared to step up and marry her?

Mary started to question everything that had happened. Had it all been in her mind? Was she projecting because she was having feelings for him? What if he didn't mean it the way it sounded?

But what other way could he have meant it?

She wanted to speak with him, to clear the air, but she

didn't know how to broach the subject. She didn't like the quiet Andrew who didn't laugh and joke with her. The Andrew who made being around Sarah bearable.

As they walked around the garden, past the rose bushes, Andrew finally spoke.

"Saturday will be dreadful for me, I should think."

Mary frowned. "Dreadful is a strong word."

"I have strong feelings." His eyes flitted over her face, and he grabbed her hands to pull her to a stop. "I truly can't stand the idea of you with another man, laughing or dancing, but if it's what you want, I'll remain silent and leave you to enjoy your night."

Mary studied him for a moment, her heart racing. His hazel eyes were soft but hurt. She'd never seen him so torn.

"Andrew...."

"Yes?"

Mary stared at him, at a loss of how to ask him about his feelings or tell him of her own. If he admitted that he loved her and wanted to be her husband, how could she make her mother see that Andrew would be good for her? She deliberately told Mary Andrew wasn't good for her and invited William to dinner. If Mary had a chance to sit and speak with her mother and be honest about how she felt, would she listen?

"I don't want to be with another man," she said softly.

He broke into a grin, studying her. "Do you mean, and I'm sorry if I'm overstepping, but you could see yourself with me?"

Mary nodded, biting her lip.

She could see herself happy, married to Andrew. He had always been so kind, so funny, and so sweet. He'd been working with his father since he was seventeen, and as their son, even if not biologically, he would inherit all their estate.

Their happiness wasn't an issue. Money wasn't an issue. So why was her mother so against it? Especially when Mary wanted it?

When she looked into his eyes, she saw a hint of some-thing she quite loved. He was hopeful and joyful, two things she'd always wanted in a husband. And when he looked at her, there was something in his eyes, something that made her heart race.

He was a good match, but convincing her mother might prove difficult.

If Mother didn't approve of the union, it wouldn't happen. Would it do any good to tell Andrew how she felt and encourage him if her mother would never allow them to marry?

"Then I should go ask for your hand right now before Mister Connell arrives expecting to meet you."

Her head hung. "I'm afraid it isn't that simple."

He lifted her chin so her eyes met his, narrowed with concern. "What do you mean?"

"Mother seems to think we aren't a good match, and every time I try to convince her, she becomes angry."

His face fell, and he sighed. He placed her hand over his arm once more and started walking again.

"Then I can try. I'll ask to speak with her, and I'll make her see reason. I'll go to my mother and tell her how much I love you and want you as my wife and that my feelings are reciprocated." He eyed her. "They are reciprocated, are they not?"

Mary swallowed, terrified of allowing him to see her com-pletely vulnerable. "I have loved you for years, Andrew."

He wrapped his arms around her, hugging her and laughing. Mary laughed, his joy contagious.

But as he released her, reality set in. It didn't matter if they loved one another unless they could convince her mother to allow their union.

Andrew didn't seem to see that as a problem. "We will talk to our parents. We'll make your mother see."

Mary recalled the look on her mother's face as she yelled at

Mary to leave it be. She wasn't so sure they would be able to convince her.

⊷⊙⊷ ⊙⊶

EVERY TIME MARY TRIED TO BROACH THE conversation with her mother about reconsidering Andrew as a husband, her mother grew angry. After the third try and the tenth time asking why, Mother told Mary not to ask again.

Andrew had suggested he speak with her, but Mary was terrified she'd say no, and they'd never get another chance. She was hoping she could convince her mother so when Andrew did ask for her hand, Mother wouldn't tell him no.

But word from William Connell and his family arrived, saying they would love to attend dinner on Saturday. Mother, of course, was over the moon, so sure she had found Mary's husband. Mary, on the other hand, was mortified.

"I'm not interested in meeting any other suiter," Mary told her. "I won't meet him. I'll stay in my room."

"Come now, Mary. You aren't a child. Stop behaving as though you are."

Mary crossed her arms over her bodice, feeling defiant and ready to ruin her mother's plans.

Her mother sighed. "Meet him. If he is terrible, I'll stop pushing him on you."

Mary thought for a moment. "And you will allow me to make my own decision?"

Her mother rolled her eyes as she walked away. Mary couldn't help but fixate on the fact that her mother didn't answer. Would she ever allow her to marry Andrew?

Thoughts swam in her mind, unsettling her stomach, of what Mr. Connell would be like. She wondered if he was kind or strict, handsome or dainty. Looks weren't the most important feature a man could have, but they made up for other shortcomings.

She hoped he was ugly and cold and her mother would hate him.

She glanced at Andrew across the dinner table. He was kind and handsome. He was everything she wanted in a husband.

Why couldn't her mother see what Mary saw?

Andrew insisted on walking with her every night. Once Mary expressed that, yet again, her mother refused to listen, they talked about happier topics, steering clear of speaking about their feelings. He hadn't mentioned anything about Mr. Connell again, but whenever Aunt Catherine and Mother talked about the dinner party, Mary saw him tense.

She wondered how he would react if her mother insisted she marry William. Would she lose her best friend?

She tried not to think too much about it. There was a chance William would be like Jeffry, and Mary wouldn't be forced to marry him.

Still, she knew her mother was eager for Mr. Connell's arrival. If Mary wasn't interested in William, would her mother still encourage their union? Did Mother's sudden interest in marrying her off to someone who lived hours away have anything to do with Uncle Isaac and Aunt Catherine inheriting the house? Perhaps Mother felt like a stranger in her own home, just as Mary did.

Would marriage give them the feeling of home again? Would becoming the lady of a house make her feel as if she belonged?

Andrew would provide them a home away from Kline Manor. He would make it everything Mary wanted, she was sure of it.

She imagined herself married to the invisible William, living in a house that wasn't hers. Would she ever learn to be happy with someone else?

After dinner, they retired to the parlor, and Andrew once again sat at the piano. He gave Mary a small smile before playing a slow, romantic tune.

"What an interesting choice of song," Aunt Catherine said.

Mary's cheeks burned as she felt Aunt Catherine's eyes on her. If Mary had to guess, she'd say Andrew had intentionally picked that song. Perhaps he wanted to show everyone how he felt about Mary.

"Again with the slow songs when there is no one to dance with," Sarah said.

"Well, I think it's lovely," Mother said. "I danced to this song with Joseph at a wedding last year before he took ill."

Mary stared at her mother, seeing tears glisten in her eyes. She hadn't thought about the many memories with her husband she would have, from parties to weddings to funerals. How much everything must remind her of him. If music could make her cry at the memory of her husband, what must living in this house do to her?

No wonder she was ready for Mary to find a husband. If she was to get married, Mother could go with her and get away from all of this.

It was time to move on. Her mother had taken care of her for twenty years. It was time she stepped up to take care of her mother now.

Was the reason Mother so against Mary being with Andrew because she could never break free of Father's memory? If Andrew was Mary's husband, Mother would always be around Kline Manor and Uncle Isaac's warm brown eyes, which were the exact same as Father's.

Andrew was sweet and funny, and as much as Mary loved talking to him and being near him, her mother was against it. If she married him, he'd be a reminder of her mother's loss.

Not being with Andrew broke her heart. How could she be with another man, with this Mr. Connell her mother was pushing on her, if her heart lay with another?

After the song was through, Andrew stood and walked over to sit in the chair near where Mary sat.

"Now your turn, Sarah," Uncle Isaac said, smiling at her.

Sarah obediently stood and walked over to the grand piano. The keys groaned with displeasure as she struck the wrong chords.

"Do you want to go for a walk?" Andrew asked Mary in a whisper.

Mary took a deep breath before nodding.

Andrew led her from the room, and when Mary turned to glance at her mother, she saw Aunt Catherine smiling and whispering to Mother, who stared with pursed lips at the two of them.

The night was cool for June. Mary could hear the insects chirping, even though it was still a little early for them to be out.

Andrew held her close to him as they walked. For the first time, Mary inhaled his woody scent and realized how much she would miss it if she were to marry someone else. Andrew smelled of nature, the thing she loved most.

Mary once again considered a future with him as her husband and felt a rush of joy. She could see them taking evening strolls after supper every day. Andrew could play the piano and Mary could gush to their guests about how talented her handsome husband was.

He would make her smile every day. She had no doubt about that.

But would her mother be happy? Would she even allow it? Mary considered begging and pleading for her mother to see reason.

They could still move away. She didn't doubt if she asked, Andrew would move them anywhere she wanted, and they wouldn't have to see Aunt Catherine and Uncle Isaac often. Mary could make sure of it. And when they did come to visit, Mother could go visit with friends. They could make it work. Mother would have to see.

"Tomorrow is the dinner party," Andrew said.

"Yes, it is."

"Are you nervous?"

She looked up at him, her heart racing. "No."

He gave her a questioning look. "Good. William will love you."

"I don't want William to love me. I want him to be mean and think I'm ugly and would make a terrible wife."

"Nobody could ever think you ugly. You are more beautiful than anyone I've ever seen. It will be love at first sight for him, no doubt."

Mary's cheeks burned at his words. He'd never called her beautiful before. He'd never acknowledged her appearance before now.

As much as she wanted William to hate her, she knew there was a chance he wouldn't. What if he asked to see her again? Mother had already told her what she thought about her future, and Mary couldn't go against what her mother wanted. It was a daughter's place to do as she was told.

Mary had to at least meet with William, even if her heart was telling her she would be happier with Andrew.

She only hoped her mother would come around and honor what Mary wanted.

"Thank you for being such a good friend, Andrew."

She felt his arm stiffen in hers, but his voice was soft. "I will always be here for you, Mary. Even if we can never be together."

Mary's heart broke as he walked her back into the house, and they parted ways. There was no doubt that he *would* always be there for her, even if she was forced to marry someone else.

Chapter Five

SATURDAY EVENING ARRIVED, AND MARY'S hands shook as she stood beside her mother, awaiting William's arrival, hoping that he had changed his mind and wouldn't arrive at all. They were gathered in the parlor, waiting for supper to be served. William was officially too late to be polite. He wasn't off to a good start in Mary's book. No doubt, Mother would want Mary to have a husband who was on time for events. A man who kept his word and arrived when he said he would.

Jeffry was there with his parents. He stood near the grand piano, talking to Sarah as Andrew softly played a slow melody. He looked thrilled at the prospect of having a captivated audience, and Mary was thrilled she wasn't required to be it.

Sarah looked glad for the attention he was giving her, and though Mary couldn't see how anyone could be happy to be talking with Jeffry, she was glad Sarah seemed happy.

Andrew glanced at Mary, his eyes soft with concern. Was he thinking what Mary was thinking? William had changed his mind about coming.

She gave him a small smile, wanting to remind him she was happy with him. William not coming would be the best outcome.

If he never arrived after promising to attend, Mother would see it as rude. Perhaps then she might see how much better Andrew was for Mary.

"I'm sure he will be here any moment," Mother said, squeezing her daughter's hand.

Mary didn't reply. She didn't trust her voice. Her stomach was in knots. If he never came, would her mother insist on their trying again?

Still, there was a chance that he would arrive late. While it wouldn't be the best first impression, it might not be enough to deter her mother from wanting them to be married.

Andrew began playing another song, more upbeat, per his father's request for Sarah, and the doorman came in to announce Mr. William Connell.

He was taller than Mary expected, with curly brown hair, chestnut eyes, and a kind smile. His clothes were untidy, with smudges of dirt on his trousers.

He bowed his head as Mother stepped forward, eyeing the mud.

"Mister Connell," Mother started. "How lovely to see you again. This is my daughter, Mary."

"It's nice to meet you." Under different circumstances, Mary might have meant it.

"It's an honor to meet you. I apologize for my tardiness and my unkempt appearance." His eyes flickered to Mary, and a small smile played on his soft, full lips. "I assure you I had every intention to be early, and I changed my clothes twice trying to find what would best impress you both. However, on my way here, my horse threw a shoe, and I had to fix it before I could continue."

That was an interesting excuse. One Mary had never heard before.

His eyes scanned the room, lingering for a moment at the

piano, where Andrew was still sitting, watching them. Mary offered him a small smile before turning back to her guest.

Mother's eyes widened. "Oh, heavens! How unfortunate. Where was your coachman? Could he not have shoed the horse?"

Mr. Connell's eyes flickered back to Mary's. "No, ma'am. I rode the horse. I didn't bring my carriage."

"Oh. Well, then." She gave him a smile. "I'm glad you are here. Tardiness can be overlooked when there is a reason. As for your clothes, Mary can show you where the washroom is." She turned to her daughter.

"Of course. Right this way."

Before she left, she caught Andrew's eye, giving him what she hoped was an apologetic look. He gave her a sad smile, and the tune slowed.

Mary led Mr. Connell down the hall.

"The washroom is right through there," she said, indicating the door in front of them.

"Thank you, Miss Kline. It's lovely to meet you."

"The pleasure is mine, Mister Connell. I'm glad you could join us tonight." Although she wasn't.

"As am I."

She politely waited for him to go inside and close the door, but he remained where he was, staring at her.

"I truly am sorry I was so late. And for the way I look. My mother suggested I take the carriage. I should have listened."

"After hearing your reason, your tardiness can be overlooked," Mary admitted, hating that he had been so determined to arrive. "I find it extremely fascinating that you can shoe a horse."

"Well, I suppose it worked in my favor, then."

Mary didn't want to admit it, but she liked his deep voice and soft smile. In another world where Andrew wasn't there, she might have admitted she found him attractive.

"I'll only be a moment," he told her, finally stepping into the washroom.

Mary stood back and waited. Thus far, he seemed charming, which was a pity because she was hoping her mother would hate him. If her mother liked him, she'd insist on a second meeting, then perhaps a third.

She felt guilty for thinking Mr. Connell was handsome and charming. She may not be Andrew's, but her heart was.

If only her mother could see that.

He stepped out of the washroom, his hands now clean, his pants as clean as he could get them, and slightly wet.

"What do you think?" he asked, holding out his arms so she could get a good look.

"You look lovely." He grinned widely, and her cheeks burned. "I mean, you seem to have gotten everything."

"Thank you, Miss Kline."

"Mary. Just Mary."

She'd always hated formalities.

"Well, then, Mary. I think it's only fitting if you call me William. Or Will."

"Is that what your friends call you?"

He took a step closer to her. "Yes. All, both of them."

Mary covered her mouth, stifling her laugh.

"What's so funny about that?"

"You only have two friends?"

"Yes, so? I was hoping after tonight I would have three." He stared at her, his eyes burning through to her, and took her hand. "What do you think, Mary? Could we be friends?"

Friends was all she wanted to be.

"I would be glad to be your friend, Will."

"Even if I admitted that I was playing and I have dozens of friends?"

"Well, now, I won't tolerate lying, but having dozens of friends isn't such a bad thing."

His eyes flickered to her lips, making her heart race. She had never been kissed before, but the way William was looking at her made it clear he was tempted. Any other woman would love his attention and lustful gaze. He was handsome and charming, and that should be enough for her to consider him.

But it wasn't.

A throat cleared behind her. She turned to find Andrew scowling in the corridor.

"Andrew," she said breathily.

"Forgive me. I don't mean to interrupt."

Mary became aware that Will was still holding her hand, and she quickly pulled it away to smooth her dress. Her heart and mind raced. What must Andrew be thinking? Why had he chosen that moment to appear?

"You haven't." She tried to sound happy, not guilty. "Will and I were just talking."

Andrew's jaw clenched as he stared at William. "Still, I feel my intrusion is most unwelcomed."

"Your presence is never unwelcome," Mary said, her eyes burning. "Will, this is my dearest cousin, Andrew."

She wished she could reassure him that her heart still belonged to him—would always belong to him.

"It's a pleasure to meet you, Andrew," he said, lips turned up in a smirk.

"And you." They shook hands, then Andrew stepped back.

"I admit, I've heard a great deal about you. Your family seems to be my father's rival in Boston. Perhaps we could find time to talk and set up a solution so we can stop stealing property out from under one another."

Andrew raised an eyebrow. "Perhaps."

William leaned back on the balls of his feet. "The way I hear it, you seem to be the one who does most of the talking, making the deals."

"I'm good at my job, Mister Connell. Would you not do the same if given the chance?"

Tongue in cheek, William let out a "Huh," before giving one shake of his head. "So you don't think we can come to some kind of arrangement?"

Andrew eyed Mary. "I think now isn't the time to talk business. It's time for supper. Everyone is waiting in the dining room."

"Quite right. Perhaps later, then. Before I leave?"

Andrew didn't answer, but averted his eyes to the floor, turned on his heel, and briskly walked away.

"He seems... interesting," William said, staring after him.

Mary sighed, trying so desperately to hide how much that interaction had upset her. "He is. He's quite lovely, in fact. He has a wonderful sense of humor."

"I'll take your word for it. Perhaps I'll get to see it one day."

Mary led him to the dining room, noticing how good he smelled. It wasn't a gentle woody smell like Andrew but still quite lovely. He had really gone to the trouble of wanting to impress them. Her chest tightened as she realized he was there to court her, and not because his mother had made him.

"Ah! There you are!" Mother said as they entered the dining room.

Mary took note that Andrew was sitting on the opposite end of the table where she and Will would be sitting. She caught his eye and frowned, trying to express her discontent. Further to her displeasure, she was straight across from Sarah and Jeffry. Since William's parents weren't there, there were two empty seats.

After the first course arrived, the group began a lively discussion that Mary didn't quite pay attention to. She didn't care about Jeffry and his business with his father.

She tried to catch Andrew's eye again, but he adamantly avoided her. He didn't bother with joining in on the conversation, and nobody but Mary seemed to notice. Her stomach tightened as she wondered if he was angry with her. Perhaps she had been wrong, and Andrew wouldn't be there if she married someone else. If he was this angry over William holding her hand, how angry would he be if they got married?

Her stomach twisted at the thought.

"Where are your parents tonight, William?" Mother asked from his other side.

"Yes, we're all dying to know why you arrived on horseback," Aunt Catherine said.

Will wiped his mouth with the napkin and set it down before answering. "Mother insisted on staying with her sister, one town over last night since we were coming to the area. She appreciated the invitation to stay here at Kline Manor, but she so rarely gets to see my aunt that she wanted to stay with her. The plan was to leave there in enough time to arrive here early. But late last night, Mother fell ill."

There were a few gasps around the table, and Mary looked at him with concern.

"I hope she is all right," Mary said.

"What's the matter with her?"

Mary shot Sarah a look telling her to hold her tongue. It wasn't their concern what was the matter with her unless William offered that information.

"She'll be fine. She suffers from headaches. Sometimes they're debilitating. She was trying to come anyway, but I told Father to keep her in bed, and Aunt Celia sent for the doctor. Mother insisted I don't miss the dinner, but I couldn't leave her without a carriage, in case she needed it, so I took a horse and came alone."

"What a shame about your mother, but I'm glad you could still be here," Aunt Catherine said.

William looked at Mary. "As am I."

Not wanting to encourage him, she quickly looked away, staring instead at the fish on her plate.

"What about your mother's sister? Didn't they have a carriage you could borrow?" Jeffry was as abrupt and rude as Sarah.

"Unfortunately not. My uncle is away on business, and my cousin departed yesterday to visit friends down south. My aunt sent their third to call for the doctor."

"Well, I'm glad everything worked out, and you could come," Mother said. "We send our regards to your parents and hope your mother gets better soon."

"Thank you," William told her. "I honestly am glad I didn't miss this."

She looked up and caught Andrew's eye, and her heart sank. Her sweet, funny Andrew. His heart was breaking as much as hers. She could see the hurt etched on his face, but what could she do? She had tried to tell her mother how she felt, but she wouldn't hear it.

If Mother wouldn't see reason, Mary and Andrew both might end up heartbroken.

Chapter Six

DURING THE REST OF DINNER, Mother and Catherine made polite conversation, while Mary listened. By the time they finished dessert, Mary had learned William was the oldest son of five children at twenty-two, and his mother was eager to see him married. His ten-year-old brother, however, wanted him to stay single so he could continue to live at home. He worked with his father in Boston, which would require him to travel for work, unless his future wife wanted to live in the city.

He eyed Mary every few minutes, as if wanting to see her reaction to what he was saying. She had to admit, she was enjoying getting to know him. He was a very likable man. But that was the problem. She didn't want him to be likable. She wanted her mother to wonder why she thought anyone but Andrew would be a good match for Mary.

As Clark set a new dish in front of them, Jeffry curled his lip before turning to Sarah to ignore him. Andrew looked him in the eye and thanked him. William didn't acknowledge they were there.

She couldn't deny this detail alone attracted her more to

Andrew. She always found men like Jeffry disgusting. The men and women who worked for them deserved their respect.

After supper, they retired to the parlor for coffee. Andrew graciously accepted his cup from Ruth, but William, again, pretended she wasn't there. This time, both Jeffry and Sarah made a face of disgust before turning back to one another.

Perhaps they deserved one another. Who else could be married to someone so completely disrespectful than someone just like them?

Aunt Catherine promptly asked Andrew to play a song on the piano. With a sigh and a glance at Mary, he reluctantly sat on the bench and began to play.

"I didn't get a chance to speak with you in the dining room," William said, taking a seat in the chair next to Mary.

"I'm more of an observer at dinner parties than the talker."

"Understood." He set his coffee cup on the table. "So if we were to throw a dinner party, I will have to do most of the talking."

Mary narrowed her eyes. "We? That's a bit presumptuous."

"I'm a confident man."

She took a sip of coffee and looked around the room. Sarah and Jeffry were talking on the sofa. Her mother was speaking quietly with Aunt Catherine, occasionally glancing at Mary and William. Uncle Isaac sat beside his wife, occasionally chiming into their conversation.

Andrew was staring at the music, except when he was staring at Mary. Her heart gave a flutter as their eyes met.

"Mary," Mother said, bringing her attention back to the conversation. "Why don't you show William around the garden? Give Andrew a break from your evening strolls."

Mary's stomach flipped, a feeling of betrayal overwhelming her, but slowly, she nodded.

"All right. Would you like to go for a walk?" she asked him.

"Please. That sounds wonderful."

Mary stood, pressing her shaking hands to her bodice, and glanced at Andrew once more. His jaw clenched, and the music grew louder, but he didn't look her way.

As they were walking out the parlor door, she heard Aunt Catherine tell Andrew to play a little softer. She wondered if he would be all right. She hated that she had to be polite and entertain a man she had no interest in. William seemed perfectly lovely, but she would never see him as anything more than a friend.

"It's a lovely evening," William said as they walked down the front stairs.

The moon was already high in the sky, casting shadows over the ground, and the insects played a soft song.

"It is. This is my favorite time of day," Mary told him. She neglected to mention that it's been even more amazing the past week with Andrew by her side.

"Then I am glad your mother suggested a walk."

"I go on one every day after supper, but I didn't think I would tonight because of the party."

"Then I am *very* glad she suggested it."

Silence fell between them once more. Mary eyed the rose bushes, and her heart ached. This garden was her's and Andrew's.

"Can I ask you something?" she asked.

"Perhaps." He laughed, his deep voice filling the night.

"Do you like flowers?"

"Flowers?" He shoved his hands in his pocket and shook his head. "Not particularly, but I suppose they are lovely in the garden."

Andrew loved flowers. He showed her how to care for them one summer when she was twelve. He'd learned how from a book he found in the staff's quarters and wanted to show his skills. Together, they cut a piece off a rose bush and planted another. She had been so convinced it wouldn't work but was thrilled when it bloomed its first bud.

"Do you like to read?"

"Yes, I quite enjoy reading. For work and pleasure. I mostly read biographies and war novels, but I'm currently reading Shakespeare's Hamlet for the dozenth time."

She looked up at him as they walked. His curly brown hair was gorgeous, his smile warmer than the night air.

"I enjoy Shakespeare."

"As do I. I've read his plays more times than I can count. Perhaps it's childish to reread classics."

"Not at all. It's comforting to read stories you're familiar with."

He eyed her. "Perhaps I can read to you sometime."

So much for hoping he wouldn't want to see her again.

"Can I ask you something, now?" he asked.

Mary looked up at him with soft eyes. "May as well."

"Did you want to meet me, or was it entirely your mother's idea?"

Mary narrowed her eyes and quickly looked away from him. He had somehow seen through the situation. What else did he see? "Honestly, I wasn't thrilled when Mother said she was writing to you. I was nervous and confused. Mother wanted me to meet you. She said we would be a good match. I felt I owed it to her to meet you before I made up my mind about whether Mother was right."

And to convince her she was wrong.

"Oh? And have you? Made up your mind?"

Her heart ached. She'd made up her mind a week ago when Andrew professed his feelings to her. "It's more complicated than that."

"Well, if you ask me, I think we would be a very good match. You are sweet and beautiful and polite and forgave me when I so rudely arrived late."

Her stomach flipped. Andrew had been right. William seemed to like her quite a bit.

"You are prepared to say you want to see me again?"

"Very much so. And you? If I asked to see you again, would you accept?"

She wanted to be honest and tell him that her heart lay with another. She wanted to end this before it started. But her mother would be furious.

"I think that would be fine."

And the more Mother avoided Mary, the more she realized no matter how much she loved Andrew, her mother would never agree to the union.

If she had to marry someone other than Andrew, William seemed a suitable husband.

She wasn't giving up on Andrew yet, though.

As he walked her back inside, Mary couldn't help but think about the implications her choice would have on those she loved most. If things worked out with William, Mother would finally get away from Kline Manor and possibly be happy again. Andrew, however, would be devastated. He cared for her as deeply as she cared for him. They would both be heartbroken.

She only hoped she wouldn't lose her best friend after this.

When they arrived in the parlor, Andrew was no longer playing the piano, but standing by the window, looking out. Mary couldn't help but notice it looked out over the gardens where she and William had been only moments ago. Had he been spying on them, or had he only just arrived?

"Well, look who's back!" Aunt Catherine said as they entered the room.

Andrew whirled around, eyeing Mary. She could tell he had questions, but he dare not ask in front of everyone.

"Did you enjoy your walk?" Mother asked.

"Yes, it's quite a lovely evening," Mary told her, taking a seat on the sofa near the door.

She couldn't help but notice William remained standing.

"It was a wonderful walk. You have a beautiful garden, Mister Kline," he said to Uncle Isaac, who nodded once. "Mary was great company. It was quite nice to have someone to share it with."

"It was my pleasure."

"Well, sit, dear boy. Have some more coffee," Uncle Isaac said. "Or perhaps I can offer you some whiskey?"

"I'm afraid I must be off." He glanced at Mary. "It's getting late, and I promised Mother I would tell her all about the party if she was up for it. She was distraught she had to miss it."

"Of course, of course."

Mary swallowed as she realized Andrew was staring at William, who either didn't seem to notice or was deliberately ignoring him.

"However, if it's all right with you, I'd like to call again tomorrow."

"Well," Mother said with a slight laugh. "I do say that would be wonderful. Don't you agree, Mary?"

Mary saw Andrew's jaw clench before she glanced at William. "That would be just fine."

"Then it's settled. I'll return tomorrow."

"Oh, William," Mother said. "If your mother is feeling better, she is more than welcome to come as well. It would be nice to see my cousin."

"Thank you, Missus Kline. I'll be sure to tell her."

William gave a slight bow to the room, then winked at Mary before taking his leave.

Mary felt stuck, pulled in two different directions. Her mother was on one side, pulling her toward William and away from her past. Andrew was on the other, pulling her toward a future they could create together.

But as Andrew stared at her, she found herself wishing she didn't have to get married at all. She wished more than anything she could be a girl again and play with her cousin in the garden, running and laughing, without thinking of marriage or children or finding a way to convince her mother she was capable of making her own choices.

Where had the time gone? How had they gone from kids chasing one another through the trees to adults who were in love with one another?

As the chatter in the room began again, Andrew took the seat next to Mary.

"Was he a gentleman?" he asked.

Mary studied him for a moment before nodding. "He was very respectable."

"Did you agree to see him again out of politeness? Or do you truly want to see him again?"

Mary stared into his hazel eyes and wished she could have told William the truth. She hated hurting Andrew. She wanted nothing more than a chance to be with him, but she was so worried her mother wouldn't allow it unless she showed her she wasn't interested in William.

"I think... I need to see him again," she said slowly.

"Right," Andrew's tone softened. "Then I hope he is everything you wish him to be."

Without waiting for her to respond, he stood and left the parlor, breaking her heart. He had clearly misunderstood, and without waiting for her to explain, he was leaving, thinking that she was interested in William.

Mary stood to follow him, wanting so desperately to speak with him and make him understand why she wanted to see him again. She wanted him to know that meeting with William was her mother's idea, and she wouldn't give up on that idea until Mary had reason enough not to marry him. She wanted to plead with him not to hate her because she loved him more than anything in this life.

"Mary, come, sit with me a moment," her mother said as she was walking from the room.

Mary looked helplessly at Andrew's retreating back before reluctantly turning back to the parlor.

Her mother wanted her with William. She was doing everything she could to keep Mary and Andrew apart. It seemed no matter how much she loved Andrew, how much she knew he would love her, it wasn't what her mother wanted.

So she sat on the sofa and pretended her heart wasn't completely shattered.

As her mother talked to her about William and their walk, Mary allowed herself to think about her feelings toward him. While she still didn't know him well enough, she didn't doubt that he could become a good friend. He was a respectable man from a prominent family and seemed to have had a good upbringing. He seemed kind, and his confidence was alarmingly charming. He was everything her mother wanted.

But there was one alarming downfall to William, something he had entirely no control over and something Mary was finding extremely difficult to get past.

He wasn't Andrew.

Chapter Seven

THE NEXT MORNING, MOTHER INSISTED Mary wear her pale pink dress because it made her look prettier and more feminine. Mary was sure William wouldn't have cared if she wore pink or blue or yellow, but she didn't argue and wore the dress her mother wanted her to wear.

It was refreshing seeing her mother so lively. It was almost as though she were the woman she was before Father had died.

It made finding a way to push William away that much harder.

As she admired her reflection, she had to admit the pink did look pretty with her pale complexion and dark brown ringlets. Would Andrew think she looked pretty?

She hadn't had a chance the night before to talk to him. After leaving the party, she went to his room, but he didn't answer when she knocked. Then after breakfast, he went to the study to work, so she hadn't had a chance to be alone with him.

She hoped sometime today they could find time to talk.

"You look beautiful."

Mary gasped and turned to see Andrew standing in the doorway. He was dressed in his traveling clothes.

"Are you going somewhere?"

He glanced at the bookshelf and writing table before meeting her eye. "This is your room? It looks just like your personality, but honestly, I was expecting more books."

"These are my favorites," she said softly. "Why are you dressed for travel?"

"I have business to attend in Boston with Father."

Mary narrowed her eyes. It was the first time she had heard of any business awaiting in Boston. Andrew had had plenty of opportunities to tell her, and Uncle Isaac hadn't mentioned anything.

It was very suspicious.

"On Sunday?"

"We want to leave a day early. We're having dinner with one of the men Father wants to do business with."

"Oh." Her heart sank. "We haven't had a chance to speak."

"Perhaps when I get home?"

Mary didn't want to wait. She wanted to tell him why she needed to see William again and reassure him that her heart still belonged to Andrew.

"When will you be home?"

"I'll be gone for a few days, at least."

"Then we must speak now."

Andrew shook his head. "I'm afraid there isn't time. Father is waiting."

There was a sad, lingering silence. Whether they wanted to admit it or not, something between them had changed. Just two days before, they were trying to plan how they could convince Mary's mother to allow their union, but now he was leaving. Because of William.

"Are you cross with me?" Mary asked in a whisper. If she hadn't agreed to see William again, would Andrew be leaving?

Andrew gave her a sad smile. "I could never be cross with you. I'm cross with myself."

"Whatever for?"

He shook his head but didn't answer. "I must be off. I didn't want to leave without saying goodbye."

He'd only been there for a week, but the idea of him leaving for a few days was breaking her heart, especially because he was leaving without knowing the truth.

"All right," she said quietly.

He stared at her for a moment longer. "You really do look so beautiful."

Her heart ached at his kindness. "Thank you, Andrew."

"I'll see you soon," he said, bowing his head.

As soon as he was gone, Mary's chest tightened. For some reason, it felt like a real goodbye. She felt as though she was losing him.

She knew it was conceited of her to think, but she truly wondered if he was leaving because she had agreed to see William again. He had expressed how much it would bother him to see her with another man, so was it so farfetched to believe he was leaving so he wouldn't have to witness it?

But he didn't know the full truth. She wasn't seeing William because she wanted to marry him. She was seeing him again to try to find a reason she couldn't be with him. She needed to prove to Mother she wouldn't be happy married to anyone but Andrew.

She shook the thoughts away. Andrew had work to do in Boston. It might not have anything to do with Mary or whatever feelings he may have toward her seeing William again.

Mary walked to the library, eager to find a distraction, but no sooner had she begun perusing the books, did her mother come in.

"He's here!" she said, grabbing her daughter's hand. "You must be at the door to greet him."

Mary felt sick. Everything felt so wrong.

She wondered if Andrew had time to leave before William arrived or if he had seen the carriage pulling up to the manor.

Mother led her to the front door, and as soon as it opened, her eyes locked with William's. He was just as handsome as he was yesterday, if not more so, dressed in more casual attire. He wore a wine-red coat, so unlike what most men wore, and wasn't wearing an ascot.

Mary looked at the short, red-haired woman next to him, who she could only assume was his mother.

Mother took her hands and greeted her, introducing her to Mary as Mrs. Connell. Mary graciously bid her hello and stepped back to let them inside.

"Where is Mister Connell?" Mother asked, taking her cousin's arm and leading her down the hall and into the parlor.

"I'm afraid he had to return to Boston for work. He's trying to buy a factory off some gentleman and is having dinner with him tonight."

"Don't you work with your father?" Mary asked William.

"Yes, but I told him I had already asked if I could call on you today, and he agreed I should stay behind to see you."

Yet Andrew had left. He couldn't have told his father he wanted to work from home today? Or he had made other arrangements?

She wasn't being fair. He took work more seriously than he took his personal life. Mary only knew him to ever have a few friends. Besides, she couldn't very well have expected Andrew to stay after she'd admitted she wanted William to call on her. How would she have felt if she were in his shoes? She would want to run too.

He let out a soft breath. "I am glad I was able to stay. I was hoping you could show me what you like to do for entertainment. Perhaps I can get to know you some more before I have to return home."

"Before you arrived, I was in the library. That's where I spend most of my time. There or in the garden. Would you like to see?"

"I would love to. Do you think Andrew would have time to chat today? I was hoping we speak business before I left."

"I'm afraid you just missed him. He's on his way to Boston, as well, for work."

She didn't miss William's jaw clench, but the moment he saw her looking at him, his features softened.

"I suppose it will have to wait, then. At least I get to spend the day with you."

She led him down the hall, then another, to the library, feeling his eyes on her more often than not. She kept her gaze ahead, hoping not to encourage him.

"I can see why you like it here," he told her when they stepped inside. He spun around, looking at the dozens of shelves lining the walls. "I see I'll need to expand my library at home if I am to make you content."

Mary's cheeks burned as he spoke of her joining his home. He was awfully forward for a man who had just met her. She hadn't expressed an interest in him yet, and he was already speaking as though a future together was set in stone.

"Who's to say we'll get that far?" she asked.

William turned and looked at her. "Do you not think we will?"

Mary shrugged, and he took a step closer to her. "You might grow tired of me."

His eyes studied her face, and he reached out, gently brushing her cheek with the back of his hand. "Do you doubt me?"

"I do not doubt you think you like me. But you will see how dreadfully boring I am and how content I am with it."

A smile played on his lips. "You are anything but boring."

"No? You hardly know me."

He shook his head. "You seem to enjoy the same things I do. Reading, taking walks after supper."

"Drawing?" she asked.

He grinned. "I paint."

"Piano?"

He nodded, taking a step closer to her. "And singing."

"I cannot sing." She hoped they could find a dealbreaker somewhere along the way.

"I very much doubt that. With a beautiful voice like yours, I bet you're a wonderful singer. Let's hear."

"I'm sorry, William, but I'm afraid if I sing, you may never have use of your ears again."

He laughed. "I truly doubt you are as bad as you are making it seem."

Mary shivered as he stepped even closer, his hand traveling to her shoulder and down her back. Nobody had ever been this close to her before. Not even Andrew. Her nerves were alive with fear and worry.

He leaned down, his breath warm on her lips, his eyes closed. Mary pulled back, prepared to tell him to mind his place, when at that instant, they heard a clatter in the hallway. William stepped back before the door opened, just barely avoiding being caught in such an inappropriate and intimate act. Mary's cheeks burned.

"Oh, William! How lovely to see you." Sarah walked in, holding Jeffry's arm. "Jeff and I were just talking about our book collections, and I wanted to show him mine."

Mary's stomach boiled with anger and disgust. *Her* book collection? She had only been there for a week. These books belonged to Mary's father, mother, and herself. Sarah didn't even like to read. Mary couldn't recall ever seeing a book in her hands that hadn't been forced into them by her mother.

"It's a lovely selection," William said. "Mary was just showing me. I think we were just about to leave, so the library is yours."

Mary let him lead her from the room, momentarily forgetting she was supposed to be cross with him.

She couldn't believe he had almost kissed her. What had he been thinking? What would have happened if they'd have been caught? Sarah would have told everyone.

And poor Andrew. What would he have thought of her if William had kissed her? Would he have ever forgiven her?

"I'm sorry," William said as they stepped outside. "I should not have done that. It was extremely rude and completely inappropriate."

"It was unexpected. We only just met."

She didn't know what to say without offending him. Just a few days ago, she was longing to kiss Andrew, and now she was nearly kissed by William. What was happening?

He stopped and looked at her, pain etched across his face.

"I promise I've never acted so foolishly before in my life."

"That's good to hear."

Even if she wasn't sure he was being completely honest. If he was willing to kiss her so soon, who was to say he hadn't kissed other women?

"You bring something out in me, Mary. Something I can't explain. I've never wanted to be so close with anyone. But you...." His hands cupped her face. "You're so beautiful, so intoxicating. It's like I've had too much wine when I've not had any."

Mary's cheeks burned. She wasn't used to being spoken to like that. The only man who had ever been that forward with her was Andrew.

Mary took his hands from her face, bringing them down to their sides.

"You are too kind," she told him, releasing his hands.

"I am being honest. When I look at you, I feel myself losing control."

"Then we should do something that doesn't require so much focus on one another."

He laughed. "Please."

She led him around the manor to the stables where she found Henry.

"Miss Kline, how can I help you?" he asked.

"Good morning, Henry. I was wondering if William and I could ride," she told him.

Henry eyed her dress, then nodded. "Of course, Miss. Does your mother know?"

Mary pressed a finger to her lips and shook her head. "I promise we'll be safe and return the horses unharmed."

"But your dress," he said.

She looked down at the pale pink silk and knew her mother would kill her if she ruined it. "You're right. Do you have any riding clothes? I wasn't expecting to go out today, so mine are in my room."

He glanced at William before nodding.

"Good." She eyed William. "You were wanting to get to know me? Truth is, Will, I sometimes sneak out to ride horses."

This was a true test. Andrew had accepted her as she was, occasionally spirited and rebellious—two traits that weren't desired in a wife. Perhaps he would be appalled and not want to marry her after this.

But to her surprise, William laughed. "Well, I have to admit, that only makes me like you all the more."

If he liked her unruliness, she wasn't sure what she could do to make him not want to see her again.

After she had changed, they mounted their horses and took off at a sprint. Mary knew her curls would be ruined, but as the wind billowed around her, she felt like she was flying, and nothing else mattered. Right then, that moment, was all she wanted and needed. She wasn't focused on how she felt about Andrew or her mother or even William. She felt alive and free.

When she reached the lake, she slowed the horse to a trot.

As William rode in pace beside her, she began to feel guilty for sharing this moment with him. Mary was supposed to be making William hate her, not fall in love with her.

Andrew had been so upset when he left. How could she tell him that she was failing to push him away?

He stared at her as if thinking. "In some ways, this is much better than walking with you. On one hand, it keeps me from putting my hands on you and kissing you." He smiled at her. "On the other, it keeps me from putting my hands on you and kissing you."

Mary swallowed. She wasn't sure how to respond. She'd never had a man speak so forward with her.

They rode slowly back to the stables, enjoying the hot afternoon sun beating down, except she couldn't shake the feeling she was betraying Andrew.

"Thank you for that," William said as they dismounted. "I never thought you'd be so fun."

"Me? Fun? Didn't I tell you I was boring?"

"You, Mary, are anything but boring."

After she had changed back into her dress, William helped her fix her curls as best as he could. Her stomach twisted at his touch, but she tried not to let it bother her. She needed to be as presentable as possible. In the end, they were better, but they weren't nearly as pretty as they had been that morning.

"I'm a mess," she said.

"A gorgeous mess."

She bit her lip as she realized how her disheveled hair would look to everyone else. "Mother's going to think we were rolling around on the ground somewhere."

He shrugged. "Perhaps we should tell her that's what we did. It might come across better than the truth."

"Don't you dare! Ladies do not roll around with men."

"Ladies don't ride horses."

"That may be true, but there are lines I won't cross, even if I'm not as ladylike as my mother wishes."

His eyes studied hers. "Then perhaps I don't want a lady. I prefer you unruly. I don't think I'd mind rolling around the grass with you."

Mary couldn't help but feel conflicted. She had thought if he could hate this side of her, they could end things, and her mother might allow her to be with Andrew. But it only made him like her more.

But then again, if her mother, or his mother, thought they were behaving inappropriately, perhaps they would put an end to it.

Or perhaps they would insist they wed at once before she became pregnant out of wedlock.

When they walked into the house, Mrs. Connell approached them. "There you are, William, dear. I'm afraid we must be off. I promised Rita we'd come to dinner."

"Rita?" Mary asked before she could stop herself. She couldn't help but wonder if Rita was another woman William was seeing. With any luck, he would fall madly in love with her and wouldn't want to bother with Mary anymore.

"My cousin's sister, dear." Mrs. Connell smiled at her. "She lives with her son and his wife. She never had daughters." She winked as though it ought to reassure her.

But she was more disappointed than anything. "That sounds lovely."

William took her hand in his. "Perhaps we can make arrangements for me to see you again."

As he walked out the door, Mary knew she was going to have to come clean about how she felt about Andrew. Otherwise, he might not understand she didn't want him to court her.

After they had gone, Mother turned to her daughter, eyebrows raised. "Your hair is a mess."

Mary self-consciously touched her messy curls. "We raced to the stables and back," she lied.

Her mother eyed her but didn't say anything else about it, even though Mary knew she would know she was lying. "He likes you."

Mary took a deep breath as they passed the library and remembered how close he had come to kissing her. She should omit that from what she tells Andrew. If he was upset with William walking with Mary, he wouldn't appreciate knowing he tried to kiss her.

"I don't think—"

"His mother and I were talking," Mother cut her off, "and she agrees you two would be an excellent match. What do you think? If he were to propose, would you accept?"

"We've only just met, Mother."

"Yes, yes. I don't mean today. But in a few weeks or months. After you've known one another for a while."

Why couldn't she be as thrilled as her mother was at the prospect of marrying him?

She looked at her mother's hopeful expression and knew what her mother wanted her to say. She knew what her mother wanted her to do. Even if her heart belonged to another man, Mary had to do what was expected of her. Even if it broke her heart.

"You know he's not who I want."

Her mother sighed and gave her a stern look. "We aren't discussing that."

"But Mother—"

"No. Absolutely not. I will not tolerate your disobedience."

Mary bit back her arguments. It didn't seem like her mother would ever listen to what she wanted.

Chapter Eight

WILLIAM VISITED AGAIN THE NEXT morning. Having been anticipating a letter, Mary was surprised when Samuel announced his arrival shortly after breakfast. She was sitting in the living room when he entered, and as soon as he saw her, he smiled.

"You look lovely," he told her.

She looked down at her plain white dress, feeling completely ordinary and not the least bit lovely. "Thank you, William."

He stared at her for a moment, as if taking her in. His face looked troubled.

"Is something the matter?" she asked.

"We are returning home this afternoon, and I couldn't leave without saying goodbye."

"Oh."

"I wish I could stay longer, but since Father is in Boston, I need to escort Mother home."

"Of course. I understand completely."

He took her hands, rubbing his thumb over it. "But there is a problem, you see. I've enjoyed my time with you immensely, and I don't want to leave."

William lived two days' travel away. She wouldn't see him for a minimum of four days, but probably longer, as the horses would need to rest for a day or two.

She wondered if now was the time to tell him she was in love with someone else.

"Can I write to you?" he asked.

She had only ever written to Andrew before. It might be weird to write to another man, especially one who wanted to court her.

"William, I need to be honest about something." It was that moment that she noticed her mother standing by the door, giving her a hard look, her eyes narrowed in warning. Fear enveloped her, and she turned back to William and tried to smile politely. "I would graciously accept a letter from you."

"Then I shall write as soon as I can. It won't be as good as seeing you, but at least I'll get to speak with you."

Mother stepped into the room, beaming wide. "Oh, William! What a lovely surprise. Would you like to stay for afternoon tea?"

"I would love to, Missus Kline, but unfortunately, Mother and I will be on our way home soon. I only came by to tell Mary I won't be able to see her for a little while."

"Oh, how dreadful. It's such a pity you can't stay longer."

"Yes, it is. It's been a wonderful visit. I've enjoyed getting to know your family."

"It was good seeing you again, dear. Thank you so much for coming. Perhaps once your mother is settled, you can come back for another visit? I'm sure Mister Kline won't mind you staying with us."

Mary's jaw clenched. Never mind asking her opinion on it, it wasn't like what she wanted would be taken into consideration.

He nodded once. "I would love nothing more, thank you."

"Then it's settled."

His eyes moved back to Mary. "I'll see you soon," he said softly.

"Travel safely."

Once he was gone, Mother rounded on her. "What did you almost do?"

Mary sniffled, unable to keep the tears from spilling. Everything was happening so fast, and she had no control over any of it.

"He deserves to know that my heart will never be his," she said softly.

"He needs to know no such thing. You are not even sure of what you're feeling. You're young. You will grow to love William and see that what you are feeling is nothing compared to what you will feel."

"I don't want to be with William, Mother."

Mother sighed heavily and looked out the window where William was no doubt stepping into his carriage.

"It doesn't matter what you want, Mary. Someday, you will see that I have made the right decision for us."

Mary buried her face in a handkerchief from her pocket, crying into it.

"Hush now. Everything will work out. You will see. I will write to his mother to further discuss your potential union. Though, I daresay he will insist since he's making a point to stop by and talk to you." She narrowed her eyes at her daughter. "Listen to me, Mary. Do as you are told, and you will live a comfortable life."

Mary wiped at her eyes but kept her face hidden. She didn't want to have a comfortable life if it meant not having Andrew in it.

"Any woman would be happy with a man like him," Mother said. "Be glad that you have captured his attention."

But she wasn't glad. She had deliberately tried to be the opposite of what men wanted in a wife.

"I'm going to go write to Josephine now so they receive my letter soon after they arrive home."

Mary remained quiet. It was really happening. Her mother was going to speak with William's mother about their union. They would be planning the wedding before Mary knew it. Marriage was forever, and once there was an engagement, there would be no turning back.

How could she be with William, knowing Andrew cared for her the way she cared for him? If she was going to be a wife, she rather be with her best friend. She would never be able to move on or love William the way a wife should love her husband.

Mother walked briskly from the room, leaving Mary still crying into the handkerchief, wondering what she was going to do when her mother wouldn't listen or allow her to tell William about Andrew. Her future was not her own.

William seemed like a good man, not to mention rich. Any woman would be more than happy to be his wife.

Mother was against her marrying Andrew, so if she didn't marry William, she could end up with someone else, possibly someone like Jeffry. What would happen to her if she kept rejecting men because they weren't Andrew and ended up alone? Wasn't marrying William better than ending up alone?

She sighed. For some reason, she wasn't so sure about that.

Mary walked to the library, eager to find a book to escape her mind for a while.

Mother was sitting at the writing desk, scribbling a letter on the parchment, and didn't look up when she entered. Mary wondered what she was saying. Would she tell Mrs. Connell Mary was eager to marry William? Or was she being less bold and enquiring if he wanted to marry her?

One thing was clear, though. Her mother was excited at the prospect of their marriage and happier than she'd been since before Father fell ill. And if Mother was happy again, shouldn't

Mary try her best to keep her that way? Perhaps she was being selfish.

She browsed the books until she came across Hamlet. William had said he was currently rereading Hamlet. Her fingers caressed the leather cover as she plucked it from the shelf. She'd read it before, but she suddenly had the urge to read it again.

She sat in a chair in the corner and opened the book. As she silently read, her mind wandered to William, wondering how he would react when Mother's letter arrived.

She'd only read about thirty pages when her mother stood.

"I believe I'll send this with the evening post," she said. "Would you like to write to William? It might be nice for him to get a letter the day he arrives."

Mary quietly let out a sigh. She hadn't wanted to write to him first, as she felt it came across as desperate. Besides, there was a part of her that hoped if she went a few days without speaking to him, he would grow bored of her and there would be no wedding.

"What should I say?"

"You can thank him for visiting. Let him know you enjoyed his company. Perhaps you can extend a personal invitation for him to stay with us. It might mean more coming from you than it had me."

She thought about him coming to stay. The idea of having him there all the time made her stomach squeeze, but it would give her a chance to tell him how she felt about Andrew.

Andrew would be coming home soon, and she didn't want to upset him more than she already had. If William came back, would Andrew leave again?

Mary sat at the writing desk and took up the quill.

William,
You've only just left. I wondered if it was too early to write,

but Mother insisted it would be nice for you to get a letter the day you arrived home. I wanted to thank you for visiting. It was a pleasure getting to know you over the past couple of days. I feel as though we have become fast friends. Mother is wanting to invite you to stay with us for a few days, if you wish. I know you are busy with work and family, so I completely understand if you can't find time to get away again so soon. I merely wanted to extend the offer. I hope this letter finds you and your family well. I look forward to hearing from you.

All my best,
Mary

Once the letter was finished, Mary folded it closed and looked up at Mother, who was standing over her, watching her. Reluctantly, she held it out to her, and she smiled.

"Thank you, sweetie. William is going to be thrilled you wrote him."

She left the room, and Mary went to be alone in her room, hoping that William would write back and say he'd be too busy to visit.

Chapter Nine

$\mathcal{T}$HE NEXT FEW DAYS PASSED with no word from William or Andrew. It was a two-day ride to William's family manor, though, so Mary hadn't expected to hear from him yet. Andrew, however, was due home, and she still hadn't seen or heard from him.

She had so much to tell him and talk to him about, but she didn't even know where he was so she could write to him. She was starting to worry that he would never come back.

Mary's nightly walks now felt lonely as she had nobody to accompany her. She used to enjoy the alone time, looking forward to it even, but now, she missed Andrew. She'd become so accustomed to their chats and his presence. She didn't know how to be without him anymore.

On the fourth day after William's departure, a letter arrived in the morning mail. Mary's hands shook as she stared down at the letter at the breakfast table.

> *Mary,*
> *I am writing to tell you I arrived home safely, and*
> *twenty minutes after walking through the door, the*

mail arrived with a letter from you. I was pleased you were already thinking of me and wanted to send me a letter, even if it had been your mother who insisted. I would love to come stay with you. Before I can, I need to arrange some things for my mother and work. I was thinking perhaps I could stay for a couple of days without being missed too much at home. It's only been two days, and I already miss you terribly. I miss your gorgeous smile and beautiful eyes. I look around my house, and it suddenly feels too big. Too empty. All I can think of is you. Your presence would fill my home and make it warm like you have my heart. You have such a beautiful energy, Mary, and now that I know you, I can't imagine not having you in my life. You're unlike anyone I've ever known. We've not had enough time to enjoy one another's company. I didn't get to read to you or play piano so you could sing to me. Perhaps in a couple of weeks, when I arrive, we can do all of it.

Until we meet again,
William

Mary folded the letter and stuffed it into her pocket with a sigh. William didn't seem to realize she wasn't as interested as he was, even though she had tried to be distant in her letter to him.

William would be coming in a couple of weeks, and that was enough to bring comfort to Mary's anxious heart. Perhaps in the time before he arrived, Mary could speak with Andrew, if he ever made it home, and her mother.

"Was that William?" her mother asked from across the table.

As much as she didn't want to admit it, Mary nodded. Every

time her mother made a comment about William, Mary found herself growing sick to her stomach.

"How lovely! I suppose you will be writing him back?"

Mary pursed her lips. She was hoping to wait a day before writing him back, wanting him to think she wasn't reliable, but with her mother watching her like a hawk, it didn't seem like it was going to be possible.

"Yes, ma'am." Mary pushed away her plate, excused herself from breakfast, and walked down the hall to the library. She sat at the writing desk and took up the quill. She stared at the parchment for a long time before she could think of what she wanted to say.

> William,
> I received your letter. I'm glad you and your mother arrived home safely. I hope she is doing well. Mother and I will prepare a room for your visit. I would appreciate your playing the piano for me, but I won't be singing. I have started to reread Hamlet. I have nearly finished it, again. I was thinking too much and went to the library to find a book and recalled you saying you were reading Hamlet. It made me realize I hadn't read it in quite some time and wanted to. I hope when you visit, we can find time to get you better acquainted with my family.
>
> Best,
> Mary

Mary sealed the letter and felt her heart quicken. She would be seeing William again soon. She wasn't sure how she was going to get herself out of this mess.

She heard hooves on the dirt road and bolted to her feet, hoping more than anything it was who she'd been waiting for.

She hurried down the hall to the front door just as Samuel was pulling it open. Mary grinned wide as she caught sight of the dark, curly hair.

Andrew had returned.

He looked tired from travel but clean and happy. He smiled when he saw Mary.

She ran to the door, leaping into Andrew's arms and squealing with delight.

"You're home!" she said, hugging him tightly.

His arms wrapped around her and squeezed.

"I've missed you," he said as she pulled away.

"And I you. It's been terrible here without you." She held his hand and led him inside. "How was it?"

Andrew stared down at her, his dark eyes warming her heart. She couldn't believe he was back, and he was looking at her like she was the only person in the world. In that moment, her heart felt so full.

"It was dreadful without you there to entertain me. I've realized I want nothing to do with traveling for work. If I could stay home with you every day, I would."

Mary smiled. "I'm glad you're home. It was so strange not having you here." She glanced down the hall, making sure nobody was around to eavesdrop. "And nobody has been here to deflect Sarah's piano playing," she whispered.

Andrew laughed. "I apologize for leaving you to suffer that horror."

"All is forgiven, now." She clutched her fist to her chest, unable to tear her eyes away from him. "We have so much to talk about. I hope we can—"

"What's that?" he asked, narrowing his eyes at the letter in her hand.

"Oh..." Her face burned. How had she forgotten she was about to send a letter to William? "A letter."

"To?"

She looked at the floor before answering, feeling somewhat ashamed, as though she were betraying Andrew. "To William, but if you could—"

"Right. Of course. Who else would it be for?" He cleared his throat and looked around the hall.

"Andrew, please, let me explain. So much has happened."

"Perhaps later we can talk. I should get settled. I'll leave you to mail your letter. I daresay you don't want to miss the evening post."

"I have hours before I need be concerned with missing the mail carrier. Won't you come sit with me and talk for a while? I want to hear about your trip, and I've wanted to speak with you since before you left."

Andrew stared at her with glossy eyes. "I don't think it wise."

"Are you cross with me?"

"No. I just think perhaps I shouldn't have come home."

Mary narrowed her eyes and released his hand, suddenly feeling betrayed. She knew he was hurt, but he wasn't giving her a chance to explain. "How can you say that? You were just saying how you didn't want to leave me again."

He studied her face. "I cannot pretend I don't feel something for you, Mary. I don't want to watch you fall in love with another man."

"There is more to marriage than love," she said, a lump forming in her throat. If she were forced to marry William, it wouldn't be because she was in love with him.

"Perhaps. But when you're in love with someone, should you not be with them?"

Her heart twinged as she realized it was an accusation. "You are not acting as though you love me."

"It is you who does not love me."

A fire burned through her, and she found herself growing

angry at his words. "You presume to know how I feel? You have not once asked me if my feelings have changed. Nor have you asked how I feel toward William."

He opened his mouth but quickly closed it. "You're right."

"I have found myself thinking of you more often than not, but I am not free to make my own decisions. I am not allowed to choose my husband myself."

He narrowed his eyes at her, then looked down the hall. Mary followed his gaze and saw her mother standing in the doorway.

"Andrew, how lovely to see you home safely. How was your trip?"

Mary swallowed, wondering how long she had been standing there and how much she heard.

"It was pleasant. Father and I closed on a property. Mister Connell's father was trying to buy it as well," he glanced at Mary, his face pale, "but we put in a higher offer."

"Oh, how wonderful for you both. Poor Mister Connell, though."

Andrew's eyes met Mary's. "Yes. Quite right," he said, his voice thick, a blow to Mary's chest. "If you'll excuse me, I really must get changed out of my traveling clothes."

He walked down the hall and up the stairs. Mary made to follow him, but her mother called after her, drawing her up short.

"You have to let him go," she said. "He will be hurt when you and Mister Connell become engaged, but he loves you, so he will be happy for you."

Mary's eyes burned with tears. Neither of them would be happy if she and William became engaged.

"I know this is hard, Mary, but it must be done. This is a very complicated situation. Most women wish to catch the eye of one wealthy gentleman, but you've captured two."

Tears escaped her eyes as she stared up at the second story where Andrew had disappeared. "I didn't want this."

"It's good to have two men who care so much."

"If it's such a good thing, why does it hurt so much?"

Her mother patted her hand. "Because you have a good heart, Mary."

Mary shook her head. It wasn't that at all. She cared for Andrew deeply, and her mother choosing William for her was killing them both. "I'm hurting him, Mother. Andrew was my first best friend. He's always been there for me."

And he was gorgeous and smart and funny and sweet.

She stared into her mother's gray eyes, silently pleading for her to see her way.

Instead of sympathy, Mother's eyes hardened. "William will make a better husband for you."

"I do not deny that William would make someone a good husband, but he is not who I want. Andrew is my best friend."

Her mother sighed. "Andrew will always be your best friend. He will find someone else and be just as happy as you and William will be."

Mary stared up the stairs, thinking of Andrew with another woman. It made her stomach roll with nausea. If she couldn't stomach the *idea* of Andrew with another woman, no wonder Andrew couldn't even be in the same room as her, knowing she was being courted by another.

But her mother wanted her to marry William. It wasn't as though Mary was choosing him.

"He isn't who I want. He isn't who makes my heart race," she said.

"Those things don't matter in a marriage, as you will come to learn. Physical attraction doesn't last forever."

"It isn't just physical, though, Mother. Andrew is everything to me. I'm in love with him. Why won't you at least consider letting me marry him?"

Her mother's lips pursed. "He isn't like us, Mary. He was

born to an impoverished woman, and his father was a black man. He may have been raised by a good family, but he isn't good enough for you."

Shock gave way to a sudden intense anger at her mother's prejudice. All the times her mother had tried to convince her that William would be better for her, what she was saying was Andrew wasn't good enough. "What bothers you more, Mother? The fact that his birth mother was poor, or his birth father was black? I didn't realize I came from such a prejudiced family."

Her mother's hand swung swiftly, slapping her across the face. "How dare you? I have never...." She took a step away from Mary, her eyes wide with a wicked ferocity. "White girls of your status do not marry black men, no matter how much money he has. Think of what the neighbors would say."

Mary's hand flew to her burning cheek. Her mother had never hit her before.

"I don't care what the neighbors say. Andrew was raised by a good, prominent family, which is what should matter to you. He is a good man."

"Our class and our name are *all* that matters. You will allow Mister Connell to court you, you will not tell anyone how you feel about Andrew, and if Mister Connell proposes, you will agree, or you will find yourself out of this family."

Mary felt sick. Never had her mother spoken so coldly to her before. But she couldn't mean it, could she?

How was she supposed to marry William when she was in love with Andrew? But how could she not when her mother was threatening to disown her?

"What is this?" Mother asked sharply, lifting the letter still clutched in Mary's hand.

Mary stared down at the letter like it was a foreign object. As though it wasn't the source of her and Andrew's dispute. She suddenly wished she could throw it in the fireplace and burn it. She almost didn't care what her mother did in retaliation.

But what would she do if she were put out on the streets?

"I wrote William back."

Her mother grinned. "See? Your heart knows who you want, even if your mind is telling you otherwise."

Mary didn't say anything. What else could she say? Mother let her know where she stood.

"Give it to me, and I'll have it mailed out for you," Mother said.

Mary thought about saying no and taking it to the library to burn it in the fireplace, but the threat still loomed over her head. Instead, she let her mother take the letter from her.

She'd never felt quite so conflicted before in her life. She wished more than anything she could be with Andrew, but would his parents allow it if they knew it didn't come with the dowry?

As she walked outside, she thought about how she could make a future with William. How could she ever be happy knowing she broke Andrew's heart?

It would break her heart, as well, to know that any prospect of a future with Andrew was over.

She only hoped that Andrew would still speak to her if she and William did get married. She didn't want to lose her best friend completely.

Chapter Ten

MARY DIDN'T GET A CHANCE to speak with Andrew for the rest of the day. Every time she tried to find him, her mother wouldn't be far behind, steering her away. At dinner, he was polite and chatty, answering everyone's questions about how his trip had gone. He even gave Mary a warm smile when she made a joke about him being a proper businessman.

Uncle Isaac would be out of town until next Friday as he had to file the paperwork for the new business. Aunt Catherine would be beside herself with boredom, so they were to expect another party on Saturday.

Mary was already dreading it, as Jeffry would surely return. She hoped Aunt Catherine wouldn't keep Andrew on the piano all night so she could get a chance to talk to him. If they were back to normal by then.

"What are your next plans, then?" Aunt Catherine asked. "Has your father mentioned what you are to do while he was away?"

"No, he hasn't. You know Father. He's reluctant to give me any independence with the business. I was thinking of going back to Boston in a few days and rejoining him."

He glanced at Mary, who nearly dropped her fork.

"You're leaving again?"

"Mary," her mother said warningly.

But Mary ignored her. "You only just got home."

"Mary!" Her mother's voice was sharper this time, quieting her protests.

She didn't want Andrew to leave again. Without him, Sarah was insufferable. Without him, the house was lonely and cold. She'd had no one to accompany her on her walks, and she had enjoyed the solitude much less than she used to. When he was gone, she felt like she was missing a piece of herself.

The chatter at the table died, and Andrew glanced at Mary. She couldn't understand why he wanted to leave her again. Hadn't he told her he didn't want to leave her again?

Her eyes stung.

Each day felt as though he were slipping further and further away from her, and it was breaking her heart.

She couldn't imagine a life without him. Especially now that he had confessed to her how much he cared.

If she chose to do what her mother wished and married William, she would lose Andrew. He was already pulling away from her, choosing to return to Boston to get away from her. If she married William, or anyone else for that matter, she'd never see him again.

But if she followed her heart and chose Andrew, she'd lose her mother.

"Excuse me," she said in a choked whisper, tossing down her napkin and standing.

Out of the corner of her eye, she saw Andrew stand, but she hurried off before anyone could protest. She gathered her skirt and ran to the door and down the stairs, hurrying around the garden and away from everyone and everything.

She wanted so desperately to hide from her family's prying eyes to feel what she was feeling without her mother telling her she would be better with time.

She sank onto a bench and wiped her eyes, begging the tears to go away.

How could it hurt so much? Andrew had never been hers. Andrew would never be hers. Her mother was adamant about it.

Since her father had died, her mother seemed as though finding a husband was the most important thing in the world. Find a good man from a proper family who would take care of her. That was the ultimate goal.

But wasn't Andrew all those things? How could she be so small as to not see past his skin color?

She sniffled and wiped her eyes again. She jumped when she saw Andrew and turned to hide her teary face.

"I beg your forgiveness, Mary," he said, kneeling in front of her, resting his hands on her knees. "I never meant to upset you. I only came to that decision a while ago and was telling everyone, not just you."

Mary remained silent. She wanted nothing to do with his sympathy. He was choosing to leave her again without allowing her to properly explain. And there was nothing he could say that would make her feel better about losing him.

When he didn't leave, she said, "I hope you have great luck in Boston and find everything you're looking for."

He reached up, his fingers gently caressing her face as he brushed the tears from her cheeks.

"How can I? When everything I've been looking for is here?"

Her heart ached as she angled away from him and choked on a sob. She wanted him so desperately, but she couldn't tell him what her mother had said. It was too horrible, too embarrassing.

"I cannot humor you, Andrew."

He touched her chin, gently pulling her attention back to his face. "Do you not love me?"

Mary licked her lips, willing herself to remain calm and not break down into tears. But her heart was aching. "My love for you is not the issue. Mother is insistent on my marriage to William."

He narrowed his sad, hazel eyes at her. "Surely, she will have to take your feelings into account. If only we could get her to listen, tell her how we feel for one another..."

She so desperately wanted to reassure him. But she couldn't. Her mother would never agree to their marriage. She already knew how Mary and Andrew felt about one another, but she still encouraged her to let him go.

"Mother insists I will grow to love William. She wants me to give him a chance."

"And you? Do you think you can grow to love him?"

Mary's heart ached. "I don't doubt that someday I could love him in some aspect."

Andrew looked at the ground, face hard.

"But my heart is yours."

His breath quickened. "It is?"

She wiped away a tear and shook her head.

"Then I'll speak with her this time. Get her to see reason. I love you, Mary, and I want to be with you."

"I've talked to her. She knows how I feel, but she...." Mary looked into his eyes, softened with pain. She couldn't tell him the truth of why Mother didn't want them together. "She doesn't care how we feel. She said if I'm with you, I can't be part of her family anymore."

"There's nothing I can say to make her agree?"

"I don't think she'll ever change her mind. She's so resolute in her decision, so sure William is perfect for me, that she doesn't see or hear anything else."

He took her hands in his. "Do you love me?"

Mary bit her lip. Of course, she loved him. More than any-thing. But love wasn't the issue. "Yes," she said, fresh tears stinging her eyes.

"Then let's run away together," he said, eyes alive with a fire she hadn't seen for a while.

Mary cocked her head, heart racing as a million thoughts of a future with Andrew crossed her mind. It would be so easy to agree. She could go pack a bag, and they could start a life together somewhere else.

But what would be the cost of that decision?

If she ran off with Andrew, her mother would disown her. She'd be humiliated. They'd become the gossip of the town, and her mother would have to live with the consequences. She would never speak to Mary again.

But for a chance to be with Andrew.

Could she lose her mother?

"It sounds like a dream," she told him.

"If Father disowns me for not asking for your hand, I will get whatever job I need to provide for you. I promise I'll be a good husband and take care of you."

"I know you would. But whatever decision I make, I will lose someone I love. Whether you or my mother." She sniffled, fresh tears stinging her eyes. "I'm sorry, Andrew, but I cannot lose my mother. If I cannot convince Mother to allow me to marry you, I'll do as she wishes and marry William. If that means I lose you, I...." Her voice cracked, and Andrew pulled her hand to his lips, kissing her knuckles.

Tears filled his eyes, and her heart ached even more. What she would give to have told him yes and ran off with him. But after the pain of losing her father, she couldn't imagine losing her mother too.

"You will never lose me, Mary. Even if you marry another man."

What should have reassured her only made her feel more guilty. Andrew was a better man than she deserved.

He had asked her to run away with him, and she all but

declined. Knowing if she stayed, she would have to marry another man to keep from losing her mother. Knowing it would mean losing him.

He was a better man than she was a woman.

Still, if he meant it, it would mean she wasn't going to lose her best friend after all. True, he wouldn't be her husband, but if she could still have him in her life, perhaps she could get past the pain of never knowing what they could have been.

"Do you promise?" she asked.

He gave her a sad smile. "I only want you to be happy, Mary. I had hoped you could be happy with me, but if you marry William, I promise to stand by your side and honor it."

She wrapped her arms around his neck, not caring if hugging him was improper. In that moment, she clung to him like a lifeline.

"Thank you, Andrew."

"I'll always be here for you, Mary. To make you laugh, to see that smile. To remind you of all the reasons you would rather have chosen me."

Mary laughed and pulled away, wiping her tears.

"Now, Andrew. What kind of lady would that make me if I were longing after a man other than my husband?"

He gently nudged her. "You, miss, are the best of ladies."

"And you, sir, are the finest gentleman."

He gave her a small smile and squeezed her hand.

Something between them had indeed changed, but that didn't mean they cared for one another any less. Andrew was still her best friend. He was still there, making her laugh when she was sad, even after she told him she would marry whomever her mother told her to. Even if that meant it wouldn't be him.

She wondered how much love it took for someone to step aside, choosing their happiness over your own. She wondered why it was so easy for Andrew but not her own mother.

Chapter Eleven

ANDREW DID AS HE SAID and returned to Boston Friday night, leaving before the dinner party on Saturday. Mary wanted to beg him not to leave her alone to entertain strangers she had no desire to talk to, but she let him go.

There was nothing more to say, and he had no reason to stay if she were never to be his.

She couldn't blame him for leaving. She wanted to run away as much as he did. The only difference was he could. Mary was trapped, waiting for a marriage she didn't want.

Mary really didn't want to attend the dinner party, especially now that Andrew was gone and she didn't have anyone to talk to. Sarah would be busy with Jeffry, and her mother and Aunt Catherine would be entertaining their guests. Mary wasn't interested in talking to any of the people from town and watching the couples flirt and chat would make her miss Andrew all the more.

She dressed in a yellow satin dress and pressed her curls to ensure they'd hold. She sighed and took one last look at herself before making her way downstairs to the parlor.

As soon as she walked into the room, she stopped, momentarily stunned, and stared at the familiar man standing just a few feet away from her.

William turned, a smile forming on his face the moment he saw her, and stepped toward her.

"William," she breathed, slowing her pace. "I thought you weren't returning for another few weeks, at least?"

For the first time since he left, Mary was glad Andrew had decided to go. If he'd have been here to see William and to be ignored by Mary as she was hosting the man who was courting her, it would only upset him further.

"I wasn't planning to, but your mother wrote to mine and said she was having another dinner party. I couldn't bear the thought of some other man trying to win your attention."

Mary laughed nervously. "What about your mother?"

"She's home and settled. Father should be home by now, so she insisted I come and see you."

Mary glanced around the room. Sarah and Jeffry were standing near the fire, talking to his parents and Aunt Catherine. They seemed to be getting on, even if Mary couldn't figure out for the life of her what anyone could see in either of them.

Her mother was sitting on a chair near the fire, talking to Mrs. Harris, a woman from town. Mrs. Harris's daughter and son were there, as well, both of age to marry. Mary wondered if it had been her mother or Aunt Catherine who had invited them to the party and what the purpose of it had been.

"Are you staying here?" she asked, turning her attention back to William.

He shuffled his feet. "If that is still all right with you."

"That sounds fine."

"Then, yes. I'm here for a week, then I'm afraid I must return home for work."

"Then we must ensure we have as much fun as we can before you have to leave again."

"In that case, would you care to dance?"

Mary stared at him, surprised at his question. She looked around the room. A man she recognized but didn't know by name was playing a soft melody on the piano, but nobody was dancing.

"We might look silly," she said.

"You don't strike me as a woman who cares what others think of her." It sounded like a challenge that Mary couldn't ignore.

"A lady would care."

He grinned mischievously. "I already told you I prefer you as you are. Proper lady or not."

Mary couldn't help but smile. It had been a particularly long past few days, and she desperately needed to clear her thoughts. Perhaps dancing was exactly what she needed. She reached out to take his hand. "That sounds lovely."

William wrapped his arm around her back and led her in a small circle, slowly twirling her around the parlor.

Mary felt eyes on them, but she didn't acknowledge them as she stared into William's eyes. He was quite the dancer. Mary felt her heart race with excitement as he sped his pace, dancing quicker in rhythm to the music.

As the song slowed, so did William. Finally, they stopped, and Mary gave him a slight curtsey.

She hadn't danced in quite some time, but that had been refreshing and exhilarating.

There were a few claps, and Mary finally acknowledged the others in the room. Her cheeks burned. She couldn't believe she'd allowed a man to hold her in front of a room full of strangers. Surprisingly, her mother was smiling at her and William. Aunt Catherine looked shocked but not entirely displeased. Sarah, on the other hand, looked appalled. Most of the guests smiled politely, but a few had turned their heads.

"Well, that was a surprise," Mother said, walking over to them.

"It was for us, as well," William told her. "I apologize if that was discourteous. I only could think of how beautiful Mary looked and how I wanted to dance with her."

Mother smiled. "That's more than fine, dear. I'm glad you two are getting on so well."

Before they could respond, they were called to dinner. William sat beside Mary, occasionally glancing her way and asking a question. Sarah and Jeffry whispered to one another, shooting Mary and William furious looks of disgust that made them both laugh.

"I think she's jealous," Mary whispered.

"Definitely jealous. She isn't half the woman you are. And he, no doubt, wants you."

Mary turned her head to narrow her eyes at him. "I was thinking she was jealous because you are by far more handsome and fun than the man courting her."

"You think I'm handsome?"

"I think most women would think you handsome."

"That's good to know. So if you decide you aren't bothered with me anymore, I can use my good looks to try to find someone else."

Mary couldn't help but laugh. He was more playful than she had thought he would be.

The rest of the party was spent in polite conversation with the others, and after dinner, as everyone was retiring back to the parlor, William steered her away from the crowd and led her outside.

The sun had already set, and the night air was colder than usual. Mary shivered as the wind blew past them and wrapped her arms over her chest.

"I'm sorry. I should have let you get your coat. Here."

He stripped off his jacket and draped it over her shoulders. Mary shrugged into it, grateful to be covered.

"Thank you," she said.

"You're welcome."

She looked out over the grounds, listening to the insects chirp and sing their nightly songs.

"I had a lot of fun with you tonight, Mary," William said. "I must admit, when Mother first told me she wanted me to come all the way here to meet you, I was worried. I wasn't looking forward to it."

His eyes met hers. She hadn't noticed how soft they were before.

"Now, I cannot imagine my life without you in it."

She immediately looked at the ground. He was growing dangerously attached to her.

"I thought you'd be different. Like most upper-class ladies who host dinner parties. But you aren't like any woman I've ever met. You've shown me that you're different. You're fun and kind." William stopped and looked into her eyes. "And while I'm being completely honest, you're the most beautiful woman I've ever seen."

Mary's cheeks warmed. "You're too kind."

"I'm only speaking the truth." He shoved his hands in his pockets and averted his gaze to the ground.

"Is something the matter?" she asked, watching his eyes narrow with concern.

"No, nothing, really, but I would like to apologize for my actions in the library the other day. I was so forward and completely inappropriate. It was wrong to try to kiss you before I've made any promises to you."

Mary's heart felt as if it was going to beat out of her chest. "I appreciate that, Will. Truly."

"I should have behaved more decently. You deserve a man

who will respect you. And trying to kiss you before we are engaged isn't respectable. Although I do say, it is difficult to be respectable when you are so beautiful."

Mary inhaled, a knot forming in her throat. He had spoken of making a promise and engagement all in one conversation. Mary wondered if he was going to make a promise now or even ask about marrying her, but wasn't it too soon? Her father had courted her mother for six months. Mary had only known William for a week.

Had he even had a chance to speak with her mother about asking for her hand?

Or perhaps he was going to end things. He had said she deserved someone better. A part of her hoped it was that. If William rejected her, she wouldn't have to leave Andrew so soon.

"Can you forgive me?" he asked.

Slowly, Mary nodded, her dark ringlet curls bobbing. "It's already forgiven and forgotten."

He smiled. "Forgotten?"

She thought back to the library and remembered how close he had been. Even if she hadn't wanted to kiss him, it was the closest she had come to kissing a man. "Well, perhaps not forgotten."

"Even if you marry someone else? Like Andrew, perhaps?"

Mary narrowed her eyes. How could he know she had been thinking of him? "Why would you think I would marry Andrew?"

"It is clear he cares for you. Desires you. When I first met him, I sensed jealousy."

Mary took a step back. She had thought that if William knew of her relationship with Andrew, knew how they felt about one another, then he wouldn't wish to court her.

"Andrew is my best friend. He only wants what's best for me." Her voice came out thick, harsh, not at all how she should sound.

William nodded. "Of course. I don't mean to upset you or overstep. I only wanted to ask because I want to know how you feel."

"How I feel? For Andrew?" She couldn't help but feel defensive. It would be so easy to tell him she was in love with Andrew, but her mother had warned her not to.

"And for me."

"Oh." Mary's gaze softened as she took him in. Concern was etched across his face. How had she missed that he'd been looking for praise and reassurance? She had been so quick to rise to Andrew's defense that she didn't consider that William might want her to admit that she wanted to be with him. But how could she be honest without going against her mother? "I cannot say I don't care for Andrew. He and I have been close for years. He's been my best friend all my life. I love him."

It was modest compared to how she truly felt, but it might sound as though she only saw him as a friend. Her mother couldn't be too angry with that response, even if she admitted that she loved him.

"Right. That's completely understandable. But what if he asked you to marry him?"

Mary's heart ached as she thought of his proposal to run away with him. What she wouldn't give to be able to accept his offer. If only it were that simple.

"If Andrew proposed, I would have to decline." Saying it aloud made her chest tighten.

William smiled and sighed with relief, not noticing how sad she had become. "Would it be rude to ask how you feel about me?"

Mary blinked away tears before faking a smile. "You have become a friend to me already. I would be lying if I didn't admit that you would make an excellent husband."

"And not just because I have money?"

Mary cocked her head, suddenly offended. "I do think wealth is an appeal for my mother, but it never has been for me. I care more about a man's personality. I want a husband who can make me laugh. Someone whose company I enjoy. I think you have more to offer a woman than money, William."

He chuckled and brought her hand to his lips, gently kissing her knuckles. "Now you are being too kind."

Mary couldn't help but feel she had just progressed their relationship. Guilt gnawed at her.

He eyed her, his gaze lingering on her lips, and her stomach twisted in knots. She was worried he would try to kiss her again, but then he turned around and walked her back into the house, where they rejoined the party.

More than once, she felt William's eyes on her. She wondered if he was thinking about what she had said. It seemed to be all she could think about.

She set something in motion, and there would be no going back now.

Chapter Twelve

WHEN MARY WENT TO BREAKFAST the next morning, William was already sitting at the dining room table. He looked smart in his suit, complete with a cravat. Apparently, she had missed the postman because he was reading a letter, and one had been set beside her plate.

Her mother sat in her usual seat, sipping her morning tea. Aunt Catherine and Sarah weren't there yet.

"Good morning, Mary," William said as she sat down beside him.

"Good morning, Will. I trust you slept well?"

"Indeed, I did. The guest suite is quite lovely."

Mary glanced at the letter beside her plate, wondering who could be writing to her.

"My mother has already written to me," he said, indicating the letter in his hands.

"Oh?" Was she wanting him home already? Mary's heart leaped with hope.

"She asks that I give her love to you and your family."

"That's lovely," Mother said. "I hope you'll send ours in return?"

"Of course," he said, setting the letter down and picking up his fork.

Mary picked up her letter and carefully slipped it open. Inside was Andrew's familiar scrawl. Immediately, her heart raced, and she smiled.

> *My Dearest Mary,*
>
> *I hope this letter finds you well. It's been all of twelve hours, and I already find myself regretting my decision to leave you. I feel as though I'm running away from something. From you, perhaps, but also rejection. After what you told me, I'm finally seeing that your mother will never let you marry me, no matter how much we care for one another. And I understand that you cannot leave her. I wish you happiness with William if, indeed, you marry him.*
>
> *Boston is busier than it was last week, but it keeps my mind occupied. Father has found me work that will keep me busy for the next couple of months. That means I won't be returning to Kline Manor for some time except for small visits.*
>
> *I want to respect your decision, and I fear if I return, I won't be able to keep from confronting your mother. I also worry about how I will act if I see you with another man. What I will say to him. I care deeply for you, Mary, and I only want happiness for you.*
>
> *So write to William and tell him you cannot stop thinking of him or something that will make him want to return to you. If he was smart, he'd be there already, making sure you didn't forget him.*
>
> *I hope you don't forget me while I am away. I'm*

still your best friend, after all. Find your happiness,
Mary. I'll see you as soon as I can.

Yours,
Andrew

Mary closed the letter, feeling a tightness in her chest. She willed herself not to cry as she closed the letter and set it on the table, tears stinging her eyes.

"Everything all right?" her mother asked.

"Mmhmm. Yes." Mary faked a smile and took a slow, deep breath to steady herself. "Andrew has taken a job in Boston and won't be home for a while."

"What a great opportunity for him!" her mother exclaimed.

Mary's heart raced furiously as she wondered how her mother could be so enthusiastic when she knew his being away was hurting him and Mary.

"That's a shame," William said. "I was hoping to get to know him. We still haven't had a chance to talk business."

Mary blinked back tears and took a sip of tea, trying to force down the lump in her throat.

She hadn't expected Andrew to be gone for so long, and she really didn't expect him to say as much as he did in that letter. She was going to talk to her mother again, but if what he was saying was true, Andrew had all but given up hope for them. What use was fighting for them if he wasn't there to help convince her mother that they were perfect for one another?

"I'm sure he will be home soon. There will be plenty of time for you to get to know the people in Mary's life."

"I certainly hope so." He glanced at Mary, but she couldn't bring herself to look at him. "Mary is a wonderful woman, Missus Kline. I've really enjoyed spending time with her. Thank you for inviting me to stay with you."

"I am thrilled you decided to accept our offer. And even happier you decided to come earlier than you originally planned."

If he was smart, he'd be there already, making sure you didn't forget him. Andrew's words floated through Mary's mind. Andrew had guessed correctly. She wondered if he had somehow known that William would be returning early.

"As am I. Last night was wonderful. It was the best dinner party I've ever gone to."

"I particularly enjoyed dessert," Mary said, her voice soft.

Her mother eyed her and sipped her tea.

"The food was good, but the company was even better."

Mary felt her cheeks burn as she stared down at her plate. She had to admit, if she could stop thinking of Andrew, she might enjoy William's company. The compliments were unexpected but very welcome.

"Do you have any plans for today, William?" Mother asked.

He glanced at Mary. "I was hoping your daughter would humor me and sing while I played the piano. Perhaps we can read before dinner. I'd love to browse your books."

"That sounds wonderful! Mary is an excellent singer, although she doesn't sing often enough for anyone but me to know. How long has it been since you sang, Mary?"

"Two years. Perhaps longer."

"That's a shame," William said. "If you are a good singer, you should sing nightly. How else will those of us who can't carry a tune entertain ourselves?"

"I'm honestly not a very good singer. Mother is partial because of her love for me."

"Then perhaps I will be partial as well."

Mary averted her gaze to her plate, unable to meet his eye. Had he just admitted he loved her? No. He couldn't have, wouldn't have. It was too soon for that. He hardly knew her.

"You are kind, William. I believe Mary is truly blessed that you have stepped into her life."

She didn't feel blessed. She felt torn in two different directions, which was sometimes unbearably agonizing.

"I suppose I can sing *one* song, but only if you promise not to make jokes about how pitchy I will inevitably be."

William placed his hand over his heart. "By my honor, I will only have nice things to say."

After breakfast, Mary excused herself to take her letter to her bedroom. She reread it, wondering how hard it had been for him to write it. She wanted to write back to him but knew that would have to wait until she had a spare moment. She tucked the letter in her copy of Romeo and Juliet, her fingers tenderly caressing the dry, darkened rose pressed between the pages before she tucked it back safely on her shelf.

Reluctantly, she went downstairs to meet William and her mother in the parlor.

She hadn't sung to an audience since Andrew played for her at his family's Christmas party two and a half years ago. Aunt Catherine had gushed about Sarah's singing, but when Mary had sung, she had done nothing but critique her.

Andrew had later told her that his mother was angry because Mary had been better than Sarah and embarrassed that she'd spent a lot of money on singing lessons and Sarah still couldn't sing, but it had really hurt Mary's feelings. It had upset her, and she'd been self-conscious about singing in front of anyone, even her mother, ever since. Andrew had tried many times to get her to sing with him, but she never could bring herself to do it. Aunt Catherine's cruel words always returned to the forefront of her mind.

William was seated at the piano when Mary walked into the room. It was odd, seeing William where Andrew usually sat, but even Mary could admit he looked particularly dashing sitting in front of the keys.

"Are you ready, my lady?" he asked.

Mary gave him a sideways look and cocked her head. "Not in the slightest, but I will do my best to prepare myself."

"There is no doubt in my mind that you will do wonderfully."

He gave her a small, warm smile, and she took a deep breath and nodded.

"All right. I suppose I'm ready."

William struck the key to a melody she was quite familiar with. She sighed out a laugh as she remembered all the times her father had sat at the piano playing this song for her mother, and the two would sing a beautiful duet.

It was the most incredible feeling for him to have chosen that song, which had meant so much to her all her life.

Mary found her voice and sang quietly at first. William's soft eyes met hers, and she found herself singing louder. He joined in, singing her father's part beautifully.

She moved closer to the piano, eyes only for William. As the song ended, she grinned wide. Singing had come back so easily, so naturally, as though she had never stopped.

That song held a special place in her heart, and singing it again was a treat she hadn't expected. She wondered if perhaps her mother had suggested it. Even if she had, Mary was glad for it.

"Well, Miss Mary, I do say your mother was right. You have a very lovely voice. You do the world a disservice by keeping it for yourself."

"I've always loved that song," she said.

"As have I. It's a beautiful duet. Perhaps we could perform it at dinner parties or just for the two of us."

"It really was beautiful," Mother said.

Mary turned to see her mother sitting on the chair near the door.

"Mother. I didn't see you come in."

"I came in when your back was turned. It really was beautiful. You sound wonderful together."

Mary looked at her feet, feeling oddly self-conscious. Though her mother had always complimented her singing voice, she hadn't sung in front of her in so long, she wasn't used to hearing her compliments.

And with everything happening, Mary had grown quite distant from her mother.

"Thank you, Mother. It was quite nice singing with you, William. You play beautifully," she told him.

"Thank you. And you? Do you play?"

Mary nodded. "My father taught me when I was just a girl. I don't play often. I much prefer to be the audience."

William scooted over on the bench. "Do you mind playing with me?"

Mary glanced at her mother, hoping she'd react negatively to the idea of the proximity, but she nodded once, giving her permission. Mary took her seat and smoothed her skirt.

William sorted through the sheet music until he found a song he was happy with, then set it on the rack for them both to see.

"Is this one all right?" he asked.

"This one will be just fine."

Together, they began the song, their fingers gently kissing each key as they played the soft, slow melody. Mary became lost in the music, lost in the song, and found herself disappointed when it was over.

"That was beautiful!"

Mary looked up to see Sarah standing by the door. She hadn't realized she had even awoken, let alone found her way to the parlor to watch Mary and William's duet.

"Play another one for me?" she asked.

"Sarah, dear, I think we should go find your mother and leave these two alone," Mother said, standing. "She'd mentioned wanting to discuss a few things with you about Mister Lawson."

Sarah frowned but followed her out of the room, shooting an envious look at Mary and William before following her aunt from the room.

"That was lovely," Mary said when it was just the two of them. "Playing together, I mean."

"It was. Thank you for humoring me and bringing a smile to my face. I must admit, I've never had as much fun as I have with you."

"You're rather fun, yourself, Will."

She looked into his eyes, only inches away, and felt her heart race. He was still so close. She thought of moving away, but the idea of offending him crossed her mind, and she resisted.

"Mary," he whispered, his breath warm on her face.

"Yes?" she asked softly.

"You have to stop looking at me like that, or I'm not going to be able to resist touching you and kissing you."

She hadn't been aware she had been looking at him in any particular way. She narrowed her eyes and quickly averted her gaze, several loose curls falling over her face as she stared down at the keys.

He slowly reached out, tilting her chin up and toward him. He brushed a strand of hair behind her ear.

His eyes were wild as he licked his lips, his chest rising and falling with each quick breath. Was he going to kiss her? She should move away before he did something they couldn't take back.

"Will...." she whispered, pleading with him.

"Yes?"

"We shouldn't...."

He licked his lips, a smile forming on them. "Perhaps just one?"

Before she could answer, he leaned forward and crushed his salty lips to hers. Her breath hitched at his boldness. She felt his hand on her bodice, pressing firmly against her, but before she could push him off her, she heard footsteps, and William pulled away.

She'd never been kissed before, not properly. She hadn't expected it to be like that. She had thought of kissing Andrew before, but she'd never known what to expect. Would it always be so hard and forced? But his hand had bothered her more than his lips had. No man had ever touched her like that.

Her cheeks burned as Ruth walked in but pulled up short when she saw the pair sitting at the piano.

"I'm so sorry to interrupt, Miss. I'll come back later."

"No, please," Mary said, silently pleading for her not to leave them alone. "We were just playing the piano. Do what you need. You won't be a bother to us."

She nodded once and walked to the opposite end of the parlor to begin cleaning.

Mary turned back to William. "Would you like to play another song?" Perhaps if she could keep his hands busy, she could keep them off her.

He stared at her for a moment.

"What is it?" she asked.

"I don't think I'll ever be able to get you out of my mind now."

Mary's stomach twisted. One thing was very certain—she wouldn't be able to get him off her mind either. But she knew for certain they would be thinking completely different thoughts when they remembered this moment.

Chapter Thirteen

*T*HE REST OF THE WEEK went by without any more stolen kisses, although it wasn't for lack of William's trying. Mary wasn't sure what had gotten into him, but every few hours he would suggest they go somewhere, but there always seemed to be someone in the room with them.

Even after dinner they weren't alone. Sarah and Jeffry had taken to walking after evening meals as well, always remaining several feet behind them. As much as Mary disliked Jeffry, she greatly appreciated his presence because without him and Sarah there, who knew what William might try again?

They talked of weddings, with Sarah hinting that she was ready for marriage. Mary tried to chime in whenever Sarah did, encouraging Jeffry to make her an honest woman. Jeffry would laugh them off every time.

Her thoughts kept returning to Andrew and how she was going to tell him about the kiss. He would be upset, no doubt.

But Andrew was gone. He'd chosen work over her, given up on the idea of them as far as she was concerned. It made her heart ache to think.

On William's final night at the house, Mother had a special

meal made up for the occasion. Mary wondered what all the fuss was about, but her mother told her to never send a man off without a proper full stomach.

"I wish you didn't have to leave," Mother said over dinner. "It's been so wonderful seeing you every day. And Mary seems to have changed since meeting you."

Mary didn't remind her how she was changing for the worse, crying every night and being kissed outside of marriage. There wasn't even a promise.

"I wish I could stay longer. Unfortunately, I must return to work. Perhaps I can get away in a few weeks, or you and Mary can come to Connell Manor to visit. I'll speak with Mother and Father, but I'm sure they would love the company."

"That would be lovely," Mother said.

But would it? How many opportunities would he have to corner her in his own home and force his lips on hers?

Perhaps he hadn't known she didn't want it. She had been frozen, after all, shocked. He might have seen that as not only acceptance but submission.

The maids cleared the plates, and they rose to retire to the parlor.

"Missus Kline, I was wondering if I may speak with you?" William asked as they walked from the room.

Mary shot him a questioning look, and Sarah broke into a fit of giggles, only to be chastised by her mother.

"I would like to work out an arrangement of when a good time for you to visit would be."

Mother looked slightly disappointed as she said, "Oh, yes, of course."

But Mary nearly let out a sigh of relief. She had been so worried he was going to ask for her hand. She wasn't ready for that.

Once she agreed to marry him, she'd never be able to marry

Andrew. And she wasn't ready to close that door yet, even if Andrew was. Even if her mother had decided it was closed before they could open it.

Sarah slid her arm around Mary's as they walked in the opposite direction of William and her mother.

"Pity. I dare say I thought for sure he was going to talk to her about marrying you."

Mary didn't reply, her stomach in knots, and Sarah took that as reason to keep talking.

"I know it's sudden, but you have spent a lot of time with him, and I daresay he seems absolutely taken with you. He is quite handsome and very wealthy. If he does ask for your hand, you would be remarkably foolish to decline."

"Two weeks aren't nearly enough time to decide if you want to get married. Men aren't as eager to settle down as women."

She was trying to convince herself. Will seemed ready for the commitment, but Mary was still trying to figure out how her life had spiraled so out of control.

She was glad all he wanted to talk about was the calendar. Mary wasn't ready to agree to be his wife.

They entered the parlor and sat down, Aunt Catherine in her seat next to the fire.

"I have to disagree with you on that, dear," she said. "Men are sometimes very keen to settle down before women. Why, your Uncle Isaac asked me three times to marry him before I said yes."

Mary narrowed her eyes, confused. "Why did you say no?"

"I wasn't ready. I was only seventeen the first time he asked. He was twenty-six. I worried he wasn't serious enough about me, so I waited to make sure he was."

"That's a risky move, Mother," Sarah said, looking absolutely stricken. "What if his eye would have been caught by another woman? Then what would you have done?"

Aunt Catherine shrugged. "I didn't want him if he wasn't serious about me. If another woman would have turned his head, he wasn't worth my time. I was a pretty girl back then, so it wasn't like I wouldn't have had other prospects, although your father was by far the best one."

Sarah smiled, and they began talking about how Uncle Isaac proposed each time. Mary tried to pay attention, but all she could think about was her mother in the other room with William. What were they talking about? Did he really want to plan the best time, or was he asking about marrying Mary?

What would she do if he asked for her hand?

She tried to shake that feeling off. They'd only known one another for two weeks. It wasn't possible for him to care enough for her that he would want to marry her, was it? It was true he had kissed her and expressed an interest in her, but that wasn't a promise. She'd heard stories of girls who kissed before marriage, even if they kept it a secret from their parents or eventual spouses.

But that didn't mean they needed to get married.

What would she do if he *was* asking for her hand in marriage? Her mother would gladly agree, but was Mary ready for what came next? If she declined, her mother wouldn't speak to her ever again. But if she declined, she could have Andrew.

Her mind was never far from Andrew, even if she were forbidden from being with him.

William returned, but Mother did not.

"Is everything all right?" she asked, peering around him and down the empty hall.

"Yes, quite. Your mother should be along any moment. I was wondering if you were ready for our walk?"

Without Jeffry there, there wouldn't be anyone to follow them and ensure William remained a gentleman. Sarah would no doubt remain in the parlor with her mother.

Mary gave him a small smile, her nerves standing on end. "Yes, of course."

He led her down the hall, stopping to allow her to get her shawl before leading her outside. It wasn't cold, but the weather had been so unpredictable with the approaching summer that Mary wanted to be prepared. Besides, adding another layer of clothing might act as a slight buffer to William.

"Did you work out when I can come stay with you?" Mary asked.

William stared ahead. "I admit, I wrote to Mother and Father days ago and got a letter this morning giving me permission to invite you and your mother anytime. I would love to have you out tomorrow, but unfortunately, I must return home to make arrangements. I was hoping you could come out as early as two weeks."

Mary's heart leaped as she realized she wouldn't be seeing him for a fortnight.

"Two weeks is a long time, but we can write every day. I never tire of hearing from you. You can tell me everything that happens."

Her chest tightened. Everything was changing.

He stopped just shy of the rose bushes—her and Andrew's rose bushes—and took her hands. "Mary, there's something I need to speak with you about."

She studied him, feeling her heart quicken. "Yes? Is something the matter?"

"Heavens, no! Everything is splendid. Perfect, even, with the exception of my leaving tomorrow."

"Oh. All right, I'm listening."

William took a deep breath and sank onto the white bench, pulling her down beside him. "You see, after we played piano in the parlor the other day, I couldn't get you out of my mind. I just knew, right then, that I wasn't just infatuated with you, Mary, but I had already fallen in love with you."

A knot formed in her throat, and she tried to swallow it down. She suddenly didn't doubt that he was going to ask her to marry him. She tried to keep her face passive.

"I've never heard any lady of the house speak to the help with so much courteousness. You were more than polite but friendly with her. I know it sounds ridiculous, out of all we've done together, everything we shared…." He stared into her eyes, and her heart raced. "But seeing how kind you are to those beneath you showed me everything I needed to know about your heart. And I'm in love with it, Mary. I'm in love with you."

Her head was swimming with thoughts and emotions. She had thought he was being kind, but to call Ruth beneath them was heartless.

"Ruth is my friend," she said, narrowing her eyes at him.

"Of course she is. And that's why I love you so. That is why I asked your mother if I could ask you to marry me."

More than ever, Mary wanted to say no. Not just because she was in love with Andrew but because of what he'd said about Ruth being beneath them. How was she expected to be with a man who thought that?

"I know we haven't been courting for long, but I know everything I need to know about you. You will make an excellent wife and lady of the house. Will you please do me the honor and give me the pleasure of being my wife?"

There it was. The dreaded question she knew would inevitably come. She had hoped for more time. She wanted to talk to Andrew about it all. She'd hoped her mother would see how unhappy she was and change her mind, even though she knew she would never agree to Mary's union with Andrew.

Her mother wanted it. She'd ordered her to accept his proposal because she wanted it so desperately. She'd be over the moon, planning the wedding. All it took was one word.

One word that was stuck in her throat, burning in her chest.

"Mary?"

Mary swallowed, tears stinging her eyes. "Yes," she whispered.

William grinned, taking her tears as tears of joy, and wrapped her in a hug. She felt his lips on her cheek and knew her life was about to change drastically. There would be no going back now.

Chapter Fourteen

ALTHOUGH MOTHER WAS THRILLED AT the proposal, Mary couldn't seem to slow her racing heart. She didn't want to say yes, but what other choice did she have? She couldn't bear to lose her mother.

Still, the idea of marriage scared her. She had always thought if the time came for marriage, she would have ended up with Andrew. Now that she was engaged, there was no hope for their future. She'd never be with Andrew. It was too late to change her mind.

She wasn't ready to start a life of her own. She would have to move away from Kline Manor and make a home somewhere else. As much as she knew her mother was looking forward to that, it terrified Mary. Kline Manor had been the only home she'd ever known.

And if she moved away, she would barely ever see Andrew. She wondered if he would still write to her and visit once she was married to another man.

William carried his bag to the carriage, and Mary stood by, waiting to say goodbye to her fiancé.

"I promise to write to you as soon as I arrive at the inn where I am staying for the night," he told her.

Mary smiled, pretending her stomach wasn't rolling with nerves. "I'll be awaiting your letter."

He stared at her for a moment, his eyes soft and warm. "I wish I didn't have to leave. Especially now."

"It's probably best to leave before I give you a reason to become cross with me and take back your promise."

"I don't think anything could make me want to go back on my promise."

She was afraid of that.

"I'll see you soon," he said.

"Travel safe."

He climbed into the carriage and waved to her one last time.

As he started down the road, her heart was torn in two. What had she done by agreeing to the marriage?

She saw Mother standing at the top of the stairs, face lit up when Mary's heart was breaking.

A lump formed in her throat as she started up the stairs and into the house, only half hearing her mother's excited chatter about William and the wedding.

She was glad her mother was happy, but she wished more than anything her mother's joy could have correlated with her own happiness and desires. Was she certain she was willing to sacrifice her happiness to keep her mother in her life?

She thought about her father and how she felt when he died. How much worse would she feel if she lost her mother too? She couldn't betray her mother's wishes.

And now that she had agreed to marry William, it was too late to reconsider.

Marrying William would pull her away from her home and family. She wouldn't see or hear much from Andrew. Although, if she were married to William, perhaps that would be for the best. Andrew had run just to get away from witnessing William court Mary.

She felt a hand on her shoulder and jumped with a gasp.

"Oh, Mother. You frightened me."

"My apologies, dear. Are you all right? You haven't seemed to have heard what I've been saying."

"Oh. I'm sorry. I was merely lost in thought."

Her mother smiled. "Good thoughts of William?"

She wanted to hear Mary gush about William and talk about how much she was going to miss him. But the truth of it was she still wasn't sure how she was going to pretend she wasn't in love with Andrew.

Mary's lack of response didn't seem to faze her.

"I am so glad the two of you get on so well. I just knew William would be a perfect match for you."

Once again, she wanted to tell her mother how much she loved Andrew and how being with William was breaking her heart.

But it was too late. She was promised to William. She couldn't go back on her word without ruining her family's reputation.

"Why don't you write him? He so loved hearing from you the day he got home."

She didn't want to write to William. She wanted to go to her bedroom and be alone. Instead, she went to the library to start her letter, feeling slightly defeated. She sat at the desk overlooking the garden and remembered how he walked with her and when he asked her to be his wife. She thought about those moments in the parlor, when they were playing piano, then when they weren't and his lips were on hers.

It truly was too late to pick Andrew and run away with him. She had to find a way to forget about the life she could have had and find a way to be happy with William. So until she felt as confident in the marriage as William, she would fake it. She would write to him as though he were Andrew.

Will,

You've been gone for only a few minutes, yet I find myself wanting to write to you already. I fear these next few weeks will be too much for me without you here. I have already grown accustomed to your constant presence. Whatever will I do without hearing the comforting sound of your voice or seeing your smile? The halls already feel empty and quiet. Whatever shall I do without your laughter to fill this manor?

Mother and Aunt Catherine insisted Sarah and I do a lesson today on etiquette. As if I don't already know how to act like a proper lady. You can attest to my perfect behavior, after all. I am at least proper enough to have captured your attention and won your affection.

This was probably the quickest engagement known to humankind, but I'm glad to have met you. I truly am excited to become your wife, even if I am a little nervous. I cannot help but worry. I worry about being a good wife, about leaving my home and family. I worry about losing the woman I am as I become a wife and, someday, a mother.

Perhaps I'm being too forward. This must be why Mother insists I take etiquette lessons. I suppose I tend to say more than I should. Please do not think I'm having second thoughts about marrying you. I want nothing more than to be your wife.

I'll write you again tomorrow. And the next day. Until you tell me you've had enough of me.

All my best,
Mary

Mary folded the letter and wrote William's address on it before taking it to Samuel to be sent out with the evening mail. Her chest pinched as she thought about how embellished her words had been. She felt guilty, as though she were lying, but if her lies would make her future husband happy, weren't they acceptable? Should a wife not say things to make her husband happy?

No sooner had she stepped away did her mother come to escort her to her lesson.

As much as she tried to pay attention, her mind wandered.

She wondered where Andrew was, how he was doing, and if he would ever forgive her. She should write to him and tell him of the engagement firsthand. She didn't want him to find out through gossip. Aunt Catherine very well may have written to tell him, but Mary should tell him, as well. She didn't want to act like she was hiding it from him, even though a part of her dreaded him finding out. She'd write to him before the evening mail went out. She didn't know how he would take the news, but she knew he would pretend to be happy for her because, just like she had, he'd made his choice when he told her he wouldn't be back for some time.

She hoped the letter she wrote didn't raise William's concern about marrying her. She hoped her worries didn't make him question whether she wanted to be with him. If she did something to ruin the engagement, would her mother blame her? Would she forgive her, or assume it was done deliberately?

"Mary, did you hear me?" Sarah asked.

Mary looked at her cousin and realized their tutor was gone, class was over, and Sarah had been speaking to her.

"No, I'm terribly sorry, Sarah. What did you say?"

She sighed. "I asked if you set a wedding date yet."

"Oh. Not yet, no. Mother and I need to speak with William's family and talk over what the next step is."

"Are you going to be married here? Or does he want it to be at his house? I heard more and more couples are getting married in churches now. Would you consider that?"

Mary shook her head and shrugged. "I'm not sure. I'll have to speak with Mother. We'll know more in a few days, I suppose."

Sarah huffed. "Well, I suppose you should run that by William's parents, as well."

Her condescending tone was beginning to aggravate Mary. She wasn't eager to be married to William, so why would she rush to discuss the details of the wedding with his parents?

"Yes, I suppose we will," she snapped back.

Sarah glared at her. "Why are you being so discourteous?"

"Forgive me, but it feels more like you are the one being discourteous."

"Because I am interested in your wedding? The question is, Mary, why aren't you? Is it because you are disappointed Andrew didn't propose?"

Mary's head snapped to her cousin, her cheeks burning. How had she known?

"Why would you think that?"

Sarah rolled her eyes. "As if I haven't known you for years? I see the way you look at one another. Mother and I thought for sure you'd be married within the next couple of years, but for some reason, you chose William. And if you don't start acting like you are in love with him, everyone is going to see right through your façade, just as I have."

"I wanted to choose Andrew," she said before she could stop herself. "But I am engaged to William. So please don't say anything. To anyone."

Sarah frowned. "I won't. But if you don't start acting like a bride in love, I won't have to."

How could she act like a bride in love? She had no idea where to even start.

She hadn't even told Andrew yet.

She still needed to write to him. She glanced at the window and realized evening was fast approaching.

"Would you excuse me, Sarah? I want to write a letter before the evening post arrives."

She eyed her for a moment, then nodded. "Yes, of course."

Mary gathered her skirts and hurried to the library. She wasn't sure how much time she had, but she knew it was getting late. She'd have to hurry if she wanted to get the letter out today, and she did. She must.

> *Andrew,*
> *I hope this letter reaches you before your mother or sister could write.*

Mary stared at the start of the letter before balling it up and sighing. That sounded as though she was only writing to tell him before someone else could. The last thing she wanted was Andrew to assume she was only telling him because she had to. She tried again.

> *Andrew,*
> *I hope this letter finds you well. I was saddened to hear that you would be in Boston for a while, but I understand why you have chosen to stay behind. The past week has been busy. You were right, in your last letter, when you said if William was smart, he'd already be here, because he was. He came for our mother's dinner party and stayed until today.*
>
> *He can be charming when he wants, which is probably how he won Mother's favor so quickly. He plays the piano, though it was strange seeing him where you usually sit. He has a pleasant singing voice, as well. Mother adores him.*

I was heartbroken after your letter. I had planned to plead with Mother until she saw reason and allowed me to choose my own husband, but William was here, and when you had told me you weren't returning for a while and instructed me to write to him, I understood that you were done trying. As you should be. You deserve much better than this life, Andrew.

I cannot lie and say it didn't hurt, but I understand your desire to run away. It's all I can think of anymore. Especially now.

Last night, while we were walking in the garden, William proposed. I accepted, as you knew I would. Mother didn't give me another option. A part of me wonders if I made the right decision. Still, it's too late to ponder on that now, isn't it?

Andrew please understand this doesn't change how I feel about you. You are my best friend, and I hope my engagement and marriage doesn't change that. It may not have been the life I would have chosen for myself, but it is what I was given. What I must do. And I hope that by obeying my mother, I do not have to lose you.

I hope you come to visit me after I move out of Kline Manor, as I cannot bear to think of life without you in it. I'm not sure when the wedding will be yet, but I truly hope you can come. I need my best friend at my side if I am to make it through the hardest day of my life.

Yours,
Mary

Mary sealed the letter and sighed. She knew the news would upset him, but what else was she to do? She had chosen William. She had to let Andrew go and had to accept that he had chosen to let her go, as well.

Still, it didn't make it any easier. It didn't make it hurt any less.

She handed the letter to Samuel, asking if he could please send it with the evening post.

As she made her way to supper, she wondered how Andrew would react when he read the letter. She wondered if he would be angry or sad or feel betrayed. She felt as though she were betraying him.

She couldn't help the sinking feeling in her stomach telling her she was about to lose her best friend.

And she couldn't stand the thought of losing Andrew.

She entered the dining room where her mother was talking amiably to Aunt Catherine about the wedding. She was looking forward to the union.

As worried as Mary was about marrying William and the consequences it would have, she was glad that her mother was no longer angry with her. She was happy, and she would stay in her life, and wasn't anything and everything worth that? Even Mary's happiness?

It was only a matter of time before she became Mrs. William Connell. The sooner she adjusted to the idea, the sooner she could find solace in it.

Chapter Fifteen

$\mathcal{W}$HEN MARY WOKE UP, SHE had a letter waiting for her from William.

He had done as he promised and wrote to her from where he stopped to stay for the night.

Before she could open the letter and read it, however, her mother entered the dining room.

"Oh, thank heavens you're finally awake. We have so much to do before the wedding. I've written to William's mother, but she won't get it until tomorrow. I thought it best to let William announce the engagement himself. I hate how far away they live. If only they were closer so we could arrange everything at once instead of waiting nearly a week to have a single conversation."

Mary stared wide eyed at her mother, wondering where she summoned so much energy first thing in the morning to discuss such life-changing matters.

"Well, have you eaten yet?" she asked, eyeing Mary's empty plate.

Mary shook her head. "I just got here."

Mother sighed. "All right. Well, eat and meet me in the library. We need to discuss the wedding."

When she was gone, Mary hung her head in her hands. If she had known it was going to be this much work to get married, she might have had second, technically third, thoughts about agreeing.

Ruth brought out her breakfast, and Mary straightened, trying to look less annoyed.

"Is everything all right, Miss?"

Mary gave her a small smile. "Yes, I suppose. I'm just nervous about the wedding. Is it horrible that I don't want to do the planning?"

Ruth laughed. "Planning a wedding is a lot of work, especially for those with money. I couldn't imagine how complicated it must be for you."

Guilt punched Mary in the gut as she thought about how simple Ruth's wedding must have been. "Oh, Ruth. I'm terribly sorry. You must think of me as horrid, complaining about how hard it is planning for my fancy wedding."

She gave her a small smile. "No, miss. I can see why you're nervous. Marriage is a big decision, and planning the wedding is more than planning some dinner party. This is the beginning of your future together. Perhaps ask your future husband his thoughts? That may ease some of the pressure you're feeling with planning."

Mary smiled and touched her hand, grateful to have her kindness when she was so overwhelmed she could hardly breathe. "Thank you, Ruth. You're wonderful."

Ruth gently touched Mary's cheek with her free hand. "As are you."

She stood and walked from the room back to the kitchen.

Mary looked down at the letter William had sent her and slowly opened it.

My sweet Mary,

I am writing, as promised, from my room at the inn. Though I admit, I had supper before sitting down to write this. I hope you are doing well and your mother isn't drowning you in wedding plans just yet. Though she seemed very eager when I left, so I daresay she may have quite a few things planned over the next few days. I regret that I had to leave you to deal with all of that on your own. Just know, whatever you decide, I will love. Choose the location and food, flowers, because you said you like them, and whatever color dress you will love. As long as you continue to choose me.

I cannot wait to get home. There is so much to do to prepare for you to join me. I need to find us a home. If there is anything you wish me to ensure we have, such as a grand library, just let me know, and I'll make sure you get it. I'll give you whatever you ask.

My only wish was that you were here with me, going with me to find our new home so we could choose it together.

The room is too quiet without your presence. I cannot stop thinking of that kiss we shared, wishing we could have had another.

I'll write when I can.

Yours always,
Will

Mary's heart thundered in her chest as she set the letter down. It was honestly happening. She was going to be married to William, and soon.

After she'd eaten, she took the letter to her bedroom, placing it in a pile next to Andrew's letters, then went to the library to find her mother.

While she wasn't ready to become immersed in all the planning, she knew her mother was, and it was the first time in months she'd taken such an interest in anything. Mary would suffer anything to keep her mother smiling.

"There you are!" she said as Mary walked in. "I was beginning to think you'd forgotten, and I was going to have to send Albert to fetch you."

"Oh, Mother. You leave poor Albert alone. He has much better things to do than to fetch me."

"Of course he does, but you certainly don't act like it."

Mary sighed and sank heavily into a chair by the window, wishing she were anywhere else in the world but in this room, preparing for a wedding she didn't want.

"Mary, sit up. Did you not just have a lesson in etiquette yesterday? Do I need to schedule another to ensure you're prepared to act decent for the wedding?"

Mary immediately straightened. "No, ma'am."

Her mother smiled. "Good. Now, shall we discuss your wedding?"

"William wrote. He said whatever I choose is fine."

"He's such a sweet boy. Though, I do say most men would say the same. Most want nothing to do with party planning. That's usually a lady's domain."

She wished she could choose to have nothing to do with party planning.

Mary zoned out as her mother began talking of fabrics and flowers, but after a while, her mother began asking her for her opinion.

She stared at Mary expectantly. Mary's mind reeled as she tried to recall what she had said. She couldn't even remember what her mother was talking about, let alone a specific question.

"What do you think, Mother? You've gone to more weddings than I have, and you've planned more parties. I'm not quite sure I could make the best decision."

That seemed to appease her mother. "Well, I think you'd look gorgeous in the lace."

Mary smiled. Andrew had once teased her about her blue dress with white lace, saying it made her look like a doll going to a tea party. He preferred silk. "Lace is perfect."

"Then it's settled. I'll contact our seamstress and have her get started on your dress. Now are we sure we want flowers? I know they're becoming more and more popular, but I think simple is better and more elegant. Flowers are so theatrical, don't you think?"

Mary loved flowers. She wanted dozens upon dozens of flowers at her wedding. But William didn't like flowers. Andrew did.

"I think William and I would love simple, Mother. No flowers."

She silently pleaded that this torture would soon be over. Her mother couldn't possibly have too much more to say on the matter, could she? Finally, after only a few more minutes of listening to her mother discussing wedding preparations and what food they should serve, she was finally dismissed.

She tried not to groan as she made her way to the garden, wanting desperately to hide from her mother. It was only the second day of her engagement, and she was already tired of it. She hoped her mother would calm down after they were finished planning, but she worried it would only get worse the closer to the ceremony it got.

Maybe Mother would get better once she was married.

But what if she didn't?

Mary had a sudden thought of her and William married and her mother insisting on her throwing parties or having children and what she should do to teach them how to be proper citizens.

Or maybe, she thought, her mother would finally see her as a woman and take a step back, letting Mary take control of her own life and home. She will be the lady of the house, after all.

But that didn't sound like her.

As she strolled around the garden, her eyes focused on the red roses. She smiled, a memory resurfacing. She had been sixteen when Andrew had given her a red rose from this very bush. They were walking around the garden, as they always had to escape the adults, and Sarah had gone back inside, insisting it was too hot to be in the sunlight when really, she wanted to flirt with the young Mr. Cavendish.

Mary had told Andrew about a boy from town who had eyed her a few times and how she thought he would want to pursue her and possibly court her when she was of age. He was a handsome boy from a good family, so she hadn't hated the prospect of courting. Andrew, however, had crinkled his nose in disgust.

"What would be so wrong with that?" Mary had asked.

Andrew stood next to the rose bush and didn't meet her eye. "You deserve someone better than a simple boy from town."

Mary had laughed. "What's wrong with the boys from town? A few of them are quite lovely, I'll have you know."

Andrew finally turned and smiled at her, his eyes finding hers. "You, Mary, are like a rose."

She narrowed her eyes as he held up the flower, but the corner of her lips turned up in a mischievous grin. "Are you saying I'm beautiful? Do you forget yourself, Andrew?"

He laughed. "Not at all. You are beautiful, but you're much more than that."

She accepted the rose, now curious. "Oh?"

"You are a wild spirit, and you require a delicate hand to

help you grow. Someone patient, who doesn't mind your thorns that will inevitably poke if not held properly."

Mary couldn't help but smile at the metaphor. It was the nicest thing he had ever said to her. It was the nicest thing *anyone* had ever said to her.

"And who could that be?" she asked in a whisper.

He grinned at her. "I don't know, but I wish him the best of luck."

Her mouth had opened with shock as he began to cackle. He took off at a sprint, and she had chased after him, still carefully holding the rose he had given her.

As the memory faded, Mary made her way into the house and up to her bedroom. She took down her copy of Romeo and Juliet. The book fell open to the middle page, revealing an old, darkened rose, pressed dry to last the years. The first and last gift Andrew had given her.

She had held it so close to her heart, hoping more than anything he would receive the love she had felt for him. Now he had, but it was too late.

She wondered if she should get rid of it now that she was engaged to another man. It was wrong for a married woman to look back on a man she could and would have married. If William were to discover the rose, he might have questions.

Still, she closed the book and put it back on the shelf. She couldn't bear to get rid of it. Andrew was a part of her story, and she wasn't willing to part with the rose and the memory just yet.

Chapter Sixteen

MARY DIDN'T RECEIVE A LETTER for another two days, then it was two at once. It was right after dinner when the evening post arrived. As Samuel handed her the letters in the parlor, Sarah gave her a knowing smile.

"Is that from William? Telling you he's home?" Mother asked.

Mary looked down at the top envelope and saw William's familiar handwriting. "Can you excuse me?"

Mother nodded, and Sarah looked slightly disappointed.

"Of course, dear."

Mary walked out of the room and out to the garden, her heart and mind racing. She walked until she was certain she was out of view of the parlor, then looked at the second letter. As she suspected, it was from Andrew.

She sat on a bench and, with shaking hands, opened the letter from Andrew.

> *Dearest Mary,*
> *I wasn't surprised to hear you accepted, although*
> *I dare say the engagement seems sudden. William*

must know what he has been lucky enough to find. My deepest congratulations to William and my very best wishes to you. I want only happiness for you, even if it isn't with me.

I knew he was smart. Or perhaps I knew what he would do because I would do the same if I were allowed. In all honesty, I knew he'd ask you to marry him when I saw the way he was looking at you that very first day.

I don't doubt that he's charming, but he still isn't good enough for you. Nobody will be. I know this is what you must do, and I respect the decision you had to make to keep what is left of your family together.

I'm sorry I gave up so easily, but truly thought it was what would be easiest for you. I know you couldn't bear the thought of losing your mother by going against her wishes. And I would never ask you to choose between her and me. I love and respect you too much.

I dread to imagine how odd Kline Manor will seem when I return and you are no longer there. If only you didn't have to leave. Who will help keep Sarah in line?

You will always be my best friend, Mary. Therefore, I will visit on occasion, though attending the wedding might prove too difficult for me. I'm not sure I have strength enough for that.

Please know I truly do wish you only the very best.

Yours,
Andrew

Mary set the letter down and wiped away a tear. She was

expecting him to be kind because that was who he was, but she didn't expect his kindness and acceptance to hurt so much.

What stung the most was that he admitted he might not come to the wedding. How could she get married without Andrew there? She wasn't sure she could go through with it without her best friend.

She sniffled and cleared her throat. She had to stop dwelling on Andrew. She would still see him, after all. It would be no different than when she was growing up and only saw him once a year. She could still write to him, couldn't she?

Or would everything change once she was married? William might not like her writing to other men, especially Andrew.

Mary took a deep breath and let it out slowly before picking up the letter from William. The man to whom she would soon be married.

She shouldn't dwell on her feelings for Andrew when she was engaged. Ready or not, it was time to move on.

She opened the letter, determined to look forward to her future with him and not back at her past with Andrew.

> *My sweet Mary,*
> *I have arrived home, and a letter from you was waiting for me. I could never tire of your letters. I must admit, I'm getting spoiled hearing from you. I quite enjoy it. It was odd arriving home and not seeing you. Even though you've never been here before. A part of me feels as though I cannot call this place home anymore. My home is with you now. I need to hurry and find a house fit for you so I can marry you and see you every day.*
> *I am sure you will find some way to entertain yourself, or your mother will find something to fill your time, such as attending more etiquette lessons,*

which I never asked for. I don't want her changing anything about you, even your slouch. I intend to find you just as wild and carefree as when I left you.

I feel like everything has changed, and nothing feels quite right without you. How can I play the piano when you will not be there to accompany me? I'm already missing our time together in the parlor.

Do not let your fears worry you, my darling. It is natural to fear the unknown. You will be the most amazing wife. I have no doubt we will have so much fun. I do not want to pull you away from your family. They will be welcome at our home as often as they wish. I understand your concerns about your life changing, but please know I would never expect you to be any different than the woman you are—the woman I fell in love with.

I like you being honest with me. You should always share your thoughts and concerns with me. Perhaps I can help ease some of them.

Mother says she will be ready for the wedding in as early as two weeks, but since your mother is making the plans, it's entirely up to her. I would gladly marry you tomorrow if I could.

I will write to you again soon. I already cannot wait until your next letter arrives.

Always yours,
Will

She folded the letters and walked back into the house, taking them straight to her bedroom to put them away. She was glad to have heard back from both William and Andrew, even if it felt as though Andrew was even farther away, and had gladly accepted that he and Mary would never be together. But Will was one step closer. At least she wasn't completely alone. William might not be who she envisioned as a husband, but he seemed to love her.

After she'd replaced her *Romeo and Juliet* book, Mary sat on the bed, careful not to wrinkle her dress. She didn't have much longer in this room. She wondered what her new bedroom would look like and if she would find it as comfortable as she had been here.

William had said his mother would be ready for the wedding in as early as two weeks.

Two weeks.

Her heart raced.

Her mother would be thrilled. She would, no doubt, agree to such a sudden wedding date. She was eager for Mary and William to marry and would think the sooner, the better.

Ready or not, it was happening. And soon.

She made her way downstairs and found her mother in the parlor with Aunt Catherine, Uncle Isaac, and Sarah. The women stared at her expectantly, but none of them said anything or asked about what was in the letters.

"William said Missus Connell would be ready for the wedding in as early as two weeks," she said, taking her seat.

The smile that appeared on her mother's face was bigger than any she'd ever seen.

"Oh, Mary! That's wonderful! Oh, we have so much to do and not much time to do it. We'll have to take you to the seamstress first thing and have the food ordered. I'll write to her straight away so we can discuss everything. I want to ensure she approves of the day and can be here for it." She rose to her feet and hurried from the room, no doubt headed for the library to write to Mrs. Connell.

Mary tried to look pleased with the news and not nauseous at the prospect of her entire life changing.

"You must be thrilled," Sarah said with a smile, a flicker of jealousy flashing in her eyes. "I cannot believe how lucky you are. Jeffry hasn't made so much as a hint of a promise yet, and you're about to get married."

Mary bit back a remark that Sarah might be better off with Jeffry not proposing. Her cousin seemed happy enough, and she had no desire to ruin it.

"It is a bit soon," Aunt Catherine said. "I'd like you to get to know Jeffry more before any arrangements are made."

Uncle Isaac peered over his paper. "I want to ensure he's good enough. What do we know of his family?"

Sarah burst into a speech about how wonderful and wealthy Jeffry's family was, how his grandfather had served in the army, and how everyone who was anyone had heard of his father.

Mary's mind wandered as she blocked out Sarah's rant. Aunt Catherine was right. It was so sudden. They knew very little of one another. Mary didn't know his parents yet. She couldn't help but wonder if William was truly happy with his decision or if he was pretending to be happier than he was, just as she was.

It had only been a few weeks, and they were engaged. It was all happening so fast it made her dizzy.

She couldn't stop thinking she was making a terrible mistake. Would she be able to fall in love with William and stay in love with him forever? Or would she forever long for Andrew and what might have been?

How much could someone learn about another person in two weeks? Were they really ready for marriage? What if they got married and they didn't like who the other was after living together for a few months?

When her mother came back, she knew that it didn't matter how well she knew William. She would have agreed no matter how she felt because her mother wanted her to. At least she didn't hate her fiancé. She could do worse.

It had to be good enough, though, because in two weeks' time, she would be married.

Chapter Seventeen

*T*HE DAYS OVER THE NEXT two weeks went by in a blur, but the nights seemed to drag by. During the day, Mother ensured Mary stayed so busy with wedding plans she didn't have time to worry about anything other than what she was currently focusing on. But at night, when Mary went to bed, she finally had time to think about Andrew and William and her future.

She hoped Andrew would come to the wedding, even if he sent word with Uncle Isaac telling her he would be working and unable to step away. Her heart ached thinking of getting married without him there. She knew it would be hard for him, but it was going to be hard for her too. Did he think she wanted to go through with it? She tried to put herself in his shoes. Would she want to attend the wedding if he were marrying another woman?

Still, it broke her heart.

Mary and her mother had just arrived home after her final fitting for her wedding dress, and as she stepped inside, she saw William standing at the end of the hall. They had been writing every day since he left, but she still wasn't used to it. When Mary saw him, she made her way down the hall, meeting him halfway.

"What a lovely surprise," she said.

He laughed and took her hands. "I told you I was coming."

"You didn't!" she said, pulling away to get a better look at him.

She had almost forgotten how handsome he was. How had he remained single long enough to meet Mary?

"I did. Two days ago. I sent the letter before I left."

She heard a small cough behind her and turned to Albert. "Excuse me, Miss. You received a letter while you were out."

Mary laughed and accepted it. "Thank you, Albert."

Sure enough, the letter was from William.

"Shall I read it now?"

Humor glistened in his eyes. "I missed you, Mary."

"I missed you too." Lying was becoming easier for her. Almost second nature. It wasn't that she didn't miss him, but that Andrew dominated most of her thoughts.

She stared into his eyes for a moment. Soon, she was going to be married to him, and she wouldn't have much of a chance to miss him. Unless he turned into the type to work all the time.

"Go on, then," he whispered, indicating the letter.

"Oh!" Mary let out a small laugh and looked down at the letter in her hands, slowly unfolding it.

Mary,

I am writing in a hurry because my carriage is waiting for me. I will be seeing you in two days' time, and I must admit, this has been the longest two weeks of my life. I cannot wait to call you mine so I can hold you and kiss you to my heart's content. I hope you still feel the same. I'd hate to arrive and be turned away.

I apologize I cannot write more, but the longer I sit at this desk with this quill in my hand, the longer

*I must go without seeing that beautiful smile. I will
see you soon, my darling.*

All my love,
William

Mary glanced up at William, feeling overwhelmed. They
would be married in a matter of a week, then he would be free
to hold her and kiss her to his heart's content. The thought made
her uneasy.

"You did tell me you were coming."

"I did. You need someone to escort you to my house this
week, and I didn't want to be without you any longer."

She smiled, feeling her cheeks burn.

"I missed your smile," he said, brushing her warm cheek
with his thumb.

"And I yours."

"Are you ready for our wedding?" he asked.

"Almost." She nearly had everything she needed for the
wedding. Her mother had ensured everything was ready and
taken care of.

She let him lead her down the hall. She didn't care where
he took her as long as they didn't have to help prepare for the
wedding.

He steered her into the garden, eyes only on her.

"I found our home."

Mary's stomach turned. Their home. "How is it? Do you
love it?"

"I do. And I think you will, as well. I hope you will, anyway.
I insisted on stocking the library with hundreds of books and a
fabulous writing desk, so you can read and write as much as you
wish. I had a grand piano placed in the parlor, so we can play
and sing."

"And the kitchen?"

"The kitchen? Can you even cook?" He wrinkled his nose.

Mary laughed, pretending not to be offended by his surprise. "Of course, I can cook. Mother doesn't like me doing it because she says that's servant's work. But I enjoy it."

"Well, now, you never told me that." He looked worried. "But I do believe your mother is right. I wouldn't want you to have to cook."

It was Mary's turn to wrinkle her nose. "Does that mean we have a small kitchen?"

"Define small."

"I don't know. Smaller than the sitting room."

He sighed, relief washing over his features. "No. It's smaller than the kitchen at my parent's home but bigger than your family's sitting room."

"Good."

"That pleases you?"

Mary nodded. "It does. I'm sure you did fine, Will."

"I hope so, but if you hate it, you can redecorate and make it so you love it."

They walked for a while, enjoying the light breeze. Mary couldn't believe he was there. She wasn't expecting him until the following morning.

Still, there was an unspoken shared nervousness between them. In exactly one week, they would be married, and everything would change.

"Are you still worried?" he asked quietly, not looking at her.

That was a big question with a complicated answer. She was worried about a lot of things. She was nervous about tripping as she walked down the aisle. She was afraid to leave home. But she was more worried about giving up Andrew forever.

"Some things still bring me concern, but you have mostly eased my worries."

"Truly?"

"Yes. I'm ready to be your wife, Will. I just pray you don't realize what a handful I am and change your mind while standing at the altar."

William gingerly touched her arm and turned her toward him, looking into her eyes. "You, my dear, will take both of my hands, and I could never change my mind about marrying you."

He gently brushed a strand of hair off her forehead, and her breath hitched.

"Are you sure?" she asked.

"I never believed in fate before, Mary. But when I saw you, I knew it had to be written in the stars that we met."

Her stomach tightened as she remembered Andrew saying he could see how Will felt on that very first day.

"You mean that?"

"Absolutely. You are more beautiful than anyone I've ever met."

She bit her lip, looking off into the distance, wondering if he loved anything other than the way she looked.

As they rounded the side of the house and made it to the front yard, she saw a carriage approaching the house. She narrowed her eyes, trying to remember if they were expecting anyone.

"Who could that be?" she asked, looking at William.

"I'm afraid I know just as much as you. Shall we go and see?"

They walked side by side as they made their way to the front of the house. The doors of the carriage swung open, and Mary felt her heart soar.

Andrew flashed her a grin as he stepped down and placed his hat on his head. It had only been three weeks since she'd last seen him, but he looked different, older and more mature, but still just as handsome as ever.

"Andrew!" she said, rushing forward.

She flung her arms around him, accidentally knocking his hat off. She couldn't help herself. She hadn't heard from him since the letter he'd written to tell her he was happy for her and her engagement, and as far as she knew, he wasn't supposed to be there for another month, at least.

She felt her feet leave the ground as he hugged her back and spun her around. How she had missed his touch and smell.

When he set her back down, she pulled away and gently shoved him. "I've written to you a dozen times, and you've not written back once!" she scolded him.

He frowned. "I'm sorry about that. I have no excuse. Do you think you can forgive me?"

"No matter. You're here now." She took his hands as though he would run off if she didn't cling to him. "Tell me about Boston. How is work? I thought you couldn't get away?"

Suddenly, Andrew pulled his hands back, slightly stiffer than he was just moments ago.

"Work is busy, which is good for business. Boston is fine. Also busy. I wasn't planning to come, but last night, I thought how I wouldn't be able to forgive myself if I missed your wedding."

Mary frowned, confused by his sudden distance. "Well, whatever the case, I'm glad you're here." She followed Andrew's gaze and turned to William, who stood only feet away, forgotten. "William, you remember Andrew?"

He stepped forward and placed a hand on the small of her back. "Yes, I do. How are you?"

Andrew's jaw clenched before he replaced it with a polite smile. "Quite well, thank you. Congratulations on your engagement. I'm glad our Mary found someone to make her happy."

Judging from the look in his eyes, he wasn't as happy as he claimed to be. Still, Mary was thrilled he was there.

She thought that would make her day better. That it would be easier to walk down the aisle if her best friend was there to support her. But as she stood between Andrew and William, she wondered how she was going to marry William while Andrew watched with accusing eyes. Already the guilt was gnawing at her.

But it was too late to go back on her word, even if she changed her mind. Even if, as she stood between the two, with Andrew looking at her with his sad, hazel eyes, she found herself having second thoughts.

Chapter Eighteen

MARY FIDGETED IN HER SEAT, trying to ignore her racing heart as Mrs. Connell once again glanced at her out of the corner of her eye. It was their first real meeting, and it wasn't going as well as they had hoped. Mrs. Connell had questioned Mary upon their arrival about her education, her plans for their future, how many children she wanted, and if her father had left her a dowry.

It was understandable that Mrs. Connell would want to ensure they were a proper family and had only good intentions, but Mary found it deplorable and insensitive to question whether her father left her a dowry. He had only been gone a few months, and Mary didn't want to think of him as merely how much money he had left them.

Besides that, Mrs. Connell seemed to think it irresponsible of Mrs. Kline to have allowed her a governess after the age of twelve.

"A woman who can think for herself is a dangerous thing, indeed," she had said. "They shouldn't bother themselves in such foolishness as education. It is the man who works, so education should be a man's burden. A woman needn't know more than how to properly run her home."

As much as she wanted to cringe, Mary had kept her face passive and polite. She had just opened her mouth to tell Mrs. Connell that ignorant women were fools when her mother caught her eye and shook her head, giving her a hard look. So Mary clamped her mouth closed and chose to sit in silence, allowing Mother to answer.

William wasn't permitted to sit near Mary. His mother had said tonight was for the families to get to know one another, not for courting. Therefore, he was to sit next to his father while the women spoke.

Mr. Connell wasn't particularly interested in the women or what they had to say. He sat in his corner of the parlor, drinking one glass of whiskey after another, speaking with William about work. The more he drank, the louder he spoke.

When it was finally time for supper, Mary breathed a sigh of relief. She was more than ready to go home and hated that they were to spend the night there. She wished they could leave right after. The more she learned about William's family, the more she wished they weren't getting married.

She had hoped William's brothers would be there, but they were away at school. She was upset to learn they wouldn't be there for the wedding either. She'd wanted to ask William if it bothered him, but she hadn't had the chance to speak with him.

At this rate, she doubted that she would be allowed to take her evening stroll. There was no doubt that Mrs. Connell wouldn't approve of William walking with her without a chaperone. She wondered how she would react if she knew that they had been alone together and walked together many times.

Mary was instructed to sit beside her mother around the middle of the table and across from Mrs. Connell, who was sitting next to William. Mr. Connell sat at the head of the table, pouring himself another glass of whiskey. Mary didn't miss the look of disgust Mrs. Connell shot her husband before her features softened, and a false smile took its place.

"The wedding is approaching quickly. William has been very busy trying to find the perfect house. Are you prepared to leave your childhood home?" Mrs. Connell asked as the servants placed bowls of soup in front of them.

The question felt almost ridiculous. How ready could anyone be to leave behind the only world they knew?

But Mary answered as honestly as she could. "I'm ready to start a life with my husband."

William smiled at her, and Mary felt the answer must have been well enough to at least appease him.

"That's good to hear. And are you ready for children?"

Mary paused, the spoon inches from her mouth. Of course she wasn't ready for children. She didn't want children, not so soon after getting married. Not with William.

But he would be expecting them sooner rather than later. Men usually did. You get married, you have babies. That was what was expected of her.

"Children would be wonderful," Mary said, setting her spoon down. "I expect William will make a wonderful father."

Maybe if she kept turning the conversation back to how grateful she was to have William in her life, his mother would stop asking so many questions.

They made it through the first course without any more questions. Mrs. Connell seemed to grow quiet as she ate.

Mr. Connell took her silence for an invitation to talk business. "I don't understand how they managed to buy that company out from under us. Especially when the boy is—"

"Father," William said, cutting him off and glancing at Mary. "Now isn't the time to talk business."

Mr. Connell huffed and shook his head, pouring himself another liberal glass of whiskey.

As much as Mary wanted him to continue his sentence, she also knew it wouldn't be wise to speak up and ask what he wanted to say. Women weren't supposed to speak over men, and since her soon-to-be husband had already asked his father to stop, Mary couldn't very well contradict him. Not in front of Mrs. Connell, who was judging Mary's every word.

No. It was best she remained quiet and try not to let her mind wander and wonder where he was going with it.

But she couldn't stop herself. The boy to whom he was referring was clearly Andrew. Unless, by some chance, someone else had bought a property out from under them, which seemed slightly unlikely to Mary. William hadn't said anything about it, at any rate.

But what was he going to say? Especially when the boy is... what? Andrew was wonderful. Smart and polite. She couldn't think of anything he could have possibly done to offend Mr. Connell and warrant gossip.

Her lips pursed slightly as she stared down at the plate that had replaced the soup during Mr. Connell's outburst.

"Well, if you ask me," Mrs. Connell said, picking at her food, "a boy like that shouldn't be allowed to work with civilized gentlemen."

Mary narrowed her eyes, anger boiling in her stomach. "A boy like what?"

Her mother placed her hand over Mary's hand and squeezed, a warning that she was overstepping. "Watch your tongue."

But she couldn't help herself. "No. I want to hear what they have to say."

"Mary!" her mother hissed.

"No, that's quite all right." Mrs. Connell wiped her hands on a napkin, a hard stare fixed at Mary. "A boy of his color."

It was more than Mary could take. She stood abruptly, her dishes clattering as she bumped the table.

"Andrew is a fine man, better than most of the white men I have known. His color—"

"Mary!" her mother scolded, rising to her feet.

"No, Mother. It isn't right to judge someone based on their skin color when it has no bearing on what kind of person they are. None of you even know him."

"Perhaps we don't know you, either, if this is how you react to the inferior race. I don't think I want William marrying such a defiant woman."

"Please," Mother said softly. "Let me explain. Mary is a sensitive girl. It's my fault, honestly. I wasn't strict enough. And she loves her cousin dearly. We didn't raise her to see him as anything but one of us."

Mary wanted to lash out and strike her. "Andrew is—"

But Mary didn't get to say what Andrew was as her mother grabbed her arm, squeezing so hard Mary gasped, having no choice but to follow as she dragged her from the dining room and down the hall.

"I had every right to speak up for—"

"Hush!" Her mother warned, forcefully shoving her into the parlor.

"But—"

"No! That is quite enough! You may have very well ruined your chance at marrying William."

"Then perhaps it is for the best." Mary glared at her.

Her mother looked stricken. "Was that the goal? To get his mother to call off the wedding?"

"No." But if she did, it wouldn't be the worst thing that could happen.

Her mother shook her head. "How dare you embarrass us like that? I have tried my best to raise you to be proper, to be a lady, but your behavior in there was anything but! It was deplorable."

Her words cut. Did she really believe standing up for someone she loved was so horrible?

"No matter what you do, even if you have completely ruined this union, I will never approve of your marrying Andrew," she hissed in a whisper. "Sit here. Do not move. Do not speak. I will go try to sort things with Missus Connell. With any luck, I can convince her you don't usually act like this."

She stalked from the room, looking angrier than Mary had ever seen.

What was it with everyone thinking Andrew was inferior because of his skin color? What did it matter when he was kind and smart? He was raised by a man of class with money and integrity. Should that not be all that mattered?

If they knew him the way Mary knew him, they wouldn't be so quick to judge. They would see how wonderful he was.

Mary wondered if her mother would be able to smooth things over. Perhaps she had gone too far. William's mother had said Mary was defiant. She might forbid them to wed, no matter what Mary's mother said.

Mary couldn't see herself as part of this family. She didn't want to think of regular visits with Mr. and Mrs. Connell. William seemed wonderful, but if having him in her life meant having them, as well, it wasn't worth it.

Mother returned, her eyes still reflecting anger. Mary's heart leapt. Did that mean the wedding was off?

"We need to go. We're heading home tonight. William has agreed to escort us back."

"We're leaving?"

"Yes. William and I managed to convince them not to call off the wedding. It's a good thing he loves you so much. He told them you are very sensitive and passionate, and he wanted to marry you anyway. I told them I should get you home. You're obviously coming down with something and are delirious." Her tone was ice, stinging.

Mary stared at the ground. Mother had convinced them to go through with the wedding. For a few minutes, she had been hopeful that the wedding would be off and it wouldn't completely be her fault.

But it wasn't. She was going to be William's wife and host dinner parties for his dreadful parents.

And William wanted to marry her regardless of her being sensitive and passionate? As though it were something negative?

What kind of person would she be if she called off the wedding herself? Her mother would disown her. It would shame their family name, and her father's memory didn't deserve that.

Even if she did call off the wedding, she couldn't be with Andrew. It would ruin his reputation.

At least if Mrs. Connell called off the wedding, they could argue the families weren't compatible.

It was too late to choose Andrew over William.

As they climbed into the carriage, waiting for the footman to load their bags, Mary wondered if she would ever be happy again.

Chapter Nineteen

FTER DINNER, THE EVENING BEFORE their wedding, William asked Mary to sing with him as he played the piano. As much as she didn't want to sing in front of Mrs. Connell, she hoped that it might make her look more feminine and earn back a little of the trust she had lost with Mother.

She glanced at Andrew as she made her way to the front of the room, feeling as though she was betraying him yet again, but he gave her an encouraging smile, giving her butterflies. Andrew hadn't heard her sing in years.

She tried to focus on William as he started playing the song, but her eyes flickered to Andrew, sitting in the chair beside the window, holding a steaming cup of coffee. His eyes stayed on hers, not acknowledging anyone else in the room.

Mary took a deep breath and began to sing, once again looking at William. She didn't trust her voice while she was looking at Andrew.

Mrs. Connell looked pleasantly surprised and watched them for a moment in silence before engaging in conversation with Sarah and Jeffry.

Mary chanced a glance toward the window again, where

Andrew was still watching her, his hazel eyes on hers, making her feel self-conscious.

She had sung this song with him when she was sixteen. He'd sat at the piano, playing almost as beautifully as he was capable of now. She'd been standing where she currently stood, and when she had looked over at him, her heart had clenched. It was the first time she'd ever looked at a boy and felt something deeper than friendship. It was the day before he had given her that rose.

He was looking at her like that now. Perhaps he was remembering that night as well. She had wondered if he felt what she had as they sang together or if those feelings had been one-sided.

That night, after Andrew had finished playing, they sat in the corner of the room and talked about the future, his taking over his father's business and Mary eventually getting married. It was something so ordinary to her then, but looking back, she wondered if Andrew was talking about his plans as though they included her. Had he been interested in a life with her even then?

As the song ended, she turned back to William, very aware she'd been staring at Andrew for entirely too long. She'd hoped William's mother hadn't noticed.

She sighed heavily and smiled as William stood and took her hand.

"I missed your voice," he said. "Have you been practicing? You sound even better than before."

Andrew walked up to them, and Mary felt her cheeks burn. "That was beautiful, Mary. I was pleasantly surprised to hear you singing again. I've missed it."

"William convinced me the last time he was here to join him. I still feel a little embarrassed singing in front of everyone, though."

"You shouldn't," William said. "You sing beautifully." He turned to Andrew, eyes wide and expectant. "Mary tells me you play the piano?"

Andrew glanced at William, a small smile playing on his lips. "She did? I do, yes, though, I daresay I'm not nearly as good as you."

Mary narrowed her eyes. "Don't be so modest, Andrew. You play wonderfully."

His smile widened. "Thank you, Mary."

"Perhaps you would like to play something?"

"Oh, no. I couldn't possibly follow that. You two were wonderful together." His voice was thick, but Mary doubted William, who barely knew him, would notice.

"Then perhaps we can get a drink? I'd like to sit with you and talk. Mary speaks of you quite often. It would be good to get to know someone she's so close with."

Andrew licked his bottom lip. Mary wondered if he was looking for a reason to say no, but being as polite as he was, Andrew nodded.

"I'll get us a drink."

William took Mary's hand. "You don't mind, do you?"

Mind? The idea of it made her pulse quicken with worry, but she couldn't very well say that.

"Not at all. I'll go sit with Mother. She mentioned wanting to speak with me."

William brought Mary's hand to his lips, lightly kissing the back of her hand, and guilt warmed her cheeks.

Mary looked away, feeling embarrassed, and caught Andrew's eye, a deep frown on his face. He quickly turned away, and her heart ached.

William released her hand and walked with Andrew to the end of the parlor where their fathers were deep in a spirited conversation and a bottle of whiskey.

Mary took a seat next to her mother and eyed the men as they each helped themselves to a glass of whiskey.

"You and William are very close," Mother said.

Not knowing how to respond, Mary gave her a small smile. She cared for William, but she wasn't sure she would consider them close. Not like she and Andrew. William had done and said several things that she was having trouble with.

"Are you ready for tomorrow?"

Tomorrow. The big day. Her wedding day. This time tomorrow, she was going to be a wife, despite almost ruining it when she met William's parents. It was hard to believe. Mary still couldn't wrap her head around the fact that it was happening. She was going to be someone's wife. William's. Someone she'd only known for a few weeks, instead of her best friend.

But it had been her mother's wish.

"I think so," Mary said softly, glancing at William and Andrew, now sitting in the corner, talking.

"No regrets?"

Mary narrowed her eyes at her mother. That was an odd question to ask when she knew how Mary felt. She glanced at Mrs. Connell, sitting across the room, and wondered if she could hear them.

"Why are you asking me this?"

She followed her mother's gaze and saw Andrew and William laughing.

"I don't doubt you care for William," she said softly, gently touching her hand. "But I question if your feelings for Andrew will get in the way of your happiness."

Mary frowned. She had those same concerns, but it wasn't as though there was anything she could do about it now. Her mother had made sure of it. "I have no intention of pursuing anything with Andrew if that's what you're worried about. You have made it quite clear what I am to do, regardless of how I feel about the situation or my happiness. Even if it was only due to your wishes, I've made a promise to him. I wouldn't do anything to dishonor him or our family, no matter how unhappy I am to become."

But as she watched them, and Andrew turned and caught her eye, she questioned whether that statement was completely accurate. She certainly wouldn't pursue anything with Andrew, but there was no denying that she was in love with him. She loved him and would give almost anything to be with him. Anything but her mother, she thought as she looked at her questioning expression.

Despite what she felt for Andrew, she was a woman of her word. She wouldn't do anything to jeopardize her relationship with him because she knew it was what her mother wanted. And now that she had accepted his proposal, there was no turning back without ruining all their lives.

As she watched the men talk, she wondered what they were saying to one another. She didn't think either William or Andrew would do or say anything that would be considered impolite, but she wondered if William would be territorial and express his claim over her. She wondered if William had guessed how she felt about Andrew. He couldn't know she was in love with him, though, even if he thought she cared for him.

"I don't think you would, I only wondered if you had any regrets about your decision."

Decision? Had she truly decided? It didn't feel as though she had been allowed to choose Andrew at all, so she wasn't sure where her mother was going with this line of questioning. Yes, she had agreed to marry William, but was that really a decision she made? Andrew had left, and her mother refused to listen to reason and insisted she marry William. So when he proposed, she didn't feel as though she were allowed to decline. If Mary had been allowed to choose of her own accord, she didn't think she'd be where she was now.

If Andrew had been allowed to court her, would she have been standing here with Andrew instead of William?

She looked back at the men and William flashed her a smile,

and in that moment, she didn't care what she would have done or any of the what-ifs. She only cared about what she *was* doing.

She was with William, and whether she or her mother chose it, she cared for him and wouldn't break the engagement no matter what she felt for Andrew.

"Everything will be fine," Mary said, not really knowing if it would be. "I'll be happy one day."

She hoped.

"Good. All I want is for you to be happy."

Mary's stomach flipped. "Is it?"

Her mother made a sound somewhere between a laugh and a sigh.

"How could you ask me that?"

Mary shook her head and stood, planning to leave, no matter what Mrs. Connell would think. She didn't want to cause a scene, and right now, with anger bubbling in her chest, she didn't trust that she could be civil. Leaving was the best thing she could do.

But her mother grabbed her wrist. "You do not walk away when I am speaking to you."

Mary looked down her nose, glaring at her mother. In that moment, she hated her. She yanked her wrist away and stalked from the room, ignoring the eyes on her retreating back and Mrs. Connell's voice of surprised disapproval.

She was halfway down the hall when her mother shouted her name. Mary turned to see her standing in the doorway. She paused, letting her mother walk toward her.

"What has come over you? You have been nothing but defiant for weeks!"

"What has come over me? What has come over you, Mother?"

She drew back as though Mary had struck her. "What do you mean?"

"You knew how I felt. You knew what I wanted, and still you pushed my feelings aside and forced me to do what you wanted.

You don't care about my happiness. You only care about your image."

"How dare you?" she hissed. "Image is everything, Mary, as you'll soon learn, but that doesn't mean I don't want you to be happy."

"That isn't how it feels."

Andrew and William walked over, concern mirrored on each of their faces. Behind them, Sarah was whispering to Jeffry. No doubt her cousin had heard enough to appease her need for gossip. This time tomorrow, Mary would be married, and everyone would know it was only because her mother wanted it.

"What is it, Sarah? If you have something to say, you can say it to all of us."

Sarah's eyes widened. Mary had never challenged her before, and right then, Mary felt as though she could hit her. Sarah let Jeffry escort her back into the parlor.

"Is everything all right?" William asked.

"Everything is fine," Mother said, her voice still thick with anger.

William studied Mary's face as though asking her.

"I'm fine," she said.

He nodded. "All right. Then if you don't mind, I'd like a word with your mother?"

Mother's eyes widened with worry.

"I want to go over a few details for tomorrow."

"Certainly." She eyed Mary before following behind William, who led her down the hall.

Mary focused on the floor, fighting back tears. Everything was falling apart.

"You aren't all right," Andrew said.

Mary's eyes found his, and the tears fell. No. As long as she was in this life with anyone but him, Mary would never be all right.

"Come on," he said, taking her hand and leading her to the door.

"Where are we going?"

They stepped outside into the night, and the fresh air was an immediate comfort. Being under cover of darkness and away from her mother and William and everyone who expected her to love William was most welcome.

"We're getting some air."

They walked for a few minutes in silence, breathing in the cool night air until the sweet smell of the rose garden hit their nose. That smell brought back so many memories. Memories of planting the rose bushes with the gardener, memories of picnics with her cousins, memories of Andrew.

But that was all a lifetime ago. Everything was changing.

Andrew indicated the rose bush directly in front of them. "This was where I picked a rose for you. Do you remember?"

"Of course I do. How could I forget? I have the rose pressed dry in a book in my room."

Andrew's eyebrows raised. "Really? You felt the desire to save it?"

"It was the first flower I ever received. The first gift a man had ever given me. The first intimate moment we shared." Mary shuffled her feet. "And I admit, I may have even loved you then."

He smiled sadly and tucked a loose curl behind her ear. "Unfortunately, life didn't work out the way I'd hoped."

"Your life isn't over yet, Andrew." She sniffled, knowing hers was. Tomorrow was the end.

"No, but it may as well be."

"Don't say that." Her voice broke as tears filled her eyes. She couldn't bear to get married knowing he didn't have any hope of finding happiness with someone else.

He shook his head. "I'm sorry. This is why I shouldn't have come. I worried I'd act like this."

Mary took a deep, shaky breath and sat on the bench, reaching out her hand. "Come sit with me."

He stared at her for a moment as if thinking it over. Mary patted the bench beside her.

"Come on."

He sighed but obliged, taking the seat beside her.

"What happened with Will?"

"William is perfectly lovely, as you said," he said. "I was hoping he'd say something rude or out of line so I could have a reason to hate him, to tell your mother he can't marry you because he's quick to anger. But he gave me no reason. He's quite funny, as it turns out."

Mary gently nudged him. "You weren't over there talking about me?"

He shrugged. "Perhaps a little. He's happy you're marrying him. He said he feels lucky you said yes. And he is."

"I know he is. I'm glad he knows it too." Because if it were up to her, she wouldn't have.

He looked at the ground and kicked at the grass.

"What were you and your mother arguing about?"

Mary frowned. "She said all that matters to her is my happiness, so I lost myself. I couldn't believe she could say that after deliberating going against what I want."

"I'm sorry," Andrew said, taking her hand.

"As am I."

"I honestly was glad for the chance to be alone with you tonight. There is just so much I wish to say to you before you get married. I'll never have the opportunity again."

Her breathing quickened. "Such as?"

"Such as how beautiful you are." Her heart skipped as he met her eye. "I'm madly in love with you, and I wish I could have courted you and asked you to marry me. I should have done so before William came into your life, but I was trying to give you time. I'm so upset I left and didn't stay and fight for you. I should have talked to your mother. To my mother."

"Andrew...."

She turned away as tears spilled down her cheeks, but his hand cupped her chin and pulled her to meet his gaze. She wasn't strong enough to hear this, not when she was so desperately wanting the same as he did.

"Please don't hate me," he whispered.

"I could never hate you."

"Do you remember last year at the wedding? We sneaked outside and got lost in the bride's garden."

Mary smiled. "I nearly fell into the pond. If you hadn't been there to catch me, I'd have been sopping wet."

"It was that moment, as you were clinging to me, your body pressed against mine, that I knew."

"Knew what?"

"That I was in love with you."

Mary's heart raced.

"That it wasn't just some schoolboy crush as I thought it had been. I was madly in love with you. And as I looked into your beautiful gray eyes, it took everything I had not to kiss you right then."

Mary subconsciously licked her lips as she thought about his lips pressing to hers. She wished more than anything he had. What might have happened if she had known he had cared for her as much as she cared for him?

Would Father have allowed her to marry him? If Andrew had asked for her hand before her father fell ill, would he have agreed?

"Mary...."

"Yes?" she breathed.

"I still want to kiss you."

Her heart hammered so fast it felt as though it was going to beat out of her chest. She couldn't deny that, in that moment, she wanted to kiss him too. She wanted to press her lips to his and show him that she loved him as desperately as he loved her.

He leaned forward, his breath hot on her lips. She wanted to lean forward and kiss him with everything she had. She wanted to change her fate.

But she couldn't, even if she kissed him. With tears in her eyes, she stood abruptly. She was to be married tomorrow, and if she kissed Andrew tonight, she didn't know if she would be strong enough to choose her mother over him.

"I'm sorry, Andrew. I'm so sorry. I can't." Her voice cracked. "Please know this has nothing to do with you and how I feel about you but everything to do with my situation. I made a promise. But if I kiss you, I'm not sure I'll be able to go through with it. So, please...." She sobbed, shaking with emotion, unable to finish her thought.

Please let me go. I'm not strong enough.

Andrew stood and wrapped his arms around her, trying to comfort her. He was so warm, so strong, and everything Mary had ever wanted.

"Don't be sorry. It is I who am in the wrong. That was highly inappropriate. I apologize for my behavior tonight."

Mary pulled away, no longer trusting herself to be near him. She loved him too much. She wanted to tell him to take her away. But that would ruin their reputation. And she'd lose her mother forever. "I must go."

He grabbed her hand, but she yanked it away, gathered her skirts, and ran toward the house, leaving Andrew calling after her.

She wiped her eyes and tried to calm her racing heart before going back into the house. William stood near the door and narrowed his eyes at her as she entered.

"Is something the matter? You look like you've been crying."

Mary shook her head. "It's nothing."

He nodded, but he didn't take his eyes off her. She couldn't bring herself to look at him.

"Did you and Mother get everything sorted?"

"Truth was, I thought you might have needed rescuing from her. You both seemed quite upset."

"Yes. I suppose I did. Thank you."

"Of course."

"I'm going to get to bed. Tomorrow's a big day."

William narrowed his eyes at her, no doubt hearing the crack in her voice as she was once again overcome with tears.

"Goodnight, Will."

"Goodnight, Mary."

As she started up the stairs, she heard the front door close. She glanced down and saw that William had gone. A part of her wished he knew why she was hurting and would leave. The other part knew that he would never go back on his word, even if he suspected she was in love with Andrew.

Chapter Twenty

*T*HE NEXT MORNING, MOTHER WOKE Mary early to prepare for the wedding. As she dragged herself out of bed, she found herself wishing she'd have asked her mother to schedule the wedding later in the day. She was too tired to get dressed and walk down the aisle.

"Can't I sleep a little bit longer?" she begged.

"Not today." Her hard tone reminded Mary of their fight the night before. "Neither you nor Andrew returned to the party last night. Mrs. Connell had quite a few questions, but William assured her you retired early. She had quite a lot to say about your outburst. Once again, she questioned if we should go through with the wedding. I told her you were upset your father isn't going to be at your wedding and were acting out. But there will be none of that today, am I clear?"

Mary swallowed. She wanted to run. But where could she go? Andrew had promised to take her away, but even if she asked him to, where could they go? If he ran off with a promised woman, his father might disinherit him. Not only would Mary lose her mother, but he could lose his family, as well.

"Yes, ma'am."

"Good. Let's get ready."

She helped her dress into something more casual that she could wear until it was time for the wedding.

"We have time for a quick breakfast, but then we need to get you ready."

"Is William up yet?" she asked, starting to make her bed. She daren't ask if she'd seen Andrew.

"Not yet." Her mother snapped her fingers. "Leave that for Ruth. You don't have time today."

Mary rolled her eyes. "It will only take a moment," she said, pulling the sheet up.

She was thrilled when she went downstairs and saw that the dining room was empty. She had half expected Mrs. Connell to be waiting at the table to interrogate her once more.

Mary had only eaten half her food when her mother informed her she only had five more minutes until they had to go because they were already running very late.

"I haven't seen Will yet," Mary said. Nor had she seen Andrew. And as much as she didn't know if she could handle seeing him, she wanted to make sure that he was all right after last night. Even if she wasn't.

"You'll see him soon enough," her mother said. "It's time to move along."

But she didn't have to wait long. William came into the dining room at that moment.

"Good morning, Mary," he said. "You're up early."

"Of course I am. I can't sleep when Mother is insisting there's still so much to do."

"That's right," Mother said. "We're about to go upstairs so Mary can get ready."

"So soon?" he asked, giving her a quizzical look.

"Is something wrong?"

"I'm sorry, I don't mean to keep you, but I was wondering

if I could have a word with Mary before she became otherwise preoccupied?"

Mother's face hardened, but she faked a smile and nodded. "Of course. I'll just leave you both and go see how the decorations are coming along."

She closed the door behind herself, and Will took the seat next to Mary. He watched her for a moment, face impassive.

"Is something the matter?" she asked, getting a cold sense of dread.

"I was hoping you could tell me. I didn't get a chance to speak with you last night. You were quite upset after you spoke with Andrew. Since you didn't feel like talking, I wanted to ask him what happened, but I couldn't find him. I know you aren't my wife yet, but I cannot stop thinking about it."

Mary's heart raced as she stared at him. "Thinking about what?"

He swallowed and looked down at his hands. "Why were you so upset?"

Mary looked down at her plate, suddenly feeling nauseous. She didn't want to admit Andrew had nearly kissed her or that she had wanted to kiss him. Nor could she tell him that they were in love with one another, but she had been forbidden from being with him.

"He told you he loves you, I presume?"

Mary's head snapped up. It was so bold, so unexpected. She had already known he loved her, but he had said it again. Slowly, she nodded.

William's jaw clenched.

"He was saying goodbye," she said hurriedly, terrified she was going to make William hate Andrew. "That was all. He knows nothing will ever happen between us. He knows how I feel. He knows I choose you."

His face softened. "You do?"

She nodded.

"If you want him, Mary, I'll step aside. I'll take the blame for the broken engagement. There will be no ill words spoken of you."

Her heart raced at his proposition. Could it be so simple? All she had to do was be honest and tell him she was in love with Andrew, and he would step aside. Her mother's reputation wouldn't be tarnished.

But her relationship with her mother would be. Mother would never forgive her and may never speak to her again.

She cupped his face in her hands and stared into his eyes. "I chose you, Will." Her heart ached. "I made you a promise, and I'm not going to go back on my word."

He smiled and sighed with relief.

"I'll see you soon," she told him, standing from the table. "Don't be late."

"I wouldn't dare." He looked much happier now.

Her mother was waiting outside. She turned to Mary when she opened the door.

"You did very good in there, Mary. I'm proud of you."

Mary stared at her, appalled she had eavesdropped.

If she did so good, then why did she feel so horrible?

As her mother worked on her hair and makeup, Mary thought about Andrew. It was still early, but she hadn't seen him yet. She hoped he was all right, and she hadn't upset him so much that he wouldn't be at the ceremony.

Or maybe that would be too hard on them both. Would she be able to go through with the wedding if Andrew was there?

"Now I know we said a lot to one another last night," her mother said after she'd finished putting her hair up, "But I don't want you to think about any of that today. Today you are getting married."

It sounded more like a warning than a reassurance.

Mary was to go through with the wedding no matter how either of them felt. Even if through her entire marriage, Mary would miss Andrew, wondering how her life would have been with him.

William would undoubtedly be upset that Andrew had told her he loved her, but she hoped he wouldn't hold a grudge. Andrew was still her best friend, after all. She hadn't told William everything that had happened, but she wasn't sure if she was trying to protect Andrew or herself.

If he knew that Mary loved Andrew, would he have called off the wedding?

Mary was quiet as Mother helped her dress in the lace wedding gown that was all the rage in Europe.

"You look beautiful."

With only a few minutes until it was time for the ceremony, Mary stood in front of the mirror, staring at her reflection, and once again pondered how she had found herself there. She had always thought if she was going to be married, she would marry Andrew.

Just a few hours ago, Andrew was telling her he loved her, and she had more than wanted to kiss him. And now she was about to marry William. She felt a lump in her throat. She didn't want to hurt Andrew. She didn't want to hurt herself.

"Are you ready?" her mother asked.

Mary met her gaze in the mirror and nodded. She didn't trust her voice.

"I'll go check on William, shall I?"

She left the room, and a moment later, Andrew stepped in.

"Wow," he breathed. "You look beautiful."

Mary's racing heart prevented her from smiling as tears filled her eyes. He was there. He was really there. He hadn't left.

"You shouldn't be back here," she said, cheeks burning.

He smiled sadly. "I know. And I don't want to ruin your

day. I just wanted to see you one last time before you belong to another man."

Mary bit her lip. She hadn't quite looked at it like that before, but it didn't mean it wasn't true. She was about to be Will's wife. Will's.

She would never again belong to herself.

"I want to wish you the very best. I promise to stand by your side like any good cousin would."

Why did that hurt worse than the idea of him running again? "Thank you, Andrew."

"But if you need anything, whether a friend or companion, or if he isn't the man you think he is and you realize you're unhappy with your life, just tell me. I'll always be there for you no matter what."

Mary studied him, considering telling him that she was ready to run away with him. But he knew as well as she that she couldn't back out now. What kind of woman would she be if she left a man at the altar? Her name would be ruined. As would Andrew's because he'd run off with her. Even if his family didn't disinherit him, he may never buy or sell another property.

"Once a wedding is set, it's done. If I back out now, or even a year from now, our family will be shamed."

"I didn't say you had to back out."

She bit her lip, her chest heaving. No. He hadn't said it, but she couldn't help but wish he would. She was always thinking about it.

"I know. I'm just trying to remind myself, I suppose."

"I told you I was willing to run away with you, Mary, and I am. If at any time in your life you decide you're unhappy, tell me, and I'll take you anywhere you want to go. To hell with what's proper. I'll take you far away from everyone who knows us, and we can start over."

She smiled and placed her hand gently on his cheek. She wanted so much to tell him to take her away.

She wrapped her arms around him, hugging him tightly, and took a deep breath to stop the tears. If only she could run away with him.

This was the last time she was going to hug Andrew as Mary Kline. Perhaps this would be the last time she ever hugged him, now that she had told William how Andrew felt.

She looked up into his hazel eyes, and her breath hitched. How many times had she looked at him and wondered what it would be like to kiss him? She nearly had allowed it last night, but she was too afraid to let him.

It would be so simple. He was right there, inches away, and they were alone.

No one would need to know.

In just a few moments, she was going to be married to William, and she'd never be able to kiss another man again.

She stood on tiptoe and firmly pressed her lips to his. He sighed as he pulled her closer, letting them melt together.

Her heart skipped as she tasted his salty, sweet kiss, so electric, tantalizing her tongue.

But then she pulled away, knowing if she let it go any further than that, she'd never go through with the wedding.

"Mary...." he said breathily.

She shook her head, tears stinging her eyes. Maybe she could. If they left right then, perhaps they could slip out to the stables and leave before anyone knew they were missing.

"I'm ready."

"Ready?" He looked at her with confusion. "For the wedding?"

Mary shook her head and opened to mouth to tell him to take her away when there was a knock on the door. Mary pulled her hands out of Andrew's just as her mother stepped inside.

"William is ready if you still are," she said, eyeing Andrew with pursed lips.

Her moment to escape was gone. She'd squandered it. Tears filled her eyes, and she shook her head.

"I'm sorry," she whispered. "It's too late."

He watched her for a moment. "It isn't if you don't want it to be."

But it was. Her mother would stop her. If not physically, then with guilt because when Mary looked at her and thought of losing her forever, she didn't want to go.

She was finally ready, but it was too late to run.

"I can't."

"I should get out there," he said softly, eyes glassy with tears.

As Mary watched him go, he looked back at her, catching her eye as if asking her one last time. Her heart skipped a beat.

She'd missed her window.

Uncle Isaac walked step for step beside Mary. Her heart ached, wishing her father was there to give her away. It was a father's place, wasn't it? She'd been denied the opportunity when her father had died. As the oldest male in the family, it was now Uncle Isaac's duty to give Mary away.

And the fact that he was Andrew's father made it that much worse—that much harder for her to walk toward a future with William.

William stood at the foot of the stairs, which had been decorated with flowers and ribbon, in front of the Justice of the Peace. He looked handsome in his best morning suit, with a satin, eggshell-colored waistcoat adorned with lilies of the valley.

Mr. and Mrs. Connell stood near their son, Mrs. Connell's lips pursed tightly, her gaze fixated on the floor. Her disapproval was visibly etched across her face. Mary wondered if they would ever manage to get along. She doubted it.

Her eyes scanned the crowd, landing on Andrew, standing

behind everyone in the hallway leading to the back door. Mary wondered if it was so he could make a quick escape if he needed. His sad eyes never left hers, further breaking her heart. She wondered how everyone would react if she ran to him and pulled him down the hall and outside. Would anyone try to stop her?

Uncle Isaac wouldn't let her go. Her mother would catch her before she could make it to Andrew.

No. She'd made her decision. She would have to try to find a way to be content with it.

She wished he was walking her down to Andrew. But would he have? Or would they have disapproved of their marriage?

He stopped in front of William and gently set her hand on top of his. Her stomach flipped at the symbolism of being given to William. She knew it was coming, but it felt surreal.

As she stood in front of William, waiting to agree to love, honor, and obey him, she once again thought of running. How could she go through with this? She was so close to the back door. All she had to do was take a step back, turn, and run. She had no doubt that Andrew would follow behind and would take her away. She didn't think William would grab her and force her to stay.

It could be so quick. And then they could leave, and she'd never have to see any of them again.

She turned slightly, wanting to seek out Andrew for comfort, to put her at ease. Or maybe she was hoping he would object and insist she was marrying the wrong man. Her mother caught her eye, giving her a hard stare, and all thoughts of running slipped from her mind. She would never let her leave.

Mary's eyes met Will's, and her breath hitched. It was really happening. She had chosen to marry Will. Andrew must stay in her past. Her love for him couldn't go beyond this day, no matter how much she cared about him.

If she had to give him up forever, at least she was able to kiss him, even if it was just once. Once would be enough to keep his love alive in her memory. Once would be enough to tame the desire that burned inside her.

Once would have to be enough. Because once was all she was going to get.

Chapter Twenty-One

*A*FTER THE CEREMONY, MARY AND Will sat at a table in the back garden, decorated for the reception. She was still feeling slightly anxious, wishing she'd have made another decision or backed out of the engagement before her mother had told everyone.

"Can you believe we're married?" Will asked softly.

"No," she said honestly. She couldn't believe she had gone through with it. "Can you?"

He shook his head. "No, not really. It happened so fast."

"Do you wish we would have waited?"

"Not at all!" He took her hand in his and squeezed it gently. "I don't think I could have been alone with you for much longer without keeping my hands off you. It was all I could do to resist you."

She raised an eyebrow. "So you married me because you wanted to touch me?"

His mouth opened, and he quickly shook his head. "No. I married you because you're the most amazing woman I've ever met. Getting to be more intimate with you physically is only one of the benefits."

"I suppose you can kiss me whenever you want now," she said.

He grinned and glanced around the bustling garden. "Then I wish we were alone right now."

She remembered Andrew's arms around her, his lips on hers, and her heart ached. She hadn't married Andrew. She'd never feel his embrace again. She was married to Will, and it was he who was to receive all her kisses for the rest of their life.

Is that what her life was going to be now? A constant reminder of those stolen intimate moments with Andrew?

Perhaps she just needed to create more intimate moments with her husband.

Husband. It didn't feel as awkward as she thought it would. It might have been because she had been prepared all her life to be someone's wife. She hoped the role and responsibilities would come just as naturally.

As Mary and William stood to thank their well-wishers, Sarah shot her a look of jealousy, turning up her nose and looking away. Mary wished she could tell her she was just as unhappy, but she couldn't. This was supposed to be a joyous occasion.

After a while, Mary grew tired of the celebrations and pretending to be happy with William and found herself going back to her kiss with Andrew before the ceremony. She wondered where he'd got to. She hadn't seen him since they'd come outside, and she wondered if he had run like she had wanted to.

She scolded herself for thinking of Andrew. She was married now, after all, to another man. And in just a few hours, she'd be in her bedroom with her husband, and Andrew shouldn't be anywhere near her thoughts.

But he was, and no matter what she did and how much she tried to remind herself that she was married to William, her thoughts kept returning to Andrew.

Toward the end of the evening, Andrew finally made an

appearance and made his way over to them. Judging by his red eyes, he'd either been crying or had a lot to drink. Or both.

Not that she blamed him. It was everything she could do to get through the service with the taste of his kiss on her lips. And most of the evening, she had wanted to go cry in her bed. She had drunk more wine than she should, only stopping because the room was starting to spin.

"I just wanted to wish the happy couple the best." His eyes lingered on Mary. "I am headed back to Boston in just a few moments, so I wanted to wish my dear cousin happiness. Thank you both for inviting me."

"Thank you for coming, Andrew," Mary said, wishing more than anything she could tell him a proper goodbye.

He took a step away, but William stood. "Andrew, I wondered if I might have a word before you go?"

Mary's heart sank. She had hoped William wouldn't say anything to Andrew, especially now that they were married, and he knew she had chosen him completely.

Andrew's jaw clenched, and he glanced at Mary before plastering on a smile. "Of course. As long as it's quick. My carriage is waiting."

"Sure, sure."

"Perhaps it can wait until he returns from his trip?" she asked, putting a hand on Will's, hoping more than anything he would let it go.

"It'll just take a moment. I'll walk him out."

"It's quite all right," Andrew reassured her. "But I suppose this is goodbye for now, Mary. I hope you write to me and tell me about your new home and how you're settling."

"Of course I will." Tears stung her eyes. "Travel safe."

Will walked beside Andrew out of the room, leaving Mary to wonder what he wanted to discuss this time, hoping more than anything that everything would be all right.

She poured herself another glass of wine, wishing she was going with Andrew.

Would Will tell Andrew off for telling her he loved her? Would Andrew tell Will that she kissed him right before the wedding? That would completely ruin her reputation and her father's name, which is the only reason she had gone through with the wedding in the first place.

She found herself regretting her moment of weakness. Her marriage was just getting started and it could be over the same day, and she would be labeled as a harlot. Not to mention, she'd be worse off than before, even because her family name would be ruined, and her mother would be a social outcast.

She absentmindedly tapped her foot, pouring herself yet another glass of wine as she waited for Will to return.

When he finally did come back, Mary felt as though her heart was going to burst with anticipation.

"Is everything all right?" she asked, trying to keep her voice level.

He gave her a small smile. "It is now. There were just a few things I wanted to discuss with him before he left."

"What was so urgent?"

He looked her in the eye, making her heart beat faster. "We can talk about it later if you like."

His eyes flickered to a few people standing nearby, reminding her that they might be overheard. As much as she wanted to know what was said, she didn't want anyone else involved. Whatever it was would have to wait.

"All right," Mary said.

Will took her hand. "Would you like to dance with me?"

She looked at him for a moment, his face starting to blur. She would be unsteady on her feet, but his arms would be around her. Besides, could she really say no?

"That sounds lovely."

Once again, there wasn't anyone dancing, but that didn't stop her and William from walking to the middle of the room. Mary felt eyes on her as he slowly led her, but she tried to focus on William, letting everyone else in the room fade away.

"You look so beautiful," he told her as he pulled her closer.

"Thank you. The seamstress did a wonderful job."

He shook his head. "I wasn't talking about the dress. It's beautiful, too, of course, but you could be wearing anything and still be radiant."

She felt her cheeks warm. "You look rather handsome, yourself."

"Thank you." He leaned closer and whispered in her ear, "I was hoping you'd find me irresistible, but you seem to be resisting me with ease. Much easier than I seem to be resisting you."

Mary swallowed. Had her feelings been that noticeable?

"Darling," he started, his voice so low only she could hear, "please don't think I'm not enjoying my time at our wedding, but when is this going to be over?"

Mary couldn't believe he was thinking exactly what she was. She was more than ready for the evening to be over. "Soon, I hope."

The song ended, and as William and Mary spun to a stop, the room erupted into applause. William held up a hand.

Mother walked over. "You two are simply beautiful together."

"Thank you, Mother."

Her mother grinned wide. "I'm happy you're happy."

Did she look happy? She didn't feel it.

She cast a sideways glance at William. "I woke up quite early this morning, and I'm rather tired. How much longer will the party go on?"

Mother looked around the bustling room. "Not long, I'd say. Give it another hour, and you can go up to bed."

Mary faked a smile. "Thank you."

Mother nodded. "Well, if you'll excuse me, I should go see if our guests need anything."

She hurried off, but not before Mary saw her eyes glistening with tears.

"What do you think?" Mary asked, turning toward Will. "Is another hour too long?"

"I think I can manage an hour. I'll go pour us some more wine."

Mary sat at the table, and as soon as William handed her the glass, she drank it down in one swallow. She waved at a servant walking by and asked for a bottle to be left at the table.

"Are you all right?" William asked, eyeing her.

Mary smiled, finally feeling like her thoughts were dimming. "I am wonderful. Let's celebrate."

She poured another glass, missing his look of apprehension.

Chapter Twenty-Two

*A*S THE HOUR DRAGGED BY, Mary found herself unable to think about anything. She watched the guests chat and eat, accepting food and wine from William when offered.

On her way back to the party after using the washroom, Mary caught sight of Sarah and Jeffry kissing fervently in the living room, his hands running down her body. Mary turned, wanting to escape before they saw her, but she was unsteady on her feet and stumbled loudly into the doorframe.

Sarah gasped and jumped back. "Mary! Oh heavens."

From what Mary could see, Jeffry looked shocked.

"Sorry," Mary said, turning away.

But Sarah grabbed hold of her arm, stopping her. "Mary! You can't say anything." There were tears in her eyes. "You just can't. Please! I kept your secret, haven't I? Please. Mother would be furious, and Father would disown me. I won't see a penny of dowry."

Mary wrapped her arms around Sarah, mostly to reassure her enough to quiet her. "I won't say anything. But please be careful."

Sarah pulled back. "You won't?"

"No." She wiped Sarah's teary cheeks, then shot Jeffry a look of disapproval. "But you should make her an honest woman before laying your hands on her."

"How dare you!" he spat.

"Jeffry, please," Sarah begged.

He backed down but glared at Mary, who couldn't help but smile at how angry she'd made him.

She returned to the party, grabbing another glass of wine before sinking down in the seat next to William. He caught her eye and smiled. She wondered what he was thinking. But then his eyes flickered to her lips, and she realized.

The kiss at the ceremony had been quick and soft. It was like an appetizer for what he would be allowed to do to her once they were alone.

Her cheeks burned at the thought, and she poured herself another glass of wine.

Finally, people began to leave. After there were only a few families left at the reception, Mother approached the couple.

"I'm releasing you from your duty for the night. I'll tell our guests you're exhausted from today's events so you both can retire for the evening."

"Thank you, Mother. It's been such a long day."

And it had. Mary had been through a rollercoaster of emotions and had enough wine that she wasn't entirely sure she was even looking at her mother. She was so tired.

"Of course. I'm so happy for you, darling. Get some rest."

She kissed her cheek and, after they said goodnight to William's parents, Mrs. Connell pursing her lips tighter as Mary approached, they slipped away from the party. As soon as she was up the stairs, she let out a heavy sigh. She hadn't realized how stuffy it had been surrounded by so many people, even if they were well-wishers.

Will's hand made small circles on her back as they walked. "Are you all right?"

She gave him a small smile. "Yes. I've had quite a bit to drink. I forgot how much energy it takes to attend such a long party."

He chuckled. "Well, I hate to tell you this, dear wife, but you'll be in charge of hosting them from time to time."

Mary groaned. "Do I have to? Can't we just have one to three visitors over at once?"

"Absolutely. At least for the first few years. Except for when my parents and siblings visit."

"Of course. I'd love to meet your brothers. They sound wonderful."

"You say that now, but you haven't met them. I apologize in advance, but they're very loud."

Mary opened her bedroom door and saw the candles had already been lit.

"This is your room?" Will asked, looking around. "It's nice. Not as feminine as I thought it would be."

Mary laughed, stumbling as she playfully shoved him. "Were you expecting me to have dolls?"

William wrapped his arm around her waist to catch her. "Well, perhaps one or two."

Mary straightened and pushed his hands off her, walking to the vanity table to begin taking off her jewelry. "Well, I hate to disappoint you, husband, but I've not played with dolls in years."

William walked up behind her and slid his hands around her bodice, making her stomach lurch. He leaned down, nuzzling against her neck, and gently kissed her bare skin.

She'd been nervous about his touch for hours, and now that she was alone with him, she felt herself afraid to feel his hands on her. She felt as though she were betraying Andrew by being with William. If she took this next step with him, she'd never be with Andrew.

But William was her husband. She'd never be with Andrew,

anyway. She'd made her decision that morning. So didn't she owe it to herself to allow William to try to make her happy as a husband would his wife?

And she was hurting so much now that she was thinking of Andrew again. She didn't want to be alone. If William was willing to hold her and comfort her, shouldn't she let him?

She spun in his arms and looked up into his gorgeous dark eyes. He leaned down and tenderly pressed his lips to hers. Her heart ached as hands that weren't Andrew's slowly slid down her arm, goosebumps pebbling at his touch.

She closed her eyes, and Andrew's face came to the forefront of her mind, his lips on hers.

His tongue played on her lips, teasing her, and she parted her own, tasting his sweetness.

He helped her undress, peeling her clothes off faster than she had ever undressed. Her cheeks burned as he slid off her slip, revealing her naked body.

He stripped off his shirt, and she slid her hands down his firm chest. It wasn't the man she'd hoped to be with, but he was the man she had married.

As he laid her on the bed, he moved slowly, rocking in rhythm with her heartbeat, holding her. She gasped as he filled her, his breath hot against her bare skin. But then he went faster, harder. She inhaled sharply. She'd never felt so vulnerable and exposed. He raised up and looked into her eyes before crushing his lips to hers, stifling her cry.

She was grateful when he backed away, finishing on the sheets instead of inside. It was her duty to be wife and mother, but she only wanted to deal with one new thing at a time.

He laid beside her, spent and breathing heavily, and Mary tugged the sheets up over her exposed breasts.

"That was beyond anything I could have expected," he said, pulling the sheet back down. "You're so beautiful, Mary."

She didn't know what to say. It wasn't quite what she expected. She closed her eyes as tears threatened to fall and concentrated on her breathing.

"Thank you for marrying me," he said. "I know that couldn't have been an easy choice for you to make."

She blinked several times as his words sank in. "I'd have been foolish not to."

"Andrew would have been a good match for you too."

Mary pulled back slightly and tugged the blanket up to cover herself once more. Of course, she'd been thinking of Andrew, but she hadn't expected William to be.

"Why do you say that?"

Will sighed and rolled onto his back. He looked troubled. That made two of them.

"He wanted to marry you. And, though I worry about making you cross with me, I believe his feelings may be reciprocated. It could just as easily have been him where I am now."

Mary sat up, wrapping the sheet tightly around her body.

"William!"

"I'm sorry. That was quite rude."

"Yes. It was."

But as rude as it was, it was true. Was Mary only cross with him because he had guessed right?

He reached out and took her hand. "Lie with me? I'll behave."

She pursed her lips, scowling, but she lay back anyway. She'd had entirely too much wine, and the room was still spinning.

"What did you two discuss?" she asked, remembering how they had gone off together before Andrew had left.

"Promise you won't be angry?"

Mary cocked her head. "I'm not sure. It depends on what was said."

"I tried to be polite. I told him now that we were married I hoped he'd respect our relationship and not cross any lines. That whatever happened before we were married is in the past."

Mary's face burned as she thought back to the kiss just moments before the wedding. It, too, was in the past, and that's where it would stay.

"What did he say?" she asked.

Will glanced at his hands, picking at his nails. "He said he respected your choice, but should you ever decide you made the wrong one, he'd be there."

Mary tried to hide the smile. "That sounds like him."

She looked over to see William staring at her. "Do you regret your decision, Mary?"

Why did everyone keep asking that? Was it true she was in love with Andrew? Yes, but she would be lying if she said she didn't care for William, as well.

But there really wasn't any choice in the matter. Her mother had made the decision for her. She had forbidden Mary from being with Andrew. Mary had to say yes to William, or her mother never would have forgiven her.

But she couldn't say that to William. He was her husband, and it was her job to make him happy.

She gently laid her hand on his cheek. "I am content with my decision."

William kissed her fingers. "Then I shall try not to be so jealous."

Jealousy was understandable, especially after everything they'd gone through. William knew that Andrew desired her. That wouldn't be easy for a man. How would she feel if William had feelings for another woman and she for him?

Of course, if he did, he'd be with that other woman and Mary wouldn't be in the situation she was in.

She had never admitted how much she cared for Andrew to William. He only suspected. But wasn't that bad enough?

"You kissed him," he said. It wasn't a question, wasn't an accusation. It was simply a fact.

"Did he say something to you?" she asked softly, feeling cold. It didn't seem like something he would do, but if he were as desperate as she was, perhaps he had.

"No. He said nothing of it. I am only assuming. You two are close. He's very hung up on you. I can only assume he had felt the same hypnotic pull I feel toward you that grew even deeper after I kissed you in the parlor that day."

A lump formed in her throat. She hadn't kissed Andrew until that day. All their feelings up until then hadn't been affected by that kiss.

She could lie. It would be so easy to lie.

But she didn't like lies. One lie always led to another, then another. And if William already suspected they had kissed, would he believe her if she lied?

Would he think less of her if she were honest? Most men would.

"We shared a kiss, yes. Only once. And he knows that's all there will ever be."

His jaw clenched. "I cannot say I blame him. You are more beautiful than anyone I've ever known. But he's not at all the type I would imagine a woman of your status with."

Mary's chest tightened. What had he meant by that?

"But you are sure he knows his place?"

Mary nodded. Andrew was a man of his word, and he'd promised not to interfere with Mary's decision.

"Then I'll do my best to ignore any jealous rage I get when he comes to visit. Though I daresay, I will not tolerate his calling while I'm out."

"I can respect that."

"Andrew is a brilliant businessman. Perhaps we could move past this and negotiate some business terms."

Mary's stomach rolled as she thought of the two of them becoming friends and working together.

"I love you, Mary," he said, leaning forward and kissing her.

She knew she cared about him, but she didn't quite know if it was love. She didn't feel for him what she felt for Andrew. It hadn't been love that made her decide to marry him. It was her mother's wishes. Still, perhaps she could fall in love with him if she would only give him a chance.

Chapter Twenty-Three

THE NEXT MORNING, MARY WAS preparing to leave, ensuring she had everything packed that she wanted to bring with her to her new home. She stared at her copy of *Romeo and Juliet* with her rose and letters pressed between the pages and debated on leaving it behind. She didn't need it anymore, after all. She was a married woman, determined to leave her feelings for Andrew in the past. And maybe if she left it behind, she would stop staring at it and thinking of what could have been.

She placed it back on the shelf with the other books she'd decided not to bring, but every time she packed something else, her eyes returned to the book.

Was she ready to leave all her memories with Andrew behind? What was the harm? He was a part of her past, and the items in that book were proof that they had loved one another.

In the end, she put it in one of her bags.

During breakfast, Will told her all about their new home and how he hoped she'd like it. She had no doubt it would be a gorgeous manor. She just wasn't sure if it would feel like home. She'd only ever lived at Kline Manor.

"Mother, we're bringing Ruth and Henry with us, right?"

Mary asked, not wanting to leave Ruth behind for Sarah to torment.

Her mother's eyes narrowed. "Why in heavens would you? Where would that leave me?"

Will glanced from Mary to her mother. "I've hired help, Mary. You won't go without."

Mary smacked her lips and turned to him. "That isn't the issue."

Andrew would have known the reason why she didn't want to leave Ruth behind. She'd loved Ruth like family, and Sarah treated her very poorly.

William held up his hand as if to back down, amusement twinkling in his eyes.

"We can't leave them here," Mary whispered, shooting a look toward the door. "Sarah is horrible to Ruth."

"I won't allow her to be."

Mary narrowed her eyes. "How can you if you aren't here to stop it?"

Mother looked taken aback. "Why wouldn't I be here?"

Now it was Mary's turn to look confused. "Aren't you coming with us?"

Her mother chuckled softly. "No, my dear. You are going out into the world with your husband to start your own family. You don't need your mother in your shadow."

Mary's heart sank. She wasn't going? Wasn't the whole point in getting close to Will and marrying him so her mother could be happy and get away from Kline Manor? Wasn't that what the urgency of getting married had been?

Had she always known that she would stay behind?

She felt betrayed, as though she'd been hoodwinked. Her mother had led her to believe she was doing this for her, hadn't she? She had taken Andrew from her, and it was for nothing? Mary was going to be without her mother anyway.

Mary suddenly felt very ill. What had she done? If her mother wasn't going to go with her no matter who she married, she should have ignored her mother's wishes and married Andrew.

She thought about Andrew in the garden, asking her to run away with him. Hadn't she been tempted to say yes? Wasn't her only reason for staying and being with William because she wanted to choose her mother's happiness over her own?

If she had known then that her mother wasn't going to be living with them, would she have still chosen to stay and marry William?

No.

She looked at her husband, and for the first time, her heart twisted with something like regret. She gingerly touched her stomach, hoping, more than anything, she could hold down breakfast. But everything felt so wrong. She felt lied to and violated.

Will was wonderful and sweet, but would she have allowed herself to go this far with him if she'd known the truth from the beginning?

Hadn't she loved Andrew first? Hadn't she loved Andrew longest? Hadn't she loved Andrew more?

It had always been Andrew right from the beginning. But her mother insisted.

Her mother had ruined her only chance at happiness.

William took her free hand. "Are you all right?" he asked. "Perhaps she can come stay if being away upsets you."

Mary blinked, her stinging eyes threatening her with tears. She didn't want her mother there. She had never felt more betrayed. She hated her for what she did.

"N-no. It's fine. It's just not what I expected."

What she expected was her mother to be packed and ready, eager even, to leave behind the painful memories of Kline Manor.

She expected to have made this decision to keep her mother happy and in her life.

But wasn't she happy? Even if she was staying behind, she was happier that Mary had chosen Will over Andrew.

Still, Mary couldn't shake the feeling that she'd been tricked, and the thought made her sick.

Mother had selfishly made this decision for Mary.

She'd broken her and Andrew's hearts for nothing.

On the way to her new home, Mary couldn't slow her racing thoughts. She wanted to write to Andrew straight away and tell him she made a terrible mistake and beg him to come to her and take her far away. It didn't matter if her mother never forgave her because in that moment she never wanted to see her again.

But she couldn't do that. She couldn't leave Will, even if Andrew would come as quickly as he could. Even if she only married him because of a lie. Even if she would rather be poor with Andrew than rich with William.

It would hurt William and ruin his reputation, as well. It would be years before he would be allowed to remarry.

No. There would be no writing to Andrew and telling him she had made a mistake. She'd made her choice, and now she must live with the consequences.

"Are you sure you're all right?" Will asked, eyeing her. "I can send someone to get your mother. She can stay as long as you need."

Mary shook her head and stared out the window, unable to meet his gaze. "I'll be fine."

Though she wasn't sure how truthful that statement was.

William had found a home for them between her family manor and his, only a day's travel away from either home, instead of two. It was just half a day outside of Boston, so he wouldn't have to be away for long for work.

Mary's heart soared as she took in the breathtaking home. Connell Manor was bigger than Kline Manor, with a large parlor with a gorgeous fireplace that someone had already lit, a grand piano, a library bigger than the one back home, and a large kitchen where she could cook. Essentially, the house was everything she could have wanted and everything she would have chosen herself.

But still, she couldn't stop thinking that it had come with a price she thought she'd been prepared to pay but wasn't.

William led the way upstairs and paused at the door at the end of the hallway.

"I wasn't sure if you wanted to share bedrooms or not, so I had a room made up for you and a room made up for the both of us."

Mary faked a smile, hoping it wasn't as off-putting as she felt.

"That was very thoughtful," she told him.

She wondered if she should decide now. It was customary to sleep in separate beds, sometimes separate rooms, but she didn't want to be alone. Even if she was upset about losing Andrew. Maybe especially because she was upset about Andrew. She didn't want to be alone with her thoughts and regrets. If she was going to be married to William, shouldn't she let him comfort her?

"I just want you to be happy here," Will said.

Mary met his eyes and swallowed. "I'm happy with you," she lied, trying to remind herself that William was everything most girls dreamed of finding.

He grinned and took her hand. "Then let's go in."

He pushed open the door, and Mary stepped inside. There was a bed for two, completely made up for them. Three wardrobes stood at the opposite end of the room. There was a vanity along the wall near the window, a bookshelf already containing a few books, two comfortable reading chairs, and a few tables around the room.

"It's beautiful," Mary said, walking around and studying the small ornaments on the tables. "You decorated?"

He nodded, then shrugged. "Well, I hired someone to."

"They did wonderful," she said, taking it all in.

"I'm glad you're happy."

Happy. Was she happy? She loved her home and was married to a prominent man, but there was still a nagging feeling in the back of her mind that something wasn't quite right. She wondered if that would ever go away.

"It's still early if you want something to eat," he said. "You must meet the staff, after all."

Mary let him lead her down to the kitchen, where a woman was bustling around the stove, and a man was sitting by the door. The man stood when they walked in.

"Good evening, Mister Connell."

"Good evening. I'd like for you to meet my wife."

George glanced at Mary, then back at Will.

Mary smiled. "Please, call me Mary."

"I'm Hannah," the maid said. "And this is my husband, George."

Mary smiled. Ruth and Henry had been married as well. She loved when couples worked together. It meant that they cared about one another enough to want to spend more time together.

"It's lovely to meet you, Hannah, George."

"And you, Mary," Hannah said.

"There is also Calvin and Jerome, but they've gone home for the day," George said.

Mary looked around, admiring the well-organized counters and cabinets. "Hannah, do you have any strict rules about me being in the kitchen?"

"Of course not, miss. It's your home."

Mary smiled. "Well, perhaps I can join you tomorrow when you make dinner? I haven't cooked in quite some time, and I admit I quite miss it."

"That sounds wonderful. Dinner is finished if you're both hungry."

Will thanked her and took the dish she was about to carry to the dining room.

"I can get it, thank you. You two can go home for the day. Thank you for staying late to make sure the house was ready for us."

"It was our pleasure, Mister Connell. Thank you."

They said their goodbyes and left Will and Mary alone, completely alone, in their big house, with no threat of someone walking in and seeing them.

"That was sweet of you," Mary said. "To allow them to go for the night."

He led the way to the dining room. "It's late enough. I don't want our help to tell everyone we're unreasonable. Besides, I have other ideas of how we can spend our evening, and I'd rather like to be alone with my wife."

His insinuation made her hesitate. After all the dark thoughts she'd had that evening, she wasn't sure if she wanted a repeat of their wedding night.

Mary was quiet during dinner, but William didn't question her. While she cleared up, Mary thought about Andrew. She wondered where he was and what he was doing and if he was all right. She hoped he wasn't as lost as she was.

Will might not have had all the memories and romantic moments that she and Andrew had shared, but maybe he was trying to have them with her now. If she would only let him. If only she could stop thinking of Andrew, she might be able to forget how alone she felt even when she was in William's arms.

After she had finished cleaning up, William took Mary's hand and led her to bed. Mary didn't argue. It was her wifely duty.

He didn't bother to close the door, but why would he? It was only them. He turned, wrapping his arms around her bodice, and pressed his lips to hers. She let him undress her, shivering as the cool air hit her bare breasts.

William was rougher than he'd been the night before, and Mary cried out twice. Perhaps this was her penance for marrying the wrong man.

Once again, he finished outside, and she was thankful. He gently kissed her cheek before rolling over, facing the wall, and fell asleep without a word to her.

Tears fell down her cheek as the loneliness overwhelmed her. This was the path she had chosen, and this was what she could always expect.

For the rest of her life.

Chapter Twenty-Four

*M*ARY DIDN'T WRITE TO ANDREW for weeks. She wanted to put as much distance and time between them as possible to give him time to get over her and to give her time to get over him.

Unfortunately, it didn't seem to be working. She couldn't stop thinking about him no matter what she did, and finally, she realized she couldn't stay away. She missed him too much.

When she finally did write to him, she tried to be friendly, but not overly personal. She didn't want to let on that she was still in love with him and how lonely and unhappy she was.

> *Andrew,*
> *Forgive me for not writing sooner. I've been busy adjusting to my new life with Will and setting up our home. The house is gorgeous and beyond anything I could have expected. I hope you can find time to visit us soon so I can give you a tour. I have already made fast friends with our maid, Hannah, although I still miss Ruth terribly and worry how Sarah is treating her without me there to intervene.*

I hope you aren't staying too busy at work. Boston is a place for parties and fun too. Don't forget. I can only imagine how lovely it is there. Perhaps I could cajole William to take me some time. You'll have to tell me the best places to visit.

I received a letter from Mother yesterday. She is planning to come visit at the end of the month to see the house. I was ever so surprised when she informed me she wasn't coming to live with me. I had thought that was the point behind the wedding, for Mother to get away from Kline Manor. Still, she's happy, and I suppose that's the same to her.

I invited Aunt Catherine and Sarah to visit as well, but Sarah doesn't want to be away from Jeffry. Could you imagine anyone wanting to be around Jeffry? I'm not sure how much she's said to you, but apparently, they're getting very close, and Sarah believes if she gives him another month or so, he'll propose.

Will has been able to work close to home mostly, but he's travelling to Boston today. He has to find another property since you and your father closed on the one they had planned to buy. Apparently if he doesn't get this one, it'll set him and his father behind. The good news is we live close enough that he can make the trip there and back in one day if everything goes well, which is great because I worry about being home alone in this big house. I asked if I could go with him—admittingly, I wanted to visit you and see your apartment—but he thinks I would keep him from working.

I hope you are keeping well, Andrew, and I truly hope you are happy.

Yours,
Mary

Mary reread the letter and sighed. There was so much more she wanted to say but knew she shouldn't. She wanted to tell him that she missed him and thought about him every day. She wanted to ask if he was all right or if he was angry with her. She wanted to tell him how used to his company she had come and how miserable she'd been without him.

She missed home and her best friend, and she wanted more than anything to tell him.

But she couldn't. Will was jealous of Andrew. She couldn't tell him she missed him without it sounding like an invitation for him to miss her, as well, and that wouldn't sit well at all now that she was a married woman. She didn't want to ruin Andrew's reputation or make a mockery of her husband.

Besides, it wasn't fair of her to say those things to him anymore. She'd married Will. She chose Will. Andrew needed the space to get over her so he could move on and find someone who could make him happy. A better woman who would choose him no matter what. Wouldn't talking to him about it all only make it worse for him?

Didn't it make it worse for her? Just thinking about it all broke her heart all over again. How could she say it all aloud?

She folded the letter, walked to the front of the house, and gave it to Calvin, asking if he could send it out with the morning post. Calvin gave a slight bow and took the letter.

Mary made her way to breakfast, wondering if Will was up yet. Sure enough, she found him sitting at the table, sipping coffee.

"Good morning, darling," he said as she sat down next to him.

"Morning. You look well rested."

"I slept very well, thankfully. Today is bound to be a very long day, indeed."

"What time do you leave today?" Mary asked.

"Soon. Straight away. Since Andrew and his father closed on another property Father was set to buy, our income has taken a dive. Father has been funneling funds into a warehouse in North Boston, but it's turned out to be a money pit. The building needs more work than it's worth."

Mary frowned. "I'm sure you'll find something."

"I hope so. But word is, the building we have our eye on is considering closing. If I don't make the sale today, we may have to start reducing staff."

Mary wouldn't mind taking care of the house herself, but she hated to think of Hannah and George out of work. Had Andrew purchasing that property really caused so much fuss?

"There was talk of another property that might be looking to sell for the right price, but that would mean staying the night and meeting for breakfast or lunch tomorrow. If Andrew doesn't beat me to it, that is."

"You won't be home tonight?"

"I'm afraid not."

That would leave her alone overnight. She'd never spent the night alone, even at home. Mother had a governess who lived with them and would stay with her when her parents were both away.

"Are you sure I cannot come? I promise to stay out of the way."

William sighed heavily. "I've told you I can't have you there. You'll distract me. How can I focus on work with a woman hanging off my arm, needing to be escorted to whatever shop she wants to visit?"

Mary's face burned at how little he thought of her. How could he think that was what she would want?

Will looked down at the paper, either ignoring or not noticing her annoyance. "I'm sure you can keep yourself entertained at home. Think of me, out there working all day, talking to men I don't care about, pretending I'm interested in keeping their businesses afloat."

Mary's eyebrows knit. "Pretend you're interested?"

He waved her off. "I don't care for this side of business. I prefer to balance the checkbooks, order supplies, and supervise renovations."

"Oh." She turned back to her toast, feeling slightly unsettled. He almost sounded cold.

He watched her for a few moments. "You *are* going to be all right, aren't you? I can arrange for someone to come stay with you if you'd like. I have a cousin not far from here."

The last thing she wanted was for someone she didn't know to come stay with her. It was frightening enough to stay alone. Staying with a stranger, even if it was William's cousin, would make her feel even more apprehensive.

Mary faked a smile. "I'll be just fine. I think it might be lovely to spend a quiet evening reading."

And for a while after he left, she was fine. She spent the morning helping Hannah tidy up and the afternoon reading in the library. But mornings and afternoons were always busy for William, who stayed in the study working on plans and budgets and whatever else he got up to that Mary wasn't involved in.

It wasn't until the evening she'd even seen him, when they'd eat dinner together and she'd read to him.

But now that he wasn't there, Mary was at a loss. The house felt so quiet without the sound of his heavy footsteps.

She wandered into the kitchen, where Hannah was already cooking dinner. Mary took one look at it and realized she wasn't going to be able to eat very much.

"Hannah, I'm so sorry. I was hoping to catch you before you

started cooking. There's no need for all of that. It's just me here tonight."

Hannah shook her head. "Oh, miss, you still need to eat, even if it is just you."

Mary waved her off. "I will. I'll have some bread and cheese. I'm not in the mood for a big dinner."

Hannah nodded. "All right."

Mary looked at the veggies already cut and the meat already cooking. "Why don't you and George stay and enjoy it?"

She shook her head. "I couldn't possibly."

"Oh, please? I insist! It'll just go to waste if you leave it."

Hannah gave her a small smile. "Well, all right, but you must join us. It'll feel so strange eating your dinner in your home if you aren't eating as well."

Mary smiled. In a way, it would be like a dinner party with friends. "Well, all right. But let me at least help. If you are to be my guests, I can't have you doing all the work."

Hannah handed her the knife to finish cutting the vegetables and went to check on the chicken.

Hannah was funny and sweet, and Mary realized she was growing close to her. She was her only friend in a world that was so new and lonely. She wouldn't know what she'd have done if Hannah wasn't there.

They sat down to dinner, and George awkwardly glanced at Mary.

"It was kind of you to invite us to dinner," he said.

"Oh, you're doing me a favor," Mary told him, lifting her water glass. "I wasn't looking forward to being alone for dinner tonight. Hannah is such a dear for agreeing to join me."

He smiled at his wife, real and genuine, a twinkle in his eye, and Mary's heart ached. Nobody had looked at her like that since Andrew. William never had that look in his eye when he looked at her. The only thing she'd ever seen in William's eyes was lust.

They talked through dinner, but, just as she expected, Mary didn't eat very much. Her mind kept going back to Andrew, wondering how he was. She hated how much she missed him.

Had he received her letter with the evening post? Would he write back? It would serve her right if he kept her waiting for a letter for weeks as she had him.

But she desperately hoped he would write her back. She wanted so much to hear from him and know how he was.

After they finished eating, George helped the women clear up.

"Dinner was lovely, Hannah," Mary said. "You really are a wonderful cook."

"She is. I got real lucky she agreed to marry me," George said, taking her hand.

Hannah's cheeks pinked.

"I agree, George. She's one of the good ones. Goodnight, you two. I'll see you in the morning."

Once they were gone, Mary wandered through each room, blowing out the candles they had lit. A crash of thunder shook the house, and she gasped. She pressed a hand to her forehead and sighed, reminding herself there was nothing to be afraid of. It was just a rainstorm.

She hoped Hannah and George would make it home all right.

It had been such a long day, and she wanted nothing more than to go up to bed. With the rain beating down outside, maybe she would sleep better.

As she started up the stairs, she heard a knock on the front door.

Her mind and heart raced. She was alone, and William wouldn't be home until tomorrow. Who would be out in this weather so late at night?

Slowly, she walked to the door and, as quietly as she could, trying to be inconspicuous, peered through the window. She gasped and hurried to unlock the door.

Andrew stood before her, eyes heavy with concern and soaking wet.

"He said he knows you, Missus Connell?" Calvin called through the rain, standing next to Andrew.

Mary nodded. "Andrew is my dear cousin."

Calvin nodded. "I'll put his horse in the stables, then."

"Thank you, Calvin."

Finally, she turned her attention to the handsome man in front of her, dressed in traveling clothes. "Andrew. What are you doing here?"

"I'm sorry to have come so late," he said. "You look stunning."

Mary glanced down at her evening gown. She didn't look any different than usual. But as she looked at him, she understood what he meant. He was devastatingly handsome. More handsome than she'd ever seen him.

"Thank you," she said. She glanced around, knowing it would be polite to invite him inside, but remembered Will saying he wouldn't tolerate Andrew calling while he was out. But Andrew had come all this way. It would be impolite to leave him outside in the pouring rain after dark – rude even. Whether William became furious with her or not, Mary couldn't leave him out there like that. Finally, she sighed and smiled. "Come in, please."

He broke into a grin, took his hat off, and stepped inside.

"Your home is lovely," he said, looking around the dark foyer. She had already blown out all the candles on the first floor, and the only light came from the moon showing through the open door.

She laughed. "That's very kind, but I daresay you can't see much of it."

"Well, the outside is lovely."

"Thank you. I agree. It's quite beautiful. Just wait until

you see it in the daylight. You're staying till morning, aren't you?"

He shuffled his feet, brushing his hand over his hat and avoiding eye contact.

"I'm not sure. Now that I'm here, I think perhaps I shouldn't have come," he said softly.

She narrowed her eyes. "Why do you say that?"

He looked at her, his eyes meeting hers, and her breath hitched.

"You really do look so beautiful."

He was so sweet, so handsome, and he was there, with her, telling her she was beautiful. She wanted nothing more than to close the distance between them and press her lips to his, to feel his hands on her and tell him how much she missed him and how happy she was to see him.

But she couldn't. Not now that she was married. She had told herself that she could only kiss him once, and that's why she did it. But there he was. Right in front of her, looking so handsome and telling her she was beautiful.

"Andrew...."

"I got your letter at dinner, and I came as soon as I read it. I rode as fast as I could. Every day that passed without word from you made me think you'd forgotten me. I missed you so much." She opened her mouth, but he held up his hand. "Please. Please. Don't tell me to go. Don't tell me I'm forgetting my place." His lip trembled. "I know I'm overstepping, but I can't keep away from you any longer. I know you chose William, but I miss my best friend."

She had never seen so much pain in his eyes. Her heart ached.

"I could never forget you, and I'm sorry I didn't write sooner," she said softly.

"I don't blame you. After what happened at your wedding, I didn't think you'd ever want to see me again."

Against her better judgment, she reached out and took his hand. "Of course I want to see you. I just thought you needed time. And perhaps I needed time too."

His thumb rubbed the back of her hand.

"Do you need more time?" he asked.

She laughed and shook her head. "Seeing you tonight has been the very best surprise."

"Truly? You aren't upset I've come unannounced?"

She shook her head. "You are always welcome in my home."

He glanced up the stairs. "Perhaps you should check with your husband before extending such an invitation."

"Oh. Will isn't home at the moment, I'm afraid."

He narrowed his beautiful hazel eyes. "You're home alone?"

Mary nodded. "Why do you look so upset?"

He rubbed his hand over his face. "Oh, Mary. Why did you let me in? Do you know how that will look if William comes home now? Or what the staff will think?" He looked over his shoulder at the open door. "Will would no doubt be furious with my being here without him, judging by our last conversation. He'd all but threatened that I remember he'd won your affection, not me. I'll take my leave. I don't want to cause you any trouble."

"You can't possibly go out there in the pouring rain!" she protested.

"But if William comes home and sees me, or someone tells him of my late-night visit, he'll think the worst."

Her heart skipped as she thought about what William would think. He might think she was having an affair. After all, he knew Andrew loved her, and she had admitted that she had cared for Andrew, as well, even if she didn't admit how much.

A fire burned in her chest as she thought about Andrew touching her the way her husband had. It was so tempting. He was there and loved her, and they were alone. Hadn't she been thinking of him every night? She wondered if Andrew would look at her while he kissed her, if he would hold her after. If he would be gentle with her.

But she had made a promise. And she couldn't break it. No matter what she felt for Andrew, she wasn't the type of woman to have an affair.

"Perhaps you're right," she whispered, taking a step back. "But you can't go back out in that storm. I'll set you up in a guest room, and as soon as William is home, I'll explain the situation. He'll understand."

She locked the door and led him upstairs, suddenly wishing she'd have waited to send Hannah and George home. She was worried about what Will would think when he got home. If he thought Andrew had said or done anything inappropriate, he'd never allow him to visit again, probably never let them write to one another. And if the past few weeks had taught her anything, it was that she couldn't go without him without her heart breaking.

The upstairs candles were still lit, so as soon as she turned toward him on the second-floor landing, she could see clearly how handsome he was. She took a candle off the wall to give him.

She led the way down the hall to one of the guest bedrooms, and her mind flashed back to months ago when he came to stay at Kline Manor when she led him to his room. He looked at her with those soft, warm eyes that held so much love for her, and her heart skipped. Just like he was doing now. Only then, she hadn't been thinking about following him into his room and staying with him.

"Well, goodnight," she said breathily.

He took her hand. "Goodnight, Mary."

Her chest ached with longing. She didn't want to say goodnight already. He had just got there. She had so much she wanted to discuss. But it wasn't just a discussion she wanted. She wanted so desperately to lean forward and press her lips to his, to follow him into the bedroom and spend the night with him.

But she was married.

She chose Will.

Her feelings didn't matter.

She took a step back, pulling her hand from his. "Goodnight, Andrew," she said again.

He swallowed and took the candle she held out for him.

She glanced back at him as she walked down the hall to her bedroom. He was still standing by the door, watching her. She gave him a small smile that she was sure he couldn't see in the darkness.

She stepped into her bedroom, closed the door, pressed her back against the hard, cold wood, and sighed heavily.

Andrew was there, just down the hall. And they were alone.

Chapter Twenty-Five

*A*FTER MARY CHANGED INTO HER nightgown and climbed into bed, she fantasized about going to Andrew's room. Would he kiss her? Hold her? Or would he tell her it was a mistake and she should return to her own chambers?

She squeezed her eyes closed, suddenly feeling very awake, wishing sleep would take her so she would stop thinking of Andrew.

It was insane, her lying in bed when they hadn't had a proper chance to talk. He'd come in, and she put him straight to bed. It was quite rude, now that she was thinking about it.

She had thought if they separated, it would give William less reason to be upset by Andrew's being there, but what if Andrew left in the middle of the night or first thing in the morning, and she missed her chance to speak with him?

Mary climbed out of bed and tiptoed to the door. She pressed her ear against it, listening as though Andrew was on the other side. She sighed and paced to the window, then back, picking at her fingernails.

She wanted so desperately to go and talk to him and learn how he'd been the past few weeks, but she was afraid. What if he kissed her again? She didn't trust that she had the strength to resist. Or worse, what if he was passive and acted as though he didn't want to kiss her? She didn't know if she could handle wanting him so desperately, only for him not to want her back.

Mary sighed and dropped her hands to her side. She couldn't just stay there. She had to see him. She was going to at least talk to him for a few minutes. No harm could come from talking, could it? If he tried something, she could control herself. She had before.

But what if Will came home while she was alone, talking to Andrew in the guest bedroom? He would assume the worst. Especially now that she was in her nightgown.

It didn't matter. She couldn't not talk to him. What if he thought she didn't want him there and left first thing in the morning?

She grabbed her dressing gown and tied it closed around herself. If she was going to be alone with Andrew, she would at least be properly covered.

Unable to bear the thought of being away from him any longer, Mary pulled the door open.

She inhaled sharply when she saw Andrew standing there, arm raised as though prepared to knock.

"Hello," she said.

He awkwardly lowered his hand and cleared his throat.

"Hello."

She laughed and took his hand. "It seems as though we had the same idea."

"You were coming to see me?"

"I was. We didn't really get a chance to speak, and I have missed you dreadfully."

He smiled as he studied her. "And I, you."

She glanced around the room she shared with Will. It felt wrong to include Andrew in this part of her life. She felt embarrassed just thinking about it.

"Will you walk with me?"

His eyes never left hers. "Anywhere."

She giggled. "Even out in the rain?"

"For a chance to be with you, yes."

She rested her hand on his arm and led him down the hall.

"How have you been? Tell me all about Boston!"

He glanced at her, his eyes intense with that spark of love Mary hadn't seen in weeks.

"Boston is... busy and bright. I like it better here, in the dark, with you."

Mary laughed. "If you're hinting at something, I can light some candles."

"Please don't. I like it better like this."

Lightning flashed, illuminating his handsome features.

"Oh? And why is that?"

He stopped walking and placed his hand on her cheek. "Because if I could see you properly, my heart might burst. I don't trust myself. If I could properly look into your eyes, I wouldn't be able to help myself from leaning forward and kissing you again."

Mary's heart leaped as she swallowed. She couldn't deny the thought of his lips on hers took her breath away.

"But I daresay," he said breathily, taking a step toward her, "Seeing you in the dim light might be just as tempting."

Mary's breath hitched. She was so sure he was going to lean in and even more sure that she was going to let him.

But, being the gentleman he was, Andrew pulled his hand away from her face and took a small step away.

"Are you happy, Mary?"

Happy. There was that word again. It was such a weighted word too. She should be happy. Any other woman in her position would be. She liked her home and had a handsome, rich husband. She had everything she should possibly want.

Everything but Andrew. But she couldn't tell him that.

"I suppose."

His lips twitched as he frowned slightly, but then they pulled into a small smile. "Good."

Her lip trembled. "Is it?"

"Of course it is. You deserve to be happy. It's all I want for you. And as long as you're happy, I won't completely regret leaving that day and giving you up."

She wrapped her hands in front of her chest and took a deep breath as she began walking again.

"I was upset when you said you weren't coming back," she told him, not able to look into his eyes. "I tried so many times to talk to Mother. Begged her to change her mind. We fought so much."

"She never would have allowed our union."

"No. You're right about that, but I had hoped if we talked to her together, perhaps she'd have seen how serious we were about one another. Perhaps she'd have seen how amazing you are and could have looked past everything else."

"You're saying I should regret choosing to stay in Boston?"

Mary finally turned to him. His eyes were on her. "No. Not regret. I don't want you to regret anything."

"I do. Not a day goes by that I don't think about what would have happened if I'd stayed and asked your mother for your hand. Maybe if I'd told William how I felt about you before your engagement, he'd have taken a step back. And if he hadn't been in the picture, perhaps your mother wouldn't have hated the idea of you with me."

She wasn't sure anything would have convinced her mother to allow them to marry, as she'd seemed adamantly against it from the very beginning. Mary should have gone against her mother's wishes, no matter what the cost.

And William had suspected from the beginning that Andrew

loved her. He had said as much after their first meeting. He didn't back down. But then again, Mary hadn't told him Andrew's feelings were reciprocated.

"You seemed to have thought about it a lot," she said.

"I have. I think about it every day. Imagine how different our lives would be if I hadn't taken the coward's way out."

"You weren't cowardly."

"I was. I was so afraid of losing you that I just let you go."

Mary's heart clenched. She didn't like hearing that he had regrets, as well. She had assumed he had the occasional regret, like she did, but she had hoped that he was moving on now that he was in Boston, surrounded by women and parties and away from her.

"Andrew...."

"I know. I'm sorry. I'm being entirely too forward. You want to hear how I'm having the time of my life in Boston, right?"

Not in the slightest. The thought unnerved her. She wanted to tell him that she felt the same and wished more than anything that they were together and that she'd have run off with him when he asked.

But Mary nodded, tears forming in her eyes.

He cocked his head and gently brushed away her tears. "Please don't cry."

But she couldn't help it. She couldn't stop.

Andrew wrapped his arms around her and gently swayed, caressing her hair with his hand.

"I'm sorry, Mary."

"Me too," she whispered. "I keep thinking if I'd have known Mother wasn't coming with me when I moved, that I might not have married William. But then I feel guilty because William deserves someone who loves him entirely. I fear I cannot ever give him that."

"Do you regret marrying him?"

Her breath caught. "Sometimes. As selfish as that sounds."

"It doesn't sound selfish at all. You aren't selfish enough if you ask me."

Mary chuckled.

"Do you want out? My option to take you far away still stands."

The offer was very tempting. And there was no one there to stop her from leaving. She could pack a bag, and they could be far away before anyone arrived in the morning and noticed she was missing.

But what would Andrew do for money? How could he get a job if he was known as a man who broke up a marriage? How could she? And William wouldn't be allowed to remarry for years, and even then, there would be rumors that made fathers reconsider if he would make a fine husband.

"I want to be with you more than anything, but I cannot do that to Will."

"I understand," he said, his voice barely a whisper.

She glanced up and saw tears in his eyes.

"I truly am sorry, Andrew."

"Should I go?" he whispered. "I can fetch my horse."

Mary took a shaky breath and shook her head. "Please don't leave. I couldn't bear the thought of you out in that storm."

"All right. I'll wait until the storm passes."

"Do you have to work tomorrow?"

"I took the next two days off."

"Then stay. I'll speak with William. Stay with me," she whispered into his chest, clinging tighter to him.

He sighed sadly and kissed the top of her head. "All right. I'll stay as long as I am able."

He held her for a moment longer, then pulled slightly away. "Hey, now. Dry those eyes. If I am to only be here for a few days visit, I suggest we do our best to make happy memories."

Mary took a step away and dried her eyes. "Very well. Quite right. Are you hungry? I can make us something to eat."

"No. I'm not hungry at all, but if you are, I can help you cook. If you show me how."

She laughed. "How about a cup of tea then?"

"Tea sounds lovely."

She started down the stairs, Andrew right behind her, and made her way to the kitchen. She found the matches and lit the candle, then started a fire to heat the kettle.

"You seem to have adjusted well to the role as lady of the house."

"I am, slightly. It's odd not having anyone to answer to, but it's honestly much better. Without Mother here to tell me what to do, I'm allowed to cook and clean and read to my heart's content. I don't have to suffer through dinner parties or lessons."

"That's one good thing that came of it, I suppose."

"Yes. I try to look at the positives. If I focus on the negatives, I daresay I'd struggle to get out of bed every morning."

She set two cups on the counter and prepared the tea as the kettle whistled.

The room was still dark but bright enough to make out Andrew's features as he watched her work.

"You're staring," she said.

"Twenty-one years I've known you, and this is the first cup of tea you've ever made me."

"That isn't true."

"No?"

"Not at all. Remember when I was four and you came to visit? I had a tea party, and you were the guest of honor."

He chuckled. "I forgot about that."

"I didn't."

"There was actual tea in the cup too."

"There. See? I've made you tea twice now."

He narrowed his eyes at her. "Did you actually make it, or did your maid make it, and you just served it?"

Mary frowned and shook her head. "All right, fine. You got me there."

Andrew laughed. "I suppose we can still count that. You did pour it."

"You see? And now that I'm serving you tea again, that's two for me and zero for you."

"Oh, is that how we're playing it?"

She nodded. "Yes. It is. Now when are you going to invite me to your home in Boston?"

He grinned. "I'm afraid my apartment is quite small. You are welcome at any time, of course, but I don't have a guest room."

"No? Well, I suppose you will have to take the sofa."

"Gladly." His soft eyes never left hers.

She took a sip of her steaming tea. "Does that mean you don't have a piano?"

"No piano, I'm afraid."

Her mouth opened. "Whatever do you do to occupy your time?"

He shrugged. "I read some. I work a lot. Mostly I write."

"You write? How long have you been writing?"

"A few weeks. Since I've been in Boston."

She swallowed. "What do you write?"

"Mostly letters to you. A few to your mother."

Mary smiled. "And were you planning to mail these letters?"

He licked his lips and shook his head. "I wouldn't do anything to risk your happiness. And if you're happy in your marriage, I plan to keep my feelings to myself." He grinned at her. "As best as I can."

"That's very kind of you."

"I've heard I'm a very kind man," he said with a wink.

"Is that so? By some lovely lady at a party in Boston, perhaps?"

"Perhaps."

Mary grinned, but her stomach clenched with jealousy. She hated the idea of other women flirting with him, but she had no right to say as much. She was a married woman. And wasn't it better if Andrew found someone else he could love?

"Then perhaps you should try to find her and get to know her."

He knit his brows and stared at his tea. "Why are you saying that?"

"Because you deserve to be happy. And because I cannot give you that happiness, someone should."

"I'm not sure I can give away a heart that belongs to someone else," he said, setting his cup on the table.

She studied him, wondering what she could say to ease his pain. She knew all too well how that felt because she was married to a man who would never fully have her heart.

"Perhaps one day you can."

"We shall see." He grinned and raised his brows, but he didn't sound entirely convinced. Mary knew he was just humoring her because she knew she could never stop loving him either.

They sat for a while, chatting about Sarah and Jeffry, who wasn't near as close to proposing as Sarah had said. Aunt Catherine had even questioned if he was courting another, as he had canceled their last meeting. That suggestion hadn't settled well with Mary as she remembered how Jeffry had clung to Sarah at the wedding.

After a while, they washed their cups and extinguished the candles before making their way upstairs. It almost felt normal.

"I'm glad I came tonight, Mary," Andrew said, standing outside her bedroom door.

"Me too." Even if it would mean a fight with her husband.

He swallowed and leaned in ever so slightly. Mary's breath caught in her throat and her eyes fluttered closed as she prepared for his kiss.

His soft lips gently pressed against her forehead. Mary sighed as he pulled away.

"Goodnight, Mary."

She opened her eyes and her lip quivered. It took everything she had not to throw herself in his arms.

"Goodnight, Andrew."

He took one step back, then another. With every foot he put between them, the easier it got for Mary to breathe. As he walked away, she wondered if it would ever get easier to be around him and not want to be with him.

Chapter Twenty-Six

$\mathcal{T}$HE NEXT MORNING, MARY AWOKE alone in her bed. William still wasn't home. She hadn't spent the night alone since before she was married. It was oddly refreshing.

She yawned and stretched as she thought about what she would have for breakfast.

Then she remembered Andrew. She jumped up, hoping he was still there. She dressed quickly, then hurried down the hall to the guest room. The door was wide open, the bed made, and there was no sign of Andrew.

Mary hurried downstairs, terrified that he might have gone while she had been sleeping. As she reached the bottom of the stairs, she heard laughing coming from the kitchen. She followed the sound and found Andrew helping Hannah with the cooking. They turned to her as she entered.

"Good morning, Sleeping Beauty," Andrew said.

"Good morning. I didn't see you in your room and worried you'd gone."

"Now, I couldn't leave without meeting Hannah. You'd made a point to tell me how wonderful she was, so I wanted to judge for myself."

Hannah laughed. "He's quite a charmer, this one."

Mary smiled and leaned back against the door. "Yes. Quite." She was so glad he hadn't left that she didn't care what Hannah thought of the fact that he was there or what excuse Andrew had given for him being there while William was out.

"Are you hungry?" Andrew asked.

Mary nodded. "Very. I couldn't eat much last night, so I'm starved." She walked over to the wood stove to see what they were making.

"Those eggs look delicious, Hannah," she said.

"I've not touched them. Andrew insisted on making breakfast himself."

"Is that so?"

"I thought since I'm going to live alone, I should know how to cook for myself. I can't save as much as I'd like if I'm going out to eat all the time."

"It sounds like you have it all planned out," Mary said as they sat down to eat in the dining room.

"Well, mostly. There's a key element missing to my plan, but I think it can still be all right."

"It will be," she said, patting his hand, but she wasn't sure.

After breakfast, Mary and Andrew cleaned up and took a stroll around the garden.

"It's beautiful here," he told her, eyeing the pond.

"Yes, but it isn't the same as Kline Manor. Especially the garden. I miss my safe place dreadfully."

"You may grow to think of this as your safe place. With time."

She eyed him as he fell silent.

"What did you tell Hannah this morning? About who you are."

He grinned as he stared at the ground. "That I'm your lover, and she can expect me whenever William is out."

Mary gasped with shock. "You didn't!"

"No. I didn't. Though I daresay, I might be willing to settle for that."

She cocked her head. "You and I both know that wouldn't be good enough. And neither of us could hurt William like that. What if word got out? All our reputations would be ruined!"

"I don't care about my reputation. I care about you."

She studied him for a moment, but he showed no sign of humor. "You didn't say that to her."

"Of course I didn't. I told her I was your cousin. I wouldn't do that, even if we would have gone too far last night."

"Gone too far?" she asked, feeling slightly disappointed in his choice of words. "Like it would be a mistake?"

"You're married. Would it not be?"

She took a deep breath and looked out over the pond. She had nearly kissed him last night, and hadn't she thought long and hard about joining him in the guest bedroom? What kind of person did that make her? Especially if he was only going to see it as a mistake.

"I suppose," she said.

Perhaps it would be a mistake. She was with William, after all, and if he ever found out that she had kissed Andrew after they'd wed, it would break his heart and ruin their marriage.

"I'm sorry if my impromptu calling has upset you."

She quickly whirled around. "It hasn't! Not at all. I'm thrilled that you are here."

"Truly? Because if my being here only makes things more difficult for you, I can stay away." He shifted, his eyes darting around the garden, then back to her. "I can try harder to stay away."

"Your being here is the best surprise. I waited to write as long as I could. I couldn't bear it if you were away for even longer."

"Then I shall try to visit as often as I can and write regularly."

Having Andrew there was more than Mary could hope for. What started off as awkward, thinking of what could have been, melted into something of normality. For a while, they were just Mary and Andrew again. There was nothing strange or sad between them as they walked the garden, talking of the mundane.

Mary had nearly forgotten everything had changed until William's carriage pulled to a stop in front of the house. From the side of the house, walking between the foliage, she stared at the door, waiting for it to open.

"William," she said, fear gnawing at her.

The thought of what he would say when he discovered Andrew was there worried her. She hoped he wouldn't be angry.

"Should I hide?" Andrew asked.

Mary laughed. "Goodness, no! Imagine what he would think if he found you hiding."

"I can leave before he sees me."

"And have George or Hannah tell him you were here while he was out? He would assume it was a planned affair."

Andrew sighed. "All right. I suppose we should go and welcome him home?"

She took his hand and squeezed, trying to reassure him, before letting go.

The door to the carriage opened, and Mary and Andrew met William as he stepped out.

His eyes flickered from Mary to Andrew, worry creased on his brow. Mary's stomach flipped as she wondered what could be going through his mind.

"How was your trip, dear?" she asked, trying her best to keep her voice steady. The pet name felt foreign in her mouth. She was accustomed to William calling her darling, but she couldn't recall calling him anything other than his name.

"It was fine, thank you. Andrew, it's good to see you again."

"And you. I apologize for arriving with no notice. I thought that you would have been home. I should have written first and arranged a time to visit. I was eager to see Mary's new home."

"Oh, Will, it was such a lovely surprise. Andrew got my letter yesterday and decided to pay us a visit. It was storming when he arrived, so I put him up in the guest bedroom for the night. He wanted to leave when he discovered you weren't home, but I just couldn't turn him away in the cold rain."

William fixed a hard stare at Andrew as though watching for a reaction. "That was awfully kind of him." His voice was harder than usual, as though it was anything but kind. "And you, my dear wife." He smiled at Mary, but it didn't quite reach his eyes.

She'd never seen him properly cross before, but she thought she might soon.

"Are you hungry? We were about to go in for dinner. Hannah mentioned making soup."

"Soup sounds delicious. Just let me go upstairs and change."

"Of course."

"Would you care to walk with me?" he asked, eyeing Andrew before smiling at Mary. "I have quite a bit to share about my trip."

"I'd love to."

She raised her brows as she shot Andrew a worried look, then followed William up the stairs and into the house. He didn't say anything as they walked, making Mary's stomach roll with nerves.

He was angry. Cold. Mary had never seen him look like this. She only hoped his anger would be short-lived and they could move on quickly.

He had every right to be angry with her and Andrew. William had specifically asked that Andrew not be over without him there. He knew about their past.

Mary only hoped that he trusted her and wouldn't accuse her of anything. Although, if she were being honest, what man wouldn't question it? Andrew had arrived the very day William had left. It did look dreadfully suspicious. Add that to the fact that he knew she and Andrew had feelings for one another and had kissed in the past, and Mary could guarantee she was about to get into her very first disagreement with her husband.

"Close the door," he said roughly as soon as they entered the bedroom.

She did as she was told and waited for an explosion she was sure was about to come. William, however, took his time undressing, his expression hard. He pulled off his coat, cravat, and his shirt.

"Do I need to worry?"

Mary shook her head. "Andrew just came for a visit. He's doing well in Boston and is planning to buy a home soon. I think there is a woman, even. He mentioned someone flirting with him at a party." Her stomach clenched at the thought, but she knew it would ease her husband's mind.

William looked as though he were thinking as he studied her. She hoped her jealousy at the imaginable woman wasn't showing on her face.

"He didn't do or say anything out of line?"

That was debatable. He had said everything he had been saying for weeks, but that would only anger William further.

"No."

He sighed. "All right. I trust you. Even if I don't trust him."

Mary bit her lip. A part of her wanted to defend Andrew, but she knew William was right. Andrew made it very clear that all she had to do was say as much, and he would take her away, consequences be damned.

But that wasn't fair on her part either. Hadn't she been the one to regret not kissing him last night? Hadn't she been the one to consider spending the night in his room?

Hadn't she wished time and time again that she had run off with him?

Perhaps William was wrong to trust her. She didn't trust herself.

"Thank you," she said to the floor, unable to look him in the eye. "It would have been easy for you to be angry and forbid Andrew from returning."

"Believe me, the thought crossed my mind as we walked up here, but if he has done nothing wrong, then I cannot be completely unreasonable. What were you to do? Turn him out in the rain? You and I both know you would never do that to anyone. It wouldn't be fair of me to be angry with you for showing him kindness. Though, I daresay it was a surprise seeing him when I arrived, and I very nearly asked him to leave the moment I saw him. He had bought the first property I went to look at before I even arrived in Boston, then I arrive home and find him alone with my wife. It took everything in me not to lose my temper then and there."

How close had they come to losing one another again?

William paced the room for a few more moments before looking at her. "I do hope you would tell me if he were to ever cross any lines."

Mary nodded. "Of course."

Although, she wasn't quite sure she would. Andrew was everything to her, and she couldn't risk losing him.

He kissed her forehead, right where Andrew had kissed her the night before. That would have been in the category of crossing the line, but she wasn't going to mention it.

"He may keep winning properties over me, but I have won you over him, and I refuse to give you up so easily."

"What do you mean?" Mary narrowed her eyes. "You won me? Like it was a contest?"

Her stomach churned.

"I admit, I first came to Kline Manor because I wanted to see the man who kept stealing properties right out from under me. It wasn't just the one, you see. He'd stolen nearly a dozen over the past two years. I'd wanted to meet with him and speak about setting up boundaries before I knew you, but he never answered my letters. I wanted to meet him to set him straight. Then about a year ago, his father had mentioned to a mutual friend that Andrew had his eye on a Miss Mary Kline and was planning to court her. I had thought he'd have started courting you, but I suppose your father's death would have delayed him. When your mother sent the letter inviting me to meet you, I thought it might have been my chance to finally meet the man who kept besting me. My father insisted I go and speak with him about business, and if he refused to see reason, to steal you out from under him."

Mary's heart raced. She couldn't believe what he was saying. It had all been an act? A contest that he was trying to win over Andrew?

Her emotions must have shown on her face because he reached out. "Mary...."

She backed away, feeling sick. "You married me because you wanted to win against Andrew?"

All this time she'd felt guilty for loving Andrew when, to William, it had just been a contest. A business arrangement. She was no different than a property to him.

He sighed. "It started off as that, but the more I talked to you, the more I saw how well you would make an excellent wife. I had gone to Kline Manor intending to make you fall in love with my charm and good looks. I hadn't anticipated you being breathtakingly beautiful. I hadn't anticipated actually wanting you as much as I did the moment I looked at you."

As he pressed his lips to hers, her stomach twisted in knots as though her body knew she was kissing the wrong man.

Her entire marriage had been built on lies, and now she was learning that it wasn't just she who had withheld the truth. She suddenly felt less guilty for loving a man she shouldn't.

"I'm glad I'm home," he told her, kissing her again and sighing heavily. "Even more so now that you're in my arms."

She took a step away. Right then, she wasn't even able to humor him and pretend to be a good, loving wife.

"You should get dressed for dinner. Hannah should have it ready by now."

"But can't we just lie down for another hour or so? I feel as though I desperately need some alone time with you."

Her skin crawled at his words, remembering all those times his hands had touched her naked flesh. She had always thought he was more lustful than loving toward her, but now not even that felt real. Had he really liked the way she looked, or had the idea of her choosing him over Andrew been the fuel to his passion?

After being alone with Andrew for nearly twenty-four hours, Mary knew she should spend some time alone with her husband to ease his worries, but she didn't want him to touch her. Not now.

"As perfect as that sounds, I'm afraid it won't be possible today. We have a guest who will be waiting for us to join him for dinner."

William raised one eyebrow, then nodded. "All right. You go be a good hostess and offer our guest a drink. I suppose this is good practice for when your mother visits. Then we can start planning dinner parties of our own, inviting friends from all over."

Mary's heart sank. She didn't want to host large dinner parties, and William knew it.

"I thought we agreed I wouldn't have to host dinner parties for at least a few years?"

He raised a brow, unbuttoning his pants. "I thought we agreed Andrew wouldn't visit while I'm out."

Mary swallowed, feeling completely lost for words.

"I'll be down in a few moments."

She found Andrew in the parlor, sitting at the piano. He didn't seem to notice her sudden appearance as he stared down at the music sheet. She stood quietly in the open doorway, watching him, mesmerized by the soft, sad tune that she hadn't heard in quite some time. It was so unlike Andrew. He usually played happy music, songs of love or passion.

She'd missed seeing him play, watching his fingers work the keys and produce the most magnificent sound.

All her life she would watch with wonder as he played the most complicated pieces. It never failed to amaze her how good he was at the piano. She had wished all her life to be able to play as well as him, better even, so she could boast about it. But she could never play even half as well.

When he played, it was as though the piano was an extension of his arm, playing the music as fast as one would think. It seemed second nature to him.

The song came to an end and Andrew sat, unmoving for a moment, staring at the keys. Then he saw Mary in the doorway and jumped to his feet.

"I apologize for not asking if I could play. I saw how lovely your piano was and didn't know how long you would be."

"Andrew, calm yourself," she said, stepping into the room. "You never have to ask if you can play. I will always welcome your music."

"Still, it's William's place. It's his home, after all."

She tried not to think about William and his coldness because if she did, she might leave right then. "William is a polite host who would love if his guest played a tune on his piano."

He glanced behind her. "Was he cross?" he asked in a whisper.

Mary cocked her head, not sure where to start or how much to say. Should she admit that it had all been an act for him to win her over Andrew? What would he say? "He was, but he seemed to understand. He only requests that I tell him if you do anything inappropriate."

And required she start hosting his friends.

A smirk tugged at his lips. "Like walk with you in the dark?" He took a step toward her. "Or kiss your forehead before bed?" He took another step toward her, and her breath caught. He was close enough to reach out and touch now. "Or tell you how much I love you and miss you?"

"Andrew...." she whispered, casting a glance over her shoulder.

"Perhaps you should tell him about all of that."

She shook her head. "I will not do anything of the sort."

Not only because she didn't want to lose Andrew, but because now she was afraid of how William would react. Just finding Andrew at his home had upset him enough to admit to her that he only married her to win over Andrew.

He took another step forward, making her heart race with anticipation, and she squeezed her eyes closed. His nearness was killing her.

But it was better than not seeing him at all, wasn't it?

Why was she starting to think that might make it harder? She wanted more than anything to be able to kiss him.

At least when he wasn't there, she wasn't as tempted.

"Sorry for my delay."

William's voice pulled her out of her stupor, and her eyes snapped open as she turned to face her husband.

"It's no problem at all," Andrew said from beside the window. When had he gotten there?

"Now that I have a moment to talk, tell me, Andrew, how is Boston?"

"Boston is wonderful. Busy. I'm considering buying a home soon to get away from all of the bustle. The city life really isn't for me."

"That sounds splendid. Have you a place in mind?"

He cocked his head. "Not in particular, but somewhere in the country, where I can grow my own fruit."

"Really? You want to be a farmer?" William laughed.

Andrew huffed out a laugh. "Uh, no. I want to continue with my father's business, but I think having a few apple and pear trees might be nice."

Mary smiled. That had been the dream. When she was thirteen, Andrew had asked her about her dream home. She had said somewhere in the country where she could have apple and pear trees. She couldn't believe he had remembered.

"That sounds lovely," she chimed in.

Andrew gave her a knowing smile before looking down at his feet.

"Well, if Mary thinks it sounds lovely, who am I to think otherwise? She has better taste than I."

"Than both of us," Andrew agreed.

"Would you like a drink while we wait?" William asked. "I do say I could go for a glass of scotch."

"Scotch sounds wonderful."

William poured them each a glass, then glanced at Mary. "Darling, would you like a glass of wine?"

"That sounds lovely."

She sipped from her glass as the men each drank theirs in one swallow. William poured them another glass.

"Easy now, boys. You haven't eaten yet," Mary warned.

"We'll be all right."

Mary watched as William had a third glass. He didn't usually drink heavily. She wondered if he would do something stupid if he drank too much.

"How was your trip? Did you get everything settled?" Andrew asked.

"I did. For now, anyway. Unfortunately, I will have to return on Monday to ensure everything has gone through. If you could stop buying properties out from under me, I may be able to stop running around so much."

"I will try, for Mary's sake, to take your business into consideration the next time I purchase something. But perhaps while you're in the city, we can get lunch. I know a quaint little bar that serves the best sandwiches."

"That could be nice."

Mary sat back in her chair, glad they were getting along for once. She was afraid to speak. She wanted to warn Andrew of William's competitiveness, but she couldn't broach the subject then.

Hannah walked in, and everyone turned to her.

"Sorry to interrupt, but dinner is ready."

"Thank you, Hannah."

✺

BY THE TIME THEY WENT TO BED, Mary was beyond exhausted. It had been a very long, very confusing day.

"Goodnight," Andrew said as they made their way up the stairs.

"Goodnight, Andrew."

"I'll be leaving early in the morning. I wanted to tell you tonight so you wouldn't think I've left without a goodbye."

"Of course," she said, hoping her sadness didn't come through her voice as William was right behind her on the landing.

"Thank you for coming," William said. "I think it's meant a great deal to Mary."

"Of course, and I apologize again for arriving unannounced. Thank you for hosting me. It was nice seeing you both. I promise next time to write first."

Mary felt William's hand on her back, then he pulled away.

"Well, I'll let you two say goodbye and go get ready for bed."

Mary turned to see him walking toward the bedroom. She wasn't expecting him to leave them alone. She had thought his jealousy would keep him tied to her until Andrew was gone.

"You'll write to me?" Andrew said.

Mary swallowed as she looked into his sad, hazel eyes. She nodded. "I will. And a lot sooner than a month, this time."

He grinned. "Good. And I promise to wait to be invited before arriving. I can't have William thinking I only want to visit when he isn't home."

She knew he was trying to make a lightness of the situation, but she couldn't bring herself to smile. Her heart was aching at the thought of him leaving her again. Especially now that everything felt strange with William.

"You should get some sleep," he told her.

Her eyes stung with tears. She didn't want to go to sleep. She didn't want to leave him and return to William. She wanted to beg him to stay, to tell him she couldn't go another month without seeing him again.

But she didn't. She couldn't. Her husband was in their bedroom, waiting for her to return.

"Goodnight, Mary," he said again.

"Goodnight, Andrew."

She resisted the urge to tell him she loved him and watched as he slowly walked to his room, turning to look at her once more before going inside and closing the door.

Now, more than anything, Mary wished she and William didn't share rooms because she wasn't entirely sure she could keep from crying herself to sleep.

Chapter Twenty-Seven

WHEN MARY WOKE UP, ANDREW was gone. Even though she knew it was coming, it still hurt. When she didn't see him in the dining room, she made her way up to the guest bedroom, hoping he was still asleep. Instead, she found it empty, the bed made, and a letter resting on his pillow.

Mary hid it in the pockets of her skirts, not wanting to risk William walking in while she was reading it. What if it made her cry? What if Andrew told her he loved her again? She would read it after William was busy poring over his work in the study.

She went to breakfast, sitting just as William walked into the room.

"Good morning," she said, trying to smile.

"Good morning. You look sad. Has Andrew gone, then?" His voice was thick.

She swallowed but bit back a retort, wishing she didn't show emotions so easily.

"He has, but I'm not sad, really. It was just nice having some comforts of my old life, my old friend, here in my new life."

"I can understand that." His tone was softer as he studied

her. "But you've been distant with me. I could only assume it was because of his presence."

"It was because of what you said to me last night."

"Oh, Mary. I am sorry if I upset you. Will you allow me to make it up to you? I can take the day off, and we can go for a ride. I know a lake not far from here I've been dying to show you. What do you say? Should I have Hannah pack a picnic?"

Mary thought about the letter in her pocket and how upset she was with William and wanted to say no. But after all that happened over the past few days, she felt like a ride to a lake was just what she needed to clear her head.

"That sounds wonderful."

"Splendid. After breakfast, you can go change into your riding clothes, and I'll have Hannah pack us something to eat for when we get to the lake."

If she was quick, she could read the letter before they left. She wondered what Andrew had wanted to tell her before he left.

Mary picked at her food, her stomach in knots. She didn't have much of an appetite.

William cast her a few glances, but he didn't comment on her not eating. She took another bite whenever she felt his eyes on her, hoping it wouldn't look too suspicious. But with every bite she took, she felt more and more nauseous.

"Well, if you'll excuse me, I'll go get dressed," Mary said after William poured himself more coffee.

"Of course."

She started toward the door, but William touched her arm, pulling her attention back to him.

"Are you still cross with me?"

She put on a smile. "No. I'm just a little tired."

He nodded, but he didn't look convinced. She would have to do better to hide her feelings.

Once she was out of his line of sight, Mary gathered her

skirts and hurried up the stairs to their bedroom. She wanted to have plenty of time to read Andrew's letter before William came to get her for their ride to the lake.

She peered down the hall to make sure she was alone before she closed the door. Her hands trembled as she pulled the letter from her skirt pocket.

My Dearest Mary,

We've only just said goodbye, and I already miss you dearly. I wasn't going to leave you a letter, but you looked heartbroken when I told you I would be gone first thing in the morning. I couldn't leave without giving you just a little more of a goodbye. A better one, I hope.

You have a good life with William. A beautiful home. You seem happy. Happier than you were at Kline Manor, at any rate. You seem in your element being the lady of the house, and I do think I shall be returning soon just to see you in action once more.

It was good to see you and speak with you. I do hope you don't stay away as long this time because I really enjoyed seeing my best friend. For a while, it felt like old times, before I ruined our friendship by telling you how I feel about you. I do hope you can forgive me for that.

I will try to keep my feelings to myself, but I hope you know that my promise to you still stands and always will.

But if that day never comes, and your love for William only deepens, then I promise to be a good friend and honor your wishes. I won't interfere.

Please know that I truly do only want what will make you happiest.

All my love,
Andrew

Mary's heart raced. He was offering to step aside and let her be happy with her husband. Mary knew how much that must hurt him because it would kill her to step aside and promise not to interfere if their roles were reversed and Andrew married another woman.

Although if it had been Andrew, Mary wouldn't have ever told him how she felt to begin with. She wouldn't visit him either. She'd suffer in silence as her best friend fell in love with his wife.

She wiped away her tears and sniffled before taking the *Romeo and Juliet* book from where it was hidden in her dresser to put the letter in with the others. Her fingers caressed the rose, as they often did when she took the book out and thought about how much Andrew had grown to mean to her since that day.

She set the book on the dresser and turned to dig her riding clothes out of the wardrobe, daydreaming of a life she and Andrew could have had if they had been braver like Romeo and Juliet. She was buttoning her shirt when William knocked once and walked in.

He whistled. "You look amazing."

Mary chuckled and waved him off. "I look amazing in men's clothes but not a dress?"

"I never said you don't look amazing in a dress, but I so rarely see you in pants that I forget how much I like it."

He leaned forward and pressed his lips to hers. She tried not to resist, waiting for him to pull away.

"Well, thank you," she said.

"Are you ready to go?"

She nodded. "Are the horses ready?"

"They should be by the time we get outside. I asked Calvin to prepare them before I came up here."

He escorted her downstairs and to the back garden, where they found two of their horses saddled and waiting for them. Mary climbed on and waited for William to lead the way.

They started at a walk, then worked into a trot. William was carrying the picnic basket, so they didn't go as fast as they had in the past.

Still, it was exhilarating, everything Mary needed to get out of her head. Riding in the summer breeze was just the cure for her overthinking. She'd have to remember to thank William later for having such a brilliant idea.

The ride was longer than she imagined. Mary had thought it would have been as close as the lake near Kline Manor, but even at a run, it took well over an hour to reach it. When they finally arrived at the lake, Mary gasped. It was at least twice the size of the one near Kline Manor and more than beautiful.

"Wow," she breathed, looking around the gorgeous lake at the flowers and cattails growing nearby. Trees surrounded the lake, nearly closing it in except for the side they had ridden in on. Yellow and purple flowers grew in patches, creating a gorgeous painted look around the lake.

"This was one of the things that sold me on the house. I know it was a long ride, but it was the best home near this lake. As soon as I saw it, I thought you might like it."

Mary climbed down from the horse, tied it to the fencepost, and made her way over to William, now standing beside his horse, tying it to the fence.

"I love it," she told him. "It's absolutely breathtaking."

He took her hand, carrying the basket in the other, and led her nearer the water.

"How about right here? Is this a good place to set up?"

"It's perfect."

She looked out over the water as a dragonfly dipped low. A frog sat on a nearby lily pad, and she grinned. She hadn't seen a frog up close in years. It croaked, and she giggled.

She turned to see William spreading the blanket over the lush green grass. "Thank you for this," she told him.

He sat the basket on the blanket and took her hands. "It was the least I could do after the horrible things I said last night. I couldn't bear to see you upset with me. Then I remembered I hadn't brought you here yet and hoped you'd enjoy it. You showed me the lake near Kline Manor, after all. I thought I should return the favor."

He brought her hand up and gently kissed her knuckles.

"Now, I know we just had breakfast, but you didn't eat much, and I never say no to more food, so I asked Hannah to pack us a few sandwiches and cakes. I hope that's to your satisfaction?"

Mary sat on the blanket and watched as William pulled things from the basket. "It looks delicious."

She wasn't lying. She hadn't been able to eat much during breakfast, but now she felt famished.

The day was warm but not as hot as it usually was. Possibly because they were near the water. After she ate two sandwiches and a cake, Mary closed her eyes and let her head fall back to face the hot sun. It was such a beautiful day. William had been smart to suggest riding today. She was grateful he had offered to take the day off and bring her.

After they ate, they sipped at some wine and watched the insects and frogs go about their lives. There was a simplicity to it that made Mary happy and relaxed. She could stay out there all day if she could. After she finished her second glass of wine, she helped herself to another cake. Hannah had packed eight, after all, so there was plenty to last the day if they chose.

"Thank you for bringing me here," she told him.

"It was my pleasure," he said.

It was the first time they had spent a full day together since they were married. William had worked every day since the wedding, only stopping for dinner.

After another hour of lying and soaking up the sun, William and Mary decided to pack up and head back to the house.

Mary made a mental note to write to Andrew to tell him about the lake. It could wait until tomorrow, though. She really should put up some boundaries between the two of them. Perhaps then she could accept that they were never to be more than friends, and she could move on.

They rode in silence, at a slower pace than before, thanks to the wine they enjoyed. Mary didn't mind. She was in no rush to get back to the manor, where everything felt big and lonely.

It would be dinner time by the time they arrived. They would have just enough time to change before Hannah would call them for supper. Mary wasn't sure she could eat very much, with as much as she had for lunch.

Perhaps she could convince William to play her something on the piano after supper to wind down from the day.

Chapter Twenty-Eight

*A*FTER DINNER, WILLIAM PLAYED A couple of songs for Mary on the piano, just as she thought he would. He seemed to be doing everything he could to see her smile. Mary greatly appreciated the effort, but a part of her was still upset with him.

Perhaps she deserved it. She was a married woman, in love with another man.

It wasn't as though she could control her emotions, though. She had tried to fall out of love with Andrew. She had tried not to think of him as much. But she couldn't. Everything reminded her of him. Even William's playing made her miss Andrew. Perhaps it had been foolish to ask him to play.

"Thank you," she said as the song came to an end. "That was absolutely beautiful."

"It isn't nearly as beautiful as you, dear wife," he said, making his way over to where she sat on the sofa.

She sucked in a breath as his fingers caressed her cheek and down her neck.

"I hope you've had a good day."

"I have. Thank you."

He smiled and leaned forward, gently pressing his lips to hers. "I think I'm going to get to sleep. Between the sun and the wine, I'm dreadfully tired, and I think I'd like to read a little before bed."

"All right. I'll be up shortly. I think I'd like to finish my wine." She held up the glass.

"Of course. I'll see you soon."

He rose and left her alone. She sipped her wine as she listened to the sounds of his footsteps on the stairs.

As the house fell silent, Mary rose from her seat, set her empty wine glass on the end table, and strode over to the piano. She sat on the bench and found the tune Andrew had played the night before. Her fingers danced over the keys as she played, not nearly as well as Andrew had done. She felt the music vibrate through her, and her chest ached with a sad longing.

As the song ended, Mary sighed and wiped away a tear. He hadn't even been gone a full day and Mary missed Andrew so much she feared her heart would break.

With a slow, shaky breath, Mary rose to her feet and made her way up to bed, extinguishing the candles as she went.

She opened the door, prepared to see William in their bed reading or fast asleep, but her heart dropped like a stone in her stomach as she saw him sitting on their bed, Mary's copy of Romeo and Juliet beside him, poring over the letters, the rose resting beside the book. She had forgotten to hide it away. How could she have forgotten when she knew he loved Shakespeare as much as she?

William's face was white as a sheet.

"You kept it all," he said quietly, not bothering to look up as she entered.

Mary didn't know what to say. Of course, she had kept it. She couldn't very well have burned it. The rose and those letters were everything she had that proved Andrew loved her as much as she loved him.

William's fingers brushed the pressed rose. "I take it he gave you this?"

Finally, his eyes met hers.

Mary's heart raced, but she nodded. "When I was sixteen."

William's eyes darkened. "You two have been in love for five years?" His voice was hard, malicious.

"No!" Mary shook her head, then shrugged as she realized she was wrong. "I don't know. The day he gave me that rose was the first time I had seen him as something more than a cousin. More than a friend." William's jaw clenched, but he didn't interrupt. He stared at her, waiting for her to go on. "I had been talking about some boy from town who had his eye on me, but Andrew had said I was too good for them, too delicate, like a rose. Then he plucked one, that very one in your hand, and gave it to me. He had been kind, unlike how he usually was with me. And for the first time, I considered what it would be like to have a future with him."

William's face hardened as he crushed the rose in his fist and tossed it on the bed. Mary gasped as her heart ached with the sudden loss. That rose was a symbol of Andrew's love for her, her first token of his affection, and now it was destroyed.

She knew she shouldn't have held onto it, but she couldn't bear to part with it. It had meant so much to her.

"Why did you bring it with you?" he asked.

Mary licked her lips, her mouth suddenly dry. How angry must William have been when he found it all? Mary had been stupid to keep it in that book, knowing how much William enjoyed Shakespeare.

"Because I couldn't bear to part with it."

"Just as you cannot bear to part with Andrew?"

Mary's chest tightened, and tears sprang to her eyes. Whether she had been ready for that or not, she had lost Andrew the moment she got married.

"I *have* parted with Andrew."

He shook his head and looked down at the letters. Mary wanted to rip them away from him, feeling as though their private life was being scrutinized and she and Andrew were being judged.

"Do you still love him?"

How on Earth could she answer that honestly? Of course, she still loved him, but she didn't want to say that to William. It was the one question he had never asked her, perhaps because he had already known the answer, but he didn't want to hear it spoken aloud. William wasn't stupid. He always knew how Mary felt, even when she didn't say anything.

"Yes," she whispered. William's eyes glistened with tears as they met hers. "But none of that matters anymore. I chose you. I married you, Will. Nothing will ever come of these feelings I have. I would never do anything to hurt you."

"What if he tries something? He says in every one of these letters how much he loves you and how he'll take you away if only you would let him. Is that what the country home is for? To whisk you off to?" His voice rose to a yell.

Mary narrowed her eyes. "I understand why you're upset, William, but you don't get to yell at me. You knew of my feelings for Andrew before we were married. What I had with Andrew is in the past. As long as I am married to you, nothing will happen."

His eyes shifted from one letter to the next, then lingered on the crushed rose. "Then perhaps you shouldn't be married to me."

"You can't mean that." Tears stung her eyes.

"I knew you cared for him. I didn't know it was love. If you've been hiding your feelings so well, how do I know you aren't hiding anything else? How do I know you haven't been having an affair with him?"

"Can you really think so low of me!"

William waved the letters in her direction. "If your love for him is this strong, why did you marry me?"

Mary closed her mouth. She wasn't going to admit that it was what her mother wanted. She couldn't say that now, after he had already threatened to leave her, because the moment the truth was out, he would leave.

"Why, Mary? I need to know."

"It would have been foolish not to marry you."

He narrowed his eyes as he studied her. "Because of my money? Because I would take care of you?"

His words stung. "Do not think me as petty as someone who marries only for money and has no regard for love."

"Then why?" he shouted, rising to his feet.

"It doesn't matter, William, I chose you!"

"WHY?"

"Because Mother wouldn't allow me to marry Andrew!" she yelled back, angry enough to throw something.

Immediately, she regretted her words. William looked as though she had slapped him across the face.

"So, you did choose him," he said, starting toward the door. "I must go."

"What? No! William, please! I'm sorry. I didn't mean it as it sounded." She walked toward him, prepared to plead with him not to leave.

He held up a hand to stop her. "Answer me this, then, and be as honest as you have been. Do you love me?"

Mary's stomach ached. "Of course I love you."

"As much as you love Andrew?"

She swallowed. That was another matter. Of course, she loved William, but hadn't she loved him more as a friend than a lover? True, she was attracted to him, but there was something about Andrew that pulled her thoughts to him. She had never thought of William the way she had Andrew.

"Yes."

But William shook his head. "That's the first lie you've told me all night."

She narrowed her eyes. Once again, he had seen right through her.

"I love you differently than I love him."

His lip trembled. "And that, I believe."

She reached out and took his hand. "So you'll stay with me?"

His sad, dark eyes stared into hers. She had never seen him so upset. "I'm not going to be the reason you aren't with the man you love. Andrew's won... again."

"But he hasn't. I married you. I love you," Mary said, wishing she could sound more convincing.

"I saw the way you are with him. The way you look at one another. You never look at me like that."

Mary's chest tightened. "I could say the same about you."

William's eyes narrowed. He looked stricken.

But Mary couldn't hold back anymore. She was too angry. "You don't look at me the way Andrew does. You look at me with longing, yes, but never with love. Never like I'm the only woman in the world. You said it yourself last night. You married me so you could finally have one over on Andrew."

The way Andrew looked at Mary, as though she were the most precious thing in existence, was entirely different from how William looked at her.

"You think I do not love you?"

"I think nobody loves me as Andrew does. You know very little about me, nor have you taken any interest in learning since our wedding. But I made my decision."

William stepped forward, the letters fluttering silently to the floor. "How could you think that? After all I have done for you?"

Mary could almost feel the anger radiating off him. He grabbed her by the wrists and pulled her to him.

"William, please...." She tried to pry her shaky hands out of his firm grip, but it was impossible. He was too strong.

"Do you think this house was for me? That garden? The maid who is entirely too friendly?"

"William, you're hurting me!"

His eyes softened with pain, and he let her go. She stumbled back, landing hard on her bottom.

"If being with Andrew will make you happy, then so be it. I'll step aside and allow you to follow your heart. I'll tell your mother it wasn't meant to be. I'll take full responsibility for our failed marriage. It's less embarrassing than the truth."

Mary hiccupped a sob. "Please don't leave me."

Her mother would blame her regardless. And what would people say if her husband left her? She'd be condemned. It wouldn't matter the reason. No judge would allow them a divorce under these circumstances.

"I'm sorry, Mary," he said, staring down at her. "I should have stepped aside the moment I suspected the two of you cared for one another. I had been foolish enough to convince myself you would change your mind and love me. I am too competitive. I never know when to quit. But I think I'm starting to."

He was leaving. There was nothing she could do to make him stay, and after hearing everything he had to say, she wasn't sure she wanted him to anymore.

As he walked out the door, Mary felt like the biggest failure in existence. Her husband was leaving because she was no different than a common harlot... in love with another man. He was right. The truth was embarrassing.

His heavy footsteps pounded on the stairs and down the front hall. Mary flinched as the door slammed.

She couldn't stop the tears from falling. She cried until it hurt to breathe. William was gone. Her marriage was over.

ഛൈ ഇൈ

SHE WOKE UP ON THE COLD FLOOR with a blanket over her. For a moment, she thought William must have come back in the middle of the night and covered her, but as she rose up and looked around and saw how tidy the room was – her letters, crushed rose, and book sitting on the end table, stacked in a neat pile—she realized Hannah must have come and found her.

Her cheeks burned with embarrassment. Had Hannah read the letters? What must she think of her? Would she have assumed that Andrew was her lover and they had had an affair when he was there without William home?

She knew she would have brought those questions on herself, but still, her heart hurt at the thought of her closest friends thinking the worst of her because she was in love with another man.

She was going to lose everyone because she couldn't control her own emotions. She was no different than a child.

Mary didn't go down to breakfast. Instead, she carefully put her letters and rose back in her book and placed it back on the end table. She lay on her bed, her blanket wrapped tightly around her, and stared at the book that had caused her so much trouble.

If she only had destroyed it when she moved, she wouldn't be going through this now. Her heart would ache with sadness over losing Andrew, but at least it wouldn't hurt because she lost William, as well. Her life wouldn't be falling to pieces.

William would be back eventually, and he would no doubt want his home. Where would that leave her? Begging Uncle Isaac and Aunt Catherine to take her in? She couldn't do that.

She wouldn't.

And there was no way she could be with Andrew now. After the way things ended with William, she would be the town gossip. Andrew would be known as the man who ended a marriage, and she couldn't subject him to that. Nobody would sell him their property, and his business would go bankrupt. And she sure as well couldn't ask him to take her far away and become a farmer when his skills lie in buying and selling homes and factories.

Mary would die an old maid. No other man would want her after this. And to be honest, if she couldn't have Andrew, she would rather be an old maid. The biggest obstacle she had was finding a home and a way to make money. Perhaps she could sell enough of her dresses and jewelry to purchase a small home in the country now that she wouldn't need them for parties. Once she became a recluse who grew her own food in her garden, she wouldn't need to talk to anyone ever again. And what did it matter how she looked if there was nobody in her life to impress?

Not even her mother would want to visit her after this.

Mary turned her head to cry into the pillow as she realized how dreadfully lonely of a future she had to look forward to. Her life was over, and all because she couldn't burn the letters and rose Andrew had given her.

Mary awoke to the sound of knocking and jumped.

"Pardon me, Miss," Hannah said in a quiet voice. "I didn't mean to startle you. I only wanted to bring you some supper." She held up a tray piled with food and a glass and pitcher of water.

Supper. Mary looked out the window and saw that the sun was already starting to set. She had stayed in bed all day, in her clothes from yesterday, no less, she thought, looking down at her crinkled dress.

"Tha—" Mary cleared her throat as her voice came out strained. "Thank you, Hannah."

"Are you ill? Should I fetch the doctor?"

Mary shook her head, then winced and touched her temple as pain shot through her head.

"I'll be all right. William and I had a disagreement is all."

Hannah brought the tray in and sat it on the end table, carefully moving the book out of the way, then poured Mary a glass of water.

"Please drink. It will help with the headache."

Mary gratefully accepted the glass and drank as much as she could before setting it back on the tray. Her throat felt much better. "Thank you."

"Of course. Would you like me to stay with you for a while? I can read to you while you eat."

Mary felt tears spring to her eyes again.

She shook her head. "No, thank you. That's very kind of you."

"All right. If you change your mind, let me know. I won't be far. I'm just dusting the stairwell."

She turned to leave, but Mary called her back. "Is William home, by any chance?"

Hannah shook her head, her eyes soft with sadness. "I've not seen him all day. Calvin said one of the horses was gone when he woke up."

Mary swallowed and nodded. "Thank you. You and George should go for the night. There's no need to dust this evening. I'm not expecting any visitors."

Hannah watched her for a moment. "You'll be all right?"

She nodded and faked a smile. "Oh, yes. I'll see you in the morning."

Hannah nodded, then slowly left Mary alone.

Mary stared at the food, and her stomach rolled. She didn't want to eat. She wanted to be sick. Everything was falling apart.

Chapter Twenty-Nine

MARY DIDN'T SEE OR HEAR from William for three days. She woke up the next morning, got dressed, and had a small breakfast in the dining room as though nothing had changed. She wrote to William every day, telling him she missed him and that the house was lonely without him, and asked when he was coming home. But, not knowing where he was, Mary just sealed them and left them at her writing desk, planning to mail them out as soon as she knew where to send them.

On the third day of his departure, Mary walked into the dining room and saw a letter sitting by her plate. She hastily tore it open and read his words.

> *Mary,*
> *I hope you are all right. I cannot deny that each passing day has me worrying more and more about how you are. I've been in Boston working over the past few days, trying to stay as busy as Andrew to keep you off my mind. I'm currently targeting a few properties that he is looking to purchase, and I do say I plan to do whatever it takes not to let these*

properties slip away. Perhaps it's retaliation, but I'm not willing to lose both my wife and my business to a man of color.

I've been intentionally avoiding him because I honestly don't trust that I can remain civil any longer. I assume you've written to him by now, telling him that I left you, and if you have, perhaps I needn't worry about running into him. Perhaps he is at my home keeping my wife company. My wife who prefers his company.

You were never really mine. Your heart has always belonged to Andrew.

I have asked Calvin to pack a bag for me as I have extended my stay for a few weeks and will need more than what I have here. I don't think I will be returning any time soon. That house is tainted for me now.

I am planning on selling the house within the next few months. I have found a nice cottage down south that you might like that will be more than comfortable for you, but as you will no longer be my wife, perhaps you should see it before I purchase it for you. I have instructed Calvin to take you this week whenever you are ready.

Do not think I am throwing you out. I made a promise to care for you, so I will ensure you receive enough alimony to get by until you are remarried, which, I daresay, won't be long after the divorce is finalized.

My father's cousin is a judge and has granted me time in his court to file for divorce. I know no judge will allow us to divorce on the grounds that you are unhappy, and I can't very well say you are in love with another man without ruining our reputations, so I am filing under the pretense of not consummating the marriage. As we have been careful, there should be no baby and no reason for anyone to think otherwise. The divorce should be final within a year.

I am sorry that things have ended this way. You truly brought me so much happiness, Mary. But that was all an act. You aren't the woman I thought you were.

I'm sending enough money for you to get by another month and pay for the staff. I'll send more next month. Please let me know if you like that cottage and would like for me to purchase it for you.

Regards,
William

Mary's heart ached. He wasn't coming home. And what's worse was he had already found her another home.

He sounded rude. She reread the letter, eyes watering at his coldness. He had been horrible to Andrew and horrible to her. He had known how Andrew had felt from the beginning, so what difference did it make? He was taking out his hurt on Andrew and his company.

She wondered what that would mean for Andrew and his father's business. If William was planning to buy his properties out from under him, would that be too hard on Andrew's business?

In that moment, she knew that William had viewed her no differently than a property, offering a better deal quicker than the competition. She wished more than ever she would have run off with Andrew.

William had already gone through the trouble of finding a judge who would hear their case. He wanted to move forward with the divorce.

She wanted to be furious with him, to shout to hell with him, but she had brought it all upon herself. She knew she should have left the rose behind at Kline Manor, but she hadn't been ready to leave Andrew behind. And now her marriage was over.

A part of her was glad for it.

She walked to the library, refusing to let her tears spill, and found the letters she had left for William. She went to the parlor and lit a fire. It was a hot day, but it didn't matter. Mary shivered as she thought of what was to come of her life. Slowly, one at a time, she tossed the letters in the lapping flames, watching them burn as her marriage had.

William wasn't coming back. If he wanted her to move into a cottage far away, so be it, but after everything that was said, she refused to accept his charity.

She wanted nothing more to do with him.

She found Hannah in the kitchen, cleaning up the breakfast mess. She asked her if she knew anyone who would be interested in purchasing jewelry and gowns, and Hannah quickly went to fetch George.

It was a two-hour ride to the store George had known about. Mary thanked him as he helped her down from the carriage. Her heart raced as the salesclerk studied her jewelry. She had brought all of it—everything she owned—besides a necklace her father had given her right before he died.

"I'll give you three hundred for the jewelry and a hundred for the gowns."

Four hundred was more than she was expecting, though her family had spent a considerable amount of money on it all. Mary graciously accepted.

"How much is it to rent a cottage, do you think?" Mary asked as George took her next door to get a drink while they let the horses rest.

"Oh, I don't know. It depends on the size. I'd say twenty to fifty a year."

Mary took a deep breath and slowly exhaled. Four hundred wouldn't stretch far at all.

"I wouldn't worry too much about it, Miss. William is a good man and will make sure you're taken care of."

"As foolish as it may be, I don't want him to."

"Beg my pardon, Miss, but I don't think it's foolish at all." He stared at her for a moment, then offered a small smile. "Drinks are on me."

He ordered them both a glass of wine and led her to the window to sit. It was a nice day out, and she had to admit, it was nice being out of the manor. All her life she had never been anywhere but home or homes of friends and relatives or church. She didn't even visit the store near her house. She had no need to.

But it was quite nice sitting at a table with a friend, having a drink, and not having to worry about hosting.

"You're every bit the woman I thought you were."

Mary narrowed her eyes. "What does that mean?"

George held up a hand. "I mean no offense. I only mean that you're a lot like my Hannah. Strong and determined."

"Oh," Mary's tone softened. If he was comparing her to Hannah, he meant it as a compliment. It also meant he didn't know the reason why William had left her. "But it is my fault William and I are separating."

"No, it isn't."

"It is. Didn't Hannah tell you about the letters?"

He smiled, proving that she had. "She did. But that doesn't mean it was your fault. You cannot help how you feel. You weren't acting on those feelings, so you aren't in the wrong."

Mary took a deep breath. It was kind of him to try to reassure her, but she didn't quite believe what he was saying. She felt as though it was entirely her fault.

Once the horses were rested, they made their way back home. Mary was more than grateful for Hannah and George, who had been nothing but kind to her during the whole ordeal. Even though she wouldn't be able to afford to keep them on when she left, she hoped they could still be friends.

When they made it back to the manor, Mary walked straight to the kitchen where Hannah was just starting supper and hugged her.

"Thank you for all of your kindness," she told her.

"Of course!" she said, hugging her back. "Did everything go all right?"

Mary nodded. "I just need to find a place to live, and I'll be fine."

Hannah eyed her. "Is there anywhere in particular you were wanting to go?"

"Somewhere in the country. Far from here where nobody will know me so I can find work."

Hannah sighed and led Mary to the seat beside the door, easing her into it. "I hope you aren't angry for my overstepping, but I wrote to a cousin of mine yesterday, and he has a cottage about four hours from here. Now, it isn't near as grand as this," she pressed when Mary's eyes and mouth widened. "It's quite small. But I think you will be comfortable enough."

"Really, Hannah? Oh, that would be wonderful! How much will he charge? Are there any jobs nearby?"

"There are always jobs, Miss. I can ask him if he knows of any. He says it's thirty a year, but there's a garden out back that a gardener has been tending for the past three years with ample fruits and vegetables, and it will be yours if you decide to take the house."

Mary's heart raced at the thought. A cottage far away and a garden?

"But why would he keep the garden if he didn't use the crops?"

"He sold them to care for the cottage while waiting for a tenant."

"And he doesn't mind renting to a woman? Especially a woman in my situation?"

"I only told him your husband left you. I didn't go into the details of your private life. But he doesn't mind renting to a woman as long as you have the means to pay rent yearly."

Mary couldn't believe her luck. All this time she was terrified of what would come of her, but Hannah had ensured she would be just fine when she finally left Connell Manor.

"Thank you, Hannah! I would love the house. Please tell your cousin I will take it!"

Hannah smiled. "I thought you might say that. I wrote him back this morning and told him you would most likely want it and to please not rent it until you said otherwise. I'll send word right away that you will come see it this week."

"Tomorrow! Please?"

Hannah nodded. "Very well."

After she finished cooking, she went to write to her cousin. Mary ate the soup and thought about her new life, far away.

Her mother would be angry about the divorce and Mary moving to a cottage, but what could she say? Mary couldn't very well force William to be married to her.

She would find a job, even if it was cooking and cleaning for some rich family in town, and the house would be hers. She might die alone, but at least she would have a home, and she wouldn't have to beg her aunt and uncle to let her come back home or take William's handouts.

After everything they had said to one another, everything that happened, she wanted nothing from him but the divorce.

Soon, she would be out of this house and away from this nightmare. She could start over and pretend that everything was fine.

Chapter Thirty

THE NEXT MORNING, MARY HAD packed away all her belongings, the things she brought with her from Kline Manor, and climbed into the carriage, prepared to go see her new home. She had already decided no matter how small it was, she would take it. She didn't need the luxuries that came with a manor. She only needed a place of her own.

As soon as she stepped out of the carriage, Mary felt an immediate difference in the air. For one, she could breathe better. Two, it was cooler up north.

She looked up the small hill at the cottage. It was quaint, made from white bricks. A white fence wrapped around the garden, which housed several small rose bushes. It was a cute, one-story home that she could feel quite comfortable in.

Mary wouldn't mind having a small home, but she hoped the inside had wood floors, at least.

A man stepped outside as she, Hannah, and George started up the hill.

"Good afternoon! It's lovely to see you again, dear cousin. And George! I do say you've aged."

George laughed and extended his hand as they met in the front garden. "As have you, Daren."

Hannah kissed her cousin's cheeks, then stepped back to introduce him to Mary.

"Daren, this is Mary. She's a dear friend of mine, so do be kind."

Daren's lip twitched as he smiled. "Now, Hannah, aren't I always kind?" He smiled at Mary. "Mary, it's lovely to meet you. I'm glad you wanted to come see the cottage. It's difficult finding good renters. Hannah tells me you'll be living alone?"

The thought of a strange man knowing she was going to be alone made her nervous. But it was Hannah's cousin. She wouldn't have recommended it if he wasn't a good man.

Mary nodded.

"Right. No need to worry. This is on private property. If you need anything at all, I'm right down the street. Though this town has been safe for as long as I can remember."

"That's good to hear."

He led them inside, and Mary felt her heart leap. It was decorated better than she would have thought. The interior was well kept, the floors a light wood, and it was completely furnished. A chandelier hung above a dining room table on one side of the house with a wood stove at the back of the room, and the sitting room was complete with a bookshelf, a small pianoforte, and flowers on the coffee table. At the back of the house were two doors.

"Now, it isn't much, but you can decorate it any way you see fit."

"It's beautiful," Mary said. "It's everything I need."

Daren laughed. "Well, surely you want to see the washroom and bedroom first?"

Mary smiled and ducked her head. "Of course."

The washroom was small, but Mary was pleasantly surprised

to find that it held a roll top tub and an indoor toilet. She had expected such a small home in the country to have outdoor facilities and a wash basin.

The bedroom was beautiful, again accented with flowers, but didn't hold more than a bed, a wardrobe, and a couple of tables, one containing yarn and knitting needles. That was fine with Mary. She had never been one to sit in the bedroom for hours.

There was a window overtop the bed, centered against the back wall, looking out at the back garden. Mary saw plants of every kind, from peppers to tomatoes, to potatoes, and a water spigot nearby. Chickens roamed around inside a fence of their own. But the best part was when she spotted the apple and pear trees.

She nearly laughed as she turned to the others, watching her from the front room.

"I love it," she said. "It's absolutely perfect."

And just what she needed to forget her life had completely fallen apart.

"Fabulous! I'll have some paperwork drawn up, and you can move in whenever you're ready."

"Tonight?" she asked, hopeful.

He smiled. "Tonight is just fine, Miss Connell."

"Kline, please."

"Miss Kline, then. The gardener is paid for the week, so he will be by the next few days. You can either choose to continue paying him or take over the garden yourself. Whatever you choose, I will be fine with."

Hannah walked around the home, admiring some of the small details, like the books that already lined the shelves.

"Are you sure you're going to be all right?" she asked.

"I'll be just fine. Look how beautiful this home is. And I have a garden. A real garden that grows food! I think I remember how to can vegetables, so I'll be able to feed myself all year."

Still, Hannah looked worried. "I have a book on canning that I will send you. And some for sewing and knitting. You can make a fine life here."

"I will. I'll find a job. I'm sure I could grow enough produce to sell the surplus. I don't need much. Don't you worry. I'll be just fine. Thanks to you." She took her friend's hands and squeezed, trying to convey how much she appreciated her help.

"Right!" Mr. Hill softly clapped his hands, getting their attention. "If you are looking for extra money, I have an offer. The missus and I are looking for a new nanny. Our previous one was married and moved away."

Mary almost couldn't believe it. "A nanny?"

"Yes. Not full-time, of course. Just when Ada and I are both away. I often have work to attend to the next town over, and Ada loves to travel. The girls are five and seven, too young to go with her, so we'll need someone to look after them on days we're both away."

Mary's heart raced as she thought how perfectly her life was coming together. She'd never cared for children before, but if it was income, she'd be more than willing to learn.

"I'll pay you fifty cents each day you work and knock your rent down to fifteen a year if you'll do it."

Mary grinned. It was better than she was expecting. Fifty cents a day could mean the world to her. She wouldn't need much to get by, especially with a garden in the back. She had no desire for fancy dresses or jewels. And if he set rent to fifteen a year, she'd have more than enough to get by for years here.

"I'd love to, Mister Hill. Thank you very much."

"You're very welcome, dear. Thank you!"

He started toward the door, then turned to face them again.

"Why don't you come by for dinner tomorrow? Around six? You can meet the girls and the missus."

"I would love to."

He grinned at her, then turned to Hannah. "Oh, and cousin, do stop by the house before you leave. Ada misses you dearly."

She promised she would be up soon, then she, George, and Calvin, who had been waiting by the door, helped Mary carry in her things.

After everyone had gone, Mary felt herself relax as she looked around her home. *Her* home. It was all hers. She owed this part of her life to no one.

Tomorrow, she would write to her mother to tell her she was no longer married to William and apologize for disappointing her, but tonight, she was going to enjoy her home and freedom.

The next morning, Mary sat at the table and wrote to her mother, informing her that she had moved to a small cottage in the country and wouldn't be able to have guests for quite a while as she was adjusting to her new life. She omitted the part where she didn't want visitors, especially her mother, because she knew she would be angry and have nothing good to say.

She didn't want her mother to ruin the place she had so quickly fallen in love with. Mother wouldn't see the charm the cottage had. She'd only see how small it was and how there was no room for guests.

But Mary never wanted more than a guest or two over at once. She'd never been one for dinner parties or hosting. She only enjoyed being in the company of a close friend or two.

Perhaps her mother could visit for Christmas. Or maybe after the new year.

Mary heard wheels creaking over the wooden road just outside and hurried to the door. Sure enough, it was a mail carrier making his way up to the Hill residence.

She waved her arm as she hurried down the hill. He stopped and smiled at her.

"Hello. I nearly didn't see you. I didn't know Mister Hill had rented the place."

She grinned wide. "It's my first morning here. I don't think I'll be writing every day, but if you want to check, perhaps once a week, I would appreciate it. If I have something urgent I need to send, I'll bring it out to you."

He laughed and accepted her letter. "I'll get this sent out first thing."

"Thank you, Mister...?"

"Jones. Harry Jones."

"Lovely to meet you, Mister Jones. I'm Mary Kline."

"Nice to meet you, Miss. Kline."

Mary went back inside, tossed a few pieces of wood in the stove, and started the fire. Next, she went to the back garden to feed the chickens and gather the few eggs they had laid. It was nothing like she'd ever done before, but she found herself enjoying it. As she turned to go back inside, she saw a few tomato plants and plucked a particularly red tomato.

She fried an egg on the stove, sliced the tomato, and cut a slice of bread. For her first breakfast here, she was thoroughly impressed. She could get used to eating like this. She only wished she lived somewhere warmer where she could have fresh produce year-round.

When the gardener arrived, Mary watched him work, asking questions about caring for each plant. He didn't seem annoyed or upset that he was about to be out of a job. On the contrary, he seemed pleased and eager to show her what to do. Apparently, he had to travel an hour to get there, and he was looking forward to being able to stay closer to home.

Mary changed into a nice dress for dinner with the Hill's, then made her way up the road to their mansion. The home was bigger than Mary would have thought, bigger even than Connell Manor. She wondered how Hannah had become a maid when her cousin obviously came from money. What had happened on her side of the family where she didn't have enough to live in a grand home?

Perhaps she hadn't made the same mistake as Mary and married for love instead of some rich man her parents chose.

The children greeted her at the door, and each had made a drawing for her. Alice, the older child, was smart and shy. Helena, the younger, had a warm smile and talked faster than any child Mary had ever met. She didn't doubt that she would have a lot of fun with the two.

Ada Hill was simply lovely. She was a perfect hostess, telling Mary wonderful stories of her travels and the girls. Mary was most interested in hearing about the girls, as she would be caring for them. Ada doted on each of them, who were, according to her, very intelligent and sweet young ladies. She informed her that they didn't have a governess because she preferred to teach the girls herself.

After dinner, Daren brought out the paperwork for her to sign, telling her he'd be by for the rent money in the morning. Mary was more than eager to pay as it would mean for the next year, at least, she wouldn't have a care in the world.

Daren also insisted she ride in his carriage home, telling her no lady should walk, especially after dark, and the next time she came to his home, he would send a coachman.

As she lay down that night, she wondered what Andrew was doing and if he had heard that William had left her. She bit her lip. Would he be angry or glad? She wondered if he would try to find her and if she should write and tell him.

She also wondered if Hannah had told William she had gone and if he would even care.

Chapter Thirty-One

THE NEXT WEEKS WENT BY in a beautiful, peaceful haze. Mary would wake up, tend to the chickens and the garden, have breakfast, then either play the piano or read. In the evening, after supper, Mary would knit. The book that Hannah had sent showed her how to create blankets and sweaters that she could sell to make some extra cash.

She had spent two days with Alice and Helena, but only during the day. Mr. Hill returned home every evening to care for his daughters and had paid Mary for her time each day. He had even seen one of the blankets she was knitting and asked if he could buy one for each of his girls.

She was growing to enjoy the monotony of her life. It was nice not having to answer to anyone and even better knowing she didn't have to worry about disappointing anyone.

When she felt inclined, Mary wrote to Hannah, Sarah, and Ruth, telling them about her home and life and asking about theirs. While Sarah didn't like the idea of living in a cottage in the country, she seemed genuinely happy that Mary had found some comfort in it.

It wasn't until night fell that she allowed herself to think of Andrew and wonder where and how he was. She wanted to write to him, but she worried about how his father would react if Andrew were to be with a divorced woman. She wasn't even divorced yet.

One morning, after Mary had tended to the chickens and garden, she walked out front and saw the mail coach, Mr. Jones, making his way up her hill.

"Good morning," she called.

He turned and saw her and waved.

"Good morning, Miss Kline. I have two letters for you today."

"Thank you, Harry. I don't have any letters for you right now, but the next time you come by, I will."

He nodded. "I'll be here tonight at six."

She thanked him and accepted her letters, making her way inside.

She set her basket of eggs and her tomato on the table, then stared down at the letters. One was from her mother, the other from Hannah. Not wanting to hear anything negative about how her life was ruined, she opened the letter from Hannah.

> *Mary,*
>
> *I hope you are settled well and enjoying your new home. The house feels so bare without you. I dearly miss my friend. Though if you are happy, then I shall bear my loneliness and be glad you have found some peace in your new home.*
>
> *Mr. Connell has returned home. He has met with a few prospective buyers. He keeps asking about you. He wants to know where you are. He's upset you won't let him help you. If you want me to tell him where you are, I will, but I won't do it unless you give me permission.*

I know you don't need the aggravation, but I do feel as though you deserve to know what's going on. When Mr. Connell was in Boston, Andrew saw him and asked what he was doing there. Mr. Connell told him what happened between the two of you, and Andrew grew angry. They got into a fight. Nobody was hurt, but neither of them made that sale.

Andrew has contacted me, begging me to tell him where you are. I told him I would write to you and ask your permission. If you want me to tell him, I will. If not, just let me know, and I'll inform him you'll tell him when you're ready. But I do say I believe he has your best interests at heart.

I love you dearly, sweet Mary, and I do hope you are well.

All my best,
Hannah

Mary set the letter on the table and sighed. She had wanted to start with Hannah's letter because she thought it would make her happy. But the news of Andrew and William fighting had upset her. She wondered what William must have said about her to get that sort of reaction from the usually calm Andrew. Judging by what he had said in his letter to her, she didn't think it could be anything good.

She didn't know if she should tell either of them where she was. She knew if she did, they'd be there. She didn't doubt that Andrew would be there, possibly wanting to whisk her away to another home. But she was happy there. She didn't want to be anywhere else.

Still, perhaps Andrew would understand and want to stay there with her. If he could live a simple, country life, then she really would have the life she dreamed. Hadn't he talked about buying a cottage in the country with a garden?

But she was scared. Her mother wouldn't approve. She had been against it from the beginning. But she didn't need Mary to care for her. And right now, Mary didn't care if her mother approved of what she was doing. Didn't Mary owe it to herself to care for herself now? To do what she knew would make her happy?

She had tried to do things her mother's way and it failed.

She picked up the letter from her mother, hands shaking as she worried about what she might say.

> *Mary,*
> *I am sorry to hear it didn't work out with William. Perhaps I can write to him and explain that what you feel for Andrew is residual childhood feelings, and he would understand. He is a good man, and I know if he could save his marriage, he will. Write to him straight away and tell him you miss him. You cannot be expected to live alone in a cottage for the remainder of your days.*

Her mother went on for three pages, telling Mary what to do to save her marriage. Mary couldn't bear it. She resolved not to write her back until she was sure she wouldn't be so condescending.

Mary was content with her life. It might not be what women usually wanted, but it was nice and more than comfortable enough for her.

Mary started the fire and made her breakfast, mulling over what she might say to William and Andrew. She had decided to write to them both, but she wasn't sure if she should give them her address. She didn't want William's money or guilt. She was ready to close that chapter of her life and pretend the past

few months had never happened. She wasn't sure she should tell
Andrew where she was either because she didn't want him to be
rejected by his family like she had been.

After breakfast, Mary sat at the table to write them both.

> *William,*
>
> *I am writing to assure you that I am fine so you will
> leave poor Hannah alone. I found a home and am
> very happy here. I have already found a job that
> will allow me to live a comfortable life without your
> money.*
>
> *I am sorry for how things ended, but I do wish
> you the very best. You have grown to mean a great
> deal to me, and I hate that I have hurt you. But you
> should know that everything you have said hurt me,
> as well. Perhaps we can call it even and go back to
> the way things were before we knew one another.*
>
> *If you need to get in touch with me, send word
> with Hannah. She can get your letters to me. I ask
> that you please respect my privacy, and I will respect
> yours. I expect nothing more from you than you
> have already given me. The home and everything in
> it belong to you.*
>
> *All my best,*
> *Mary*

She reread the letter, hoping she didn't sound disrespectful.
She wanted William to know she was putting up boundaries.
She wasn't interested in being his friend. Not after how he had
treated her. She may have loved another man, but that didn't
mean she wasn't the best wife she knew how to be. She'd never
acted on her feelings. She'd tried her best to fall in love with her
husband. And in the end, he resented her for it.

After she was satisfied with her letter to William, she wrote to Andrew.

Dearest Andrew,
Hannah tells me you have asked about me. I am doing wonderfully. My home is in the country, and it's beautiful. It has a full garden, complete with apple and pear trees. I know you would love it, if only because I do. Perhaps soon you can visit. Although, I must tell you, I only have one bedroom, so we will have to fight over the bed.

William found your letters that I had saved. And the rose you gave me. It was stupid of me to keep them, but I couldn't bring myself to throw them out. It was like I was losing you forever if I did that.

Please know I am not angry with him or hurt. I was at first, but I'm fine now. I don't even mind if he tells everyone our dissolution was my fault as long as he doesn't mention you. Please try to let William's words go over your head. I am sorry if our fight caused you aggravation at work.

For the first time since I left Kline Manor, I can breathe. Hannah and George have been a tremendous help, and I owe it to them that I have found the home of my dreams.

I hope you are well, Andrew.

Yours,
Mary

Mary reread the letter, then sealed it. In the end, she wrote her address on her letter to Andrew but not to William. She wasn't ready to see him.

She wrote another letter to Hannah, thanking her for the

update and telling her of her decision and that she had written to both William and Andrew.

She truly was grateful to Hannah and George for everything.

By the time Harry arrived to get the mail, Mary was shaking with nerves. She offered him a couple of apples, and he thanked her. Having a garden really was at the top of her favorite things she'd ever owned.

That night before bed, she opened her Romeo and Juliet book and reread all of the letters Andrew had written her. As she pressed what was left of the rose to her lips, she realized she hoped more than anything Andrew would come to her.

Chapter Thirty-Two

THE NEXT EVENING, MARY WAS tending to her garden, picking a few of the ripe fruits and vegetables, when she heard a carriage out front.

She narrowed her eyes, wondering if it was Harry again. Could her letters have had time to get to William and Andrew, then back again? She didn't think so.

Perhaps Mr. Hill had sent a carriage for her. It was possible he had forgotten to tell her she was requested again. He had one day last week.

She walked around the front of the house, gently rocking her basket back and forth, and saw a carriage waiting at the bottom of the hill. It didn't look like the one that came to fetch her for Mr. Hill, though.

She stood back, hesitant.

The carriage door opened, and a familiar face popped out.

Mary smiled and ran down the hill, dropping her basket to the ground in her haste to get to him.

Andrew grinned up at her as he ran to meet her. As soon as she was close, she jumped into his arms, wrapping hers around his neck and laughing and crying.

"You're here! You're truly here!"

"Course I am. You didn't think for one second I wouldn't come as soon as I found out where you were hiding?"

He didn't let go as he eased her to the ground. She couldn't calm her racing heart as she clung to him, never wanting to let go.

Eventually, however, she pulled back. She looked into his hazel eyes and her heart skipped as she saw that familiar glisten that showed her how much he loved her.

"Come inside. Let me show you my home."

Andrew didn't argue as she pulled him up the hill. They gathered the discarded basket and Andrew carried it for her, holding onto her hand so tightly she wondered if he was worried she would run off.

She showed him around her home, pointing out her favorite aspects. He was also impressed by the fact that she had indoor plumbing in such a quaint country cottage.

"Your home is beautiful, Mary. You've done well."

She smiled, her breath hitching as he looked her in the eye.

"I love it. It's everything I've always wanted."

"Can I stay with you?" he asked. "I promise to pull my weight and help with everything, from rent to tending the garden to cooking and cleaning."

"I would love to say yes, Andrew, but what would the neighbors think? An unwed man and woman living together? Why, that would absolutely ruin my already tainted reputation."

His eyes glistened with humor, but he took her hand. "What if we weren't unwed?"

Mary's pulse quickened. Was he really asking her to marry him?

"Andrew...."

"No, hear me out, please."

Mary closed her mouth and nodded.

"I know I've not been the most reliable, and I've run more often than I've been there for you, but if you allow me this last chance, I promise I won't run. I'll be here for you through everything."

Mary could no longer see clearly as tears filled her eyes and blurred her vision. She blinked them away, and he wiped her cheeks.

"I'm still married to William. The divorce won't be finalized for at least a year. I cannot marry until then."

"I can wait a year. I'll wait ten years if you'll have me."

Mary laughed through her tears.

"Mary, will you please allow me to be your husband and share your life with me?"

In a matter of two weeks, Mary's life had flipped completely upside down. Finally, after months of trying to be the woman her mother wanted her to be, Mary was allowing herself to make decisions that would make her happy, regardless of her mother's wishes and their reputation.

So for once, Mary didn't think about anyone but herself as she said, "Yes!" and flung herself into his arms.

She knew it was too soon after her marriage was over, but she didn't care. All that time with William was time she could have had with Andrew. She hated that her marriage had gone horribly with William, but hadn't she wanted to be with Andrew more than anything? Wasn't she finally getting everything she'd ever wanted?

It didn't matter that it was soon. It only mattered that she had him, finally, and she didn't have to answer to anyone for her decision.

Who cared what her mother would say? As far as Mary was concerned, if her mother loved her, she would just be happy that her daughter was happy. If that wasn't enough for her, Mary didn't want her in her life.

❦

OVER THE NEXT YEAR, SO MUCH CHANGED. William got engaged to a girl in Boston three months after their separation. Mary hoped he would be happier with her. Andrew had found a small cottage twenty minutes from Mary's and walked over every day for lunch, leaving only when she was ready for bed. Hannah and George began working for the couple who had bought Connell Manor.

Sarah and Jeffry had separated, but Sarah had found solace in the arms of a man from her church, who was studying to be a doctor. Sarah was hopeful he would propose.

One month after William had written to Mary that their divorce was final, Mary and Andrew were married. The wedding was small. Mary invited the Hill's, Hannah and George, Ruth and Henry, and Sarah and her guest of choice. Ruth and Henry couldn't make it, but they sent their congratulations and best wishes. Sarah brought her doctor friend, Mr. Jacob Noble, and Mary had to admit, he did seem to be falling for her, and he was much kinder than Jeffry.

Mary plucked flowers from her garden to use in her bouquet. Red roses. The symbol of her and Andrew's love.

After their guests had left, Mary sat at the table and wrote to tell her mother that against her wishes, she had wed Andrew and they were happy at their cottage in the country.

She received a letter two days later from her mother, telling her that although she would have chosen a different path for her, she would try to be content knowing that Mary was happy.

Mary finally took a deep breath and let herself feel that everything would be all right.

Chapter Thirty-Three

M ARY STOOD IN FRONT OF her and Andrew's cottage, rubbing her swollen belly as she watched the carriage pull to a stop. Andrew gently touched the small of her back then walked down the short path to open the carriage door. He held out his hand and helped Mother from the carriage.

Her heart froze. What if her mother hated the cottage and tried to convince them to move somewhere bigger? Had she truly accepted Mary's decision to marry Andrew, or was her prejudice against him still controlling how she felt about him?

Mary wouldn't tolerate her mother treating Andrew badly in his own home. She had chosen Andrew over her mother this time, and she would be bold enough to tell her off if need be.

Mother stepped down from the carriage and her gaze locked with Mary's. She smiled and accepted Andrew's arm, letting him lead her up the path to the cottage.

Mary didn't miss her mother's jaw tightening as she took in the small property.

When she made it to where Mary stood, Mother wrapped her in an embrace.

"Oh, my dear, Mary. Look at you!" She pulled back, taking

both of Mary's hands in hers, raising them up so she could take in Mary's pregnant belly.

"I know. I'm huge."

Her mother released her hands and Mary rubbed her belly.

"Nonsense. Let's see if we can fatten our little one up a bit more before she's born, shall we?"

Mary raised her eyebrows. "She?"

Her mother waved her off. "Or he."

When Mary had married Andrew, she had never thought her mother would be coming to stay with them. But when she had learned that Mary was expecting, she insisted she come to stay with them until the baby was born, and shortly after to help Mary when Andrew had to work.

"Your home is beautiful, but it seems to be under construction?" Mother tilted her head back to look at the second story.

"The cottage was only one story when I arrived. Andrew's been doing some renovations, expanding the cottage for our growing family."

Andrew had been busy for the past six months, building a second story onto the cottage with the help of Mr. Hill and a few men from town Andrew had befriended, when they had time to spare. They had finished two rooms and were working on a third, but it was more than enough for Mother and the baby. Besides, Mary wanted the baby with her for the first few months.

She looked at her husband, now getting her mother's bags from the carriage, and wondered what she had done to deserve him. Nothing that she could recall.

"Will you show me around?" Mother asked. "I'm dying to see your garden. Sarah said you have the most beautiful roses."

"Andrew takes good care of my roses."

Her mother stared at her for a moment. She tucked a strand of hair behind Mary's ear and pressed her palm to her cheek. "Andrew takes good care of you, it seems."

Mary laughed and looked down at the ground. "Yes. He does."

"I'm sorry for not thinking he was good enough," Mother whispered. "What William did was deplorable. Andrew is the better man."

It was all Mary had wanted to hear.

"I am curious, though," Mother said as they walked down the cobblestone path to the back garden. "When did you first realize you were in love with Andrew?"

The red rose bushes came into view.

"I was sixteen. And it started with a rose."

.

About the Author

DONISE SHEPPARD IS A ROMANCE and horror writer residing in southern West Virginia with her husband and four children. Donise found her passion for books at an early age and has been chasing stories ever since. She is an author, editor, and co-owner of Pixie Forest Publishing. Love and romance are her first passions, but who can resist a scary story? When she isn't working, she's reading for pleasure, baking, or singing off key.

www.ingramcontent.com/pod-product-compliance
Lightning Source LLC
Chambersburg PA
CBHW030656260626
47157CB00007B/2674